THE
BROKEN
RAVEN

JOSEPH ELLIOTT

WALKER
BOOKS

First published 2021 by Walker Books Ltd
87 Vauxhall Walk, London SE11 5HJ

2 4 6 8 10 9 7 5 3 1

This book has been typeset in Sabon, Old Claude, Toolbox Mustache

Printed and bound by CPI Group (UK) Ltd, Croydon CR0 4YY

British Library Cataloguing in Publication Data:
a catalogue record for this book is available from the British Library

ISBN 978-1-4063-8587-8

www.walker.co.uk

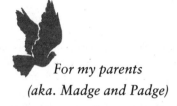
For my parents
(aka. Madge and Padge)

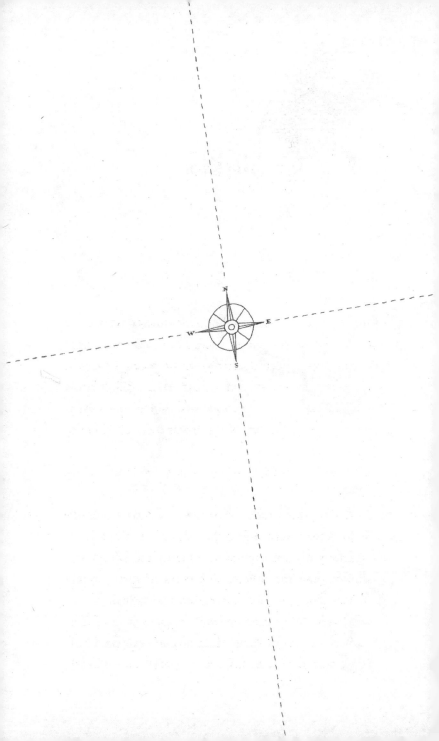

SIGRID

MY FACE IS ON FIRE BUT I'M NOT GUNNA SCREAM. I don't think I could even if I tried. I need water but can't ask for it; my mouth doesn't work no more. I knew it was gunna hurt. It's *sposed* to hurt. Still, I didn't know it was gunna hurt as much as this. Somethin's gushin down my cheek. I dunno if it's ink or tears or blood or what. Praps it's a mix of all three.

"I'm movin on to your neck," ses the man. "Keep still."

As if I'm gunna move with that hek massive needle close to skewerin me. I grip the sides of the stool, lettin its splinters dig into my skin. One of the stool's legs is shorter than the others, so I gotta hold my weight slanted to stop it wobblin. Evrythin's hek skittin in this shack. I knew soon as I came in that this was a bad idea, but it was too late by then. Mamma'd already paid him.

He looms over me, his breath harsk as milkreek.

Dark blue ink drips from the end of the needle. I close my eyes as the stabbin starts again.

A forever time later, the man pulls away and tosses the needle on the side.

"Done," he ses.

I'm hot all over. Swear Øden I never been so hot. Even breathin hurts.

"Þokka," I say, although it seems hek foolin to thank him, given how he's done nothin but stab me with a needle for the last however long.

My mother is waitin for me outside. Soon as I step out, the man slams the shack door shut without sayin goodbye or nothin.

"Well," ses my mother, "let's see it." She grabs my head to steady herself and leans in for a better look. Her face is too close to mine. Bits of sweaty hair are stuck to her forehead and her eyes are faraway and wild. "Ha!" is all she ses.

"What?" I say. "What's wrong with it?"

"Nothin," ses my mother, but she's smilin wicked. She could at least pretend it looks all right. It was her what convinced me this was a good idea, after all. I was far too keen, but who wouldn't want their first ink early? This wasn't how I imagined it happenin, though. All of my mother's ideas are bad ones; you'd of thought I would've learnt that by now.

"Did it hurt?"

"Yes," I say. No point in lyin.

"It'll heal soon," she ses, pretendin she cares.

The walk back to our shack is a blur of throbbin. The ground's sodden from where it's been spewin all afternoon, and the wet finds my toes through the holes in my shoes. I tried fixin the shoes yesterday but I guess I didn't do a very good job. I'll try again tonight, do them better.

Soon as we're back, my mother crashes on her sleepin mat and asks for water. There's a mirror by the water bucket, so while I'm fillin up the horn I see my new ink for the first time. The mirror's cracked, which doesn't help none. Has been ever since I knew it. Probly my mother did it before I was born, or maybe it was my pa before... Well, before what happened to him happened. One of the mirror cracks goes right through my reflection. My face is diffrunt now. I keep starin at it, but I can't find the person I was before. First inkin is sposed to make you look brave. On me, the way that sickweasel done it, it doesn't look nothin but ugly. There's no other word for it. It's swollen red and crusty with blood. Mamma thinks he was lyin about used to bein a *tatovmaðr*. I coulda told her that. He woulda told her anythin to get his greedy hams on our money.

The ink's sposed to be a raven. Mamma let me choose, probly cuz she couldn't be bothered thinkin of somethin herself. It don't look nothin like what I was hopin, though. It clings to my neck with its head stretchin over my jaw like it's tryin to peck out my cheek. It looks dead, like someone clean snapped its neck. It looks like it's cryin on my cheek but it's not got no tears. Oh well, isn't nothin I can do about it now. We just gotta hope it's good enough to fool whoever my mother's plannin on showin it to. Now I'm inked I should be able to get work on one of the larger farms, diggin up crops or somethin. It'll be hard grind, but I don't mind that none. Anythin's better than spendin all day bein pushed around by Mamma.

I cross over to her now and hand her the water horn. She takes it without sayin nothin and doesn't even open her eyes. I try to slip out, but of course she hears.

"Where you goin?"

"Granpa Halvor's," I say.

"What you goin there for?"

"I wanna show him my ink." That's a lie. He's gunna be hek grieved when he sees it. I shoulda told him we were gunna do it. I didn't cuz I knew he'd tell me not to.

"You spend too much time with that old man," ses my mother. "It's not normal." She doesn't hardly speak to Granpa Halvor. I think cuz he reminds her too much of my pa. "Don't be long. My head's throbbin and I'm hungry," she ses.

I'm already out the door before she's finished speakin. Granpa Halvor's shack isn't far from ours. Close enough to run to when my mother's turned sour from neckin. I knock on his door and, soon as he opens it, first thing he ses is, "What has she done to you?"

"She didn't do nothin," I tell him.

"She may not have held the needle, but I bet it was her idea."

His face is tight with so much concern, I feel my own face crumplin. "I shouldn't of done it," I say. "It's my fault. I knew it was a sickrotten idea."

"Hey, shush, girl. Come inside and I'll make you some sweetmilk."

He puts his arm around my shoulders and leads me in. Granpa Halvor's shack isn't nothin like ours. It's hek poky, but everythin's put neat and tidy clean. Best of all is the twistknot rug on the floor what's nearly as big as the whole place. Granpa made it himself when he was a kidlin out of bits of old clothes and scraps. He cleans it every day so it isn't never dusty. I sit on it and run my fingers through the scruffs.

He brings me over a bowl of sweetmilk and while I'm drinkin, he dabs at my face with a wet rag. I hold in the wince that's wantin to come out.

"Who's the grotthief what did this to you?" he asks me.

"I dunno, Granpa," I say.

"Sure as hellfire wasn't no proper *tatovmaðr*."

"I know, Granpa."

"How much'd you pay him?"

"I dunno, Granpa."

"It wouldn't of come cheap, gettin him to do it with you bein only twelve and all. What was your mother thinkin? What's her game? And what sort of a lyin, thievin scoundrel would do this to a girl? I feel like trackin him down and ... and..."

I can't help smilin at that. The thought of Granpa hurtin anyone is hek smirks.

"What you laughin for?" he ses. "If I was twenty years younger ... I'll have you know I was a force to be reckoned with in my time."

"Sure you were, Granpa," I say. I slurp down the rest of the sweetmilk. It's hek creamin on my insides. "I thought you didn't agree with fightin anyways?"

"Depends who's fightin and what they're fightin for. If it's sendin away our kidlins to be slaughtered on foreign lands for nothin but pride and power, then no, I don't agree with fightin one speck."

He's talkin about his son, my pa. I don't hardly remember him. He died over the seas somewhere when I was a little kidlin, fightin for the king in some blood-splash invasion.

"What about if Mal-Rakki came back?" I ask. "Would you fight for him?"

"That's diffrunt and you know it. His fight has purpose. The day he returns, I'll be the first to stand by his side."

What if Mal-Rakki never comes back? I think, but I don't say it. I draw lines in the dregs of the sweetmilk with the tip of my finger.

"Here, I got this for you." Granpa Halvor throws somethin at me.

I catch it quick, and my gawpers open hek wide.

"Where'd you get this?" I ask. The plum is bright yellow, soft as a babkin's foot, perfectly ripe.

"I pulled it out my nose hole; where d'you think I got it?"

"But I thought you had to give them all up to the king?"

"I did, but I sneaked one away, just for you."

I smile, and for a speck I forget about the wreckmess of my face and all its hurtin. The tree behind Granpa's shack is a scraggin old knot, but it grows the most hek *ríkka* plums in the whole of Norveg. I bite into the one in my hand and it's good – so good! Its juice trickles down my arm, and I lick it up, not wantin to waste none. I take another bite, then offer the rest to Granpa.

"No, girl, it's yours. I want you to enjoy it," he ses.

I don't need tellin twice. I put the rest of it in my mouth, stone and all, and chew down, lettin the sweetness burst inside my cheeks. I should slow down, take my time scrammin, but it's too good for bein slow. Once all the flesh has gone, I keep the stone in my mouth, suckin on it for any last drips.

"I think you enjoyed that," ses Granpa Halvor.

I nod. "Thanks, Granpa." I spit out the stone and bury it in one of my trouser pockets. "Once I'm earnin, I'll buy us fruit evry day."

"What you talkin about, earnin?" His forehead creases, makin the ink rabbit what's there crumple into a slackdead heap. Granpa's got hek loads of ink, but the rabbit on his forehead has always been my favourite.

"Mamma says I can earn good pennies workin on one of the big farms. That's why I got the ink done."

"You don't wanna be workin down there. You'd have to get up before the sun to arrive on time. Earnin isn't evrythin, Sigrid. Specially when the king's men come take it all from us anyways."

"What choice have I got?"

"What do you mean what choice? There are always choices. It's knowin which are the right ones that's the hard part."

I dunno about that. Far as I see it, I haven't got no choices, sept doin what Mamma tells me. Which reminds me...

"I gotta go, Granpa," I say. "Mamma's not feelin too good. She'll be hek skapped if I'm not back cookin somethin soon."

Granpa scowls hard, like a beaver what's been bit. He's always scowlin when I mention Mamma. "Well, don't let her talk you into no more brainrot plans," he ses. "And keep that ink of yours clean. If it gets any redder, come straight back to see me."

"Yes, Granpa."

Before I go, he holds my chin between his thumb and finger and turns my head sideways to get another gawp at my ink. "My little Sigrid, growin up," he ses. "A raven was a perfect choice. He may not have been no proper *tatovmaðr* what done it, but I think he did a good job. I like it."

He strokes my other cheek with his knuckles. It's nice of him to lie.

AGATHA

"Again, again," all the children are saying.

I ask Milkwort if he wants to do it again and he does. He likes it. He is going to do the fastest one ever.

"Okay," I say to the children. "Get r– ready."

They put their hands on the table in a line. I give Milkwort two taps on his head and put him next to the first hand. The children are smiling.

"Here he comes... G– Go!" I say, and I say it to Milkwort in my head as well.

As soon as he hears it, Milkwort runs up the first girl's arm, around her neck and down her other arm. Then he moves on to the boy next to her, then the next one and then all the other children in the row. They like it because it tickles and they laugh. It is good to laugh. Some of the children are from Clann-a-Tuath which is my clan and some of them are from Clann-na-Bruthaich which is a different clan. I am their favourite and so is Milkwort.

"Again!" they say after Milkwort has gone around all of them.

"No more. Agatha has a meeting to attend," says a person behind me who is Maistreas Eilionoir. I did not know that she was there and was watching.

"Oh, yes," I say. "I d– do."

I tell Milkwort it is time to go and he runs up my arm and into my pocket. It is okay that Maistreas Eilionoir saw me talking to him, even though he is a vole. Speaking to animals is not *dùth* but Maistreas Eilionoir says I am allowed to do it now. I say goodbye to the children and they all shout, "Goodbye, Agatha" and "Goodbye, Milkwort" very loud.

I walk with Maistreas Eilionoir to the meeting bothan. It is different here because we are in Clann-na-Bruthaich's enclave which is not our enclave. We're on our island Skye but it is more south and a different place. The people from Raasay are still living in our enclave and they won't leave because they are mean. We tried to get them to go by asking them and talking to them lots but they won't. That is why there is the meeting to decide what we should do.

The meeting bothan is big. Some people from Clann-na-Bruthaich are inside it already and are talking in groups. There are chairs in a square shape and I count them and there are eighteen.

"Take a seat," says Maistreas Eilionoir.

I sit on the chair that is the closest one. It is hard and not comfortable. Maistreas Eilionoir goes away to speak to the Clann-na-Bruthaich people so I am on my own.

I am here because I am important. I am the hero. Maistreas Eilionoir said it and so did the other people. I was so brave to go all the way to Norveg in the ship with Jaime and I did the clever plan in the mountain room. I talked to the bats in my head and asked them to put out all the fires so the shadow things could come in and it worked and all the nasty deamhain were killed. That means our clan was free and I did it.

More people come into the meeting bothan who I don't know. It is boring to wait for them all. Milkwort wants to go out of my pocket so I let him. I stroke him for a little bit and then he runs down my leg and goes off to do exploring. He likes looking in new places. He will come back to me soon.

The next person to come in is Jaime. He stops near the door and looks at all the people. When he sees me he does a little wave. I wave back to him and smile a big one. Jaime is my good friend. He walks to where I am.

"Hi, Aggie," he says.

"Hello, Jaime," I say. "You can sit by m– me if you like?"

"Thanks." He sits on the chair next to my chair. Jaime is allowed to be in the meeting because he is the hero too.

All the other people sit down which means the meeting is going to start. A man called Kenrick is the only person who does not sit down. He is the clan chief of Clann-na-Bruthaich. All of the other elders from

Clann-na-Bruthaich were killed by the deamhain so he is the only one left. I thought they should call him "Maighstir" Kenrick but they don't use that word here. He has lots of creases on his face and dark hair which only grows on his beard and the sides of his head and not on the top.

"*Fàilte,*" he says, which is to mean "welcome" in the old language, "particularly to our honourable guests from Clann-a-Tuath. This meeting was requested by Eilionoir on behalf of her clan, so perhaps you would like to speak first?"

Maistreas Eilionoir nods and stands up at the same time as Kenrick sits down.

"*Mòran taing,* Kenrick," says Maistreas Eilionoir. I don't know what that one means. "And thanks to all of you for your hospitality during this last moon. It has been a difficult time for us all, but particularly for my clan, as I'm sure you can appreciate. While we are enormously grateful to be able to stay here, what we really want is to go home." Her voice is scratches. She stops and does two coughs. "Despite our best efforts, negotiations with the people of Raasay have come to nothing; they are resolute in their decision to remain in our enclave. So now we must decide upon a new course of action. This isn't about pride; this is about what's right. It is our home, and it was taken from us.

"We have been here nearly a month now, and we are beginning to feel like we're outstaying our welcome. Some of you are not keen for us to remain here indefinitely – that much has been made clear – and I understand your concerns. This is your home and you are protective of it, just as we are of ours. But if we do not reclaim our enclave, we have nowhere else to go.

"I implore you to pledge your support, to take up arms and march north by our side. It was always agreed that we would try and resolve this conflict without bloodshed, and that is still our intention. The Raasay islanders are not as skilled at fighting as we are, so will not wish to engage in combat if it can be avoided. A fierce show of force should be enough to convince them to leave. With your help, I have every confidence we will be successful."

She sits back down with a big nod.

"Your voice is heard with respect," says Kenrick. "I can only apologize if you feel our hospitality is waning. You know you have our full support, but – after all we've been through – it's difficult for me to ask my people to put their lives in danger again so soon."

"May I respectfully point out that if it wasn't for Agatha and Jaime, you wouldn't have any people *to* risk," says Maistreas Eilionoir. "They'd all still be rotting in a prison cell in Norveg."

"We would have found a way out," says Catriona. She's another important one from Clann-na-Bruthaich. She is young but her hair is not nice and her face is angry. "You cannot make demands of us now in recompense for assistance we never requested."

Maistreas Eilionoir does a humph.

"I disagree," says a different woman who is thin and has sad eyes. "Clann-a-Tuath wants what's theirs by right, and they deserve nothing less. While we were prisoners in the mountain, I dreamt of nothing but home. I'm sure it was the same for us all. Is it fair that we should be granted our dream yet deny them theirs? I, for one, am willing to risk my life to help them."

"Your support is received with heartfelt gratitude," says Maistreas Eilionoir.

"If you're so convinced that threatening the Raasay islanders will work, why didn't you do it weeks ago?" asks a Clann-na-Bruthaich man.

"We needed time to regain our strength," says Lenox. He is the Hawk from my clan who taught me how to be a good Hawk. The deamhain killed all the other elders from our clan so Maistreas Eilionoir had to choose new people to do the deciding for Clann-a-Tuath just for now. Lenox is one of them and so am I and so is Jaime. "The time to act is now. The longer we leave it, the more time they have to bolster their defences. We've already given them too long to prepare."

"But what if your plan doesn't work? What if they're not scared into leaving, as you predict?" asks Kenrick. "We will have no option but to fight. Do we really want to risk more death? I know you don't consider this your home, but it could be. After the losses we suffered in the mountain, there is plenty of room for all of us here. There's no reason why you can't just stay."

"I'm afraid that's incorrect," Catriona says to Kenrick,

"and you do not speak for us all." Everyone looks at her. "Our food supplies are disastrously low. You've all seen it – the meal rations have been getting increasingly smaller for weeks, and they will continue to do so. Our crops failed while we were in the mountain and, since the deamhain burned most of our boats, even fishing is proving problematic. The truth is simple: we will not survive the winter with this many mouths to feed."

"So you want us to leave yet are unwilling to help us do so?" says Maistreas Eilionoir.

Catriona sucks in her cheeks and does not reply.

A man speaks next, then a woman and then Lenox again. When Lenox talks I watch his eyebrows going up and down and up and down. The meeting is getting more boring. I'd rather be up on the enclave wall doing the looking out. I'm a Hawk again now and that is the best ever. Maistreas Eilionoir said I'm allowed to be one because I am the hero. I promised to do the best looking ever. It is a different wall because it is Clann-na-Bruthaich's wall but it is still being a Hawk.

After lots more talking, Kenrick says that everyone has been heard. That is not true. I have not been heard.

"What about— me?" I say. Everyone looks at me and now I wish I didn't say it.

"You are at liberty to say whatever you like, Agatha," says Kenrick. "What are your thoughts on the matter?"

"I think we should f– fight them. I am not afraid. I am the hero. It is our— home and they are wr– wrong to— to be there."

23

"Enlightening," says Catriona.

"Thank you, Agatha," says Kenrick. "If no one has anything further to add, I draw this meeting to a close. Let us sleep on the matter and we will vote at dusk tomorrow. The majority decision will be final."

People start to leave the bothan. Everyone is talking to each other about the things that were said.

"I'm going to the cookboth," I say to Jaime. "Do you want to come— with me?"

"No thanks, Aggie," Jaime says. "I'm pretty tired. That meeting exhausted me."

"Okay. See you later, Jaime."

I leave the bothan and walk to the cookboth. I'm hungry. Evening meal was a long time ago and it was a very small one because we have to do the rations. I will smile my biggest smile at the Stewer and say please and then he will give me something to eat. They always say okay to me because I am the hero. I will get some food for Milkwort too.

I tell Milkwort where we are going, but he doesn't answer. At first, I am panic that I can't speak to him again like in Scotia when I couldn't do it. Then I remember that he is still in the meeting bothan. I left him and I forgot. I hope he will not be cross with me. I run back to the meeting bothan as fast as I can which is not very fast but I am trying. No one is outside any more. Everyone has gone.

I open the door. The lanterns are still lit inside but no one is there. Before I even call for Milkwort he runs up my leg. He saw me come in. It tickles only a little bit. He is a good vole. I say sorry for leaving him here and tell him my plan which is to get some food for both of us and he is happy about that.

Wait. Someone is talking in whispers. I only just heard it. It's coming from the room next to this one. I didn't know there was a room there. I go to the door of it. It is open only a little bit. I look in and there are two people there who are Kenrick and Catriona. They cannot see me. It is rude to listen to other people when they do not know that you are there. I am not rude but I do listen.

"This is a democracy, Catriona, not a dictatorship. I respect your opinions and – for the most part – I agree with you, but I will not silence anyone's right to speak."

"You're stuck in the past," says Catriona. "Times have changed. We've all seen what happens as a result of weak leadership."

"I don't know what you are implying," says Kenrick, "but I do not appreciate the tone of your voice."

"I'm not implying anything. What I am quite clearly stating is that sometimes hard decisions need to be made. After all we've been through, you should be putting the needs of our own clan first."

"That's exactly what I am doing," says Kenrick.

"What? By giving Clann-a-Tuath half of everything we own? Half of all our food?"

"Clann-a-Tuath are earning their keep. What would you have me do? Turn them out to fend for themselves in the wild?"

"Precisely that, yes. All I care about is our clan – what precious few of us there are left – and I refuse to be manipulated by these bullish outsiders."

"You will have your vote tomorrow, the same as everyone else. Until then, I suggest you hold your tongue. Clann-a-Tuath are our guests here, and for as long as I am the chief of this clan, they will remain so." Kenrick turns to leave.

I need to hide or he will find me. Oh, it's okay, there is a different door and he is going out of that one.

"One more thing," he says to Catriona. "If you undermine me in public again, there will be consequences." Then he is gone.

Catriona is staring at the door where he left. She is not happy. I should go too but I can't stop doing the watching. She taps her fingers on the back of a chair. She looks around her even though there is no one in the room. I duck away from the door crack so she won't see me. When I look back, her hand is going under her clothes by her neck. She moves her hand around like she is searching for something. Then she finds it and she pulls it out.

I cannot even believe it.

It is Nathara's necklace. The one with all the shadow things inside. It is on Skye and that lady Catriona is holding it in her hand.

JAIME

"How did it go?" Aileen asks after I say goodbye to Aggie and step outside the meeting bothan. She's been waiting for me, eager to hear any news.

"I don't think I'm any good at playing elder," I say.

"Was anything decided?"

The other people from the meeting mill around us, continuing the debates in irritable little groups.

"Not really," I say.

"Come on, I want to hear about it."

I shrug. I don't know what to say.

"Right, come with me," she says. She grabs my hand and leads me away.

I flinch at her touch; I'm still not used to her being here, back on Skye, safe from the deamhain.

We weave in and out of bothans and around the loch that lies at the heart of Clann-na-Bruthaich's enclave. We've been here nearly a month now, but I still struggle to find my way around. Aileen appears to be navigating it just fine. She stops by the giant oak tree that Clann-na-Bruthaich use for their meetings. It's the biggest and the oldest tree in the enclave. By the light of the moon, its autumnal leaves shimmer midnight red. Aileen starts to climb.

"Wait. Surely we're not allowed...?" I say, hovering below her. I've seen people tending to the tree as if it's sacred.

"Probably not." She looks over her shoulder and gives me a conspiratorial grin.

"What if someone sees us?"

"Well, the longer you stand there dawdling, the more likely that is to happen."

I shake my head, glance behind me to check no one's watching, and then place my hands on the trunk. The first few steps are easy; hand- and footholds have been chiselled into the bark, all the way up to what they call the *speaker's branch* – a long, sturdy branch which has been cleared of its leaves. It's where Kenrick stands when he leads their meeting circles. Although they don't call them meeting circles here, because they don't stand in a circle. They just gather below him at the base of the tree.

From the speaker's branch upwards, the climbing becomes trickier. I try to copy the route Aileen's taking, but she's already several yards above me. Damp leaves slap me in the face and the rough bark crumbles away beneath my fingers. My arms start to ache. While we were at Dunnottar, Cray told me that if I kept practising with my sword it'd increase my upper-body strength. I've been training every day, but my arms still feel like weeds as I pull myself from branch to branch. I'm out of breath by the time I reach Aileen, who's settled herself on a neat perch with enough space for both of us.

"Did we really have to come all the way to the top?" I ask her.

"Shhh. Look at the view."

Now I see why she wanted to bring me here. We're so high, we can see straight over the enclave wall, for miles around. The pitch-black water between us and the mainland shimmers with a mesmerizing glow as it tears up the reflection of the moon.

Clann-na-Bruthaich's enclave is closer to the mainland than ours is, but in this light Scotia is nothing but a gloom in the distance. What happened there already feels like a lifetime ago. Whenever I think about it, my heart aches with ... I don't know what. Grief or fear or longing or something. I can't quite work it out.

"So, tell me everything," says Aileen.

"There's not much to say, really." I recount the arguments that went back and forth without any resolution, and explain about the vote that's been agreed for tomorrow night.

"Which way are you going to vote?"

"I don't know. It's too much pressure. I preferred it when the elders made all the decisions for me." A small bird flies towards us, as if to land in the tree, then changes its mind, altering direction at the last moment with a dramatic swoop. "How would you vote?"

"All I know is that this will never feel like home," she says. "I'm as desperate as everyone else is to go back to our enclave, and some members of Clann-na-Bruthaich clearly aren't happy with us staying here any more. Like Catriona; she's made it obvious she wants us gone."

"She didn't hold back at the meeting. She's worried there won't be enough food for both clans over the winter. If it was up to her, we'd be turfed out by morning."

"Miserable *gobhar*. And ungrateful too; we've been working our hands raw here. Maybe we should just go back to Norveg. At least they wanted us there…"

I don't laugh. I don't even give her a polite smile.

"Oh come on, it was a joke," she says. She knocks my side with her shoulder, then starts laughing, either at her own joke or at my unwillingness to acknowledge it.

Her laughter cracks right through me. I can't bear it. Ever since we came back, we've been pretending that nothing happened, that everything is the same between us, but it's not.

"What happened in Scotia, Jaime?" she says as if she knows that's what I'm thinking about. I can't help feeling that's the real reason she's brought me up here: to ask me that question. It's not the first time she's asked.

"I don't want to talk about it."

"Maybe it would do you good. I know it's hard, but it might help."

"Sorry, Aileen. I … I just can't right now."

"I only want to help. I'm supposed to be your best friend. But since we've come back—"

"I said no."

We sit in a silence as thick as cold stew. I want to talk to her about it. I do. But I can't. There's no room in my head for it all. If I tell her what happened to me, she'll tell me what happened to her, and I can't face hearing about that, either. The reality of everything she suffered would engulf the positivity of the rescue.

"It's getting cold. Are you ready to head back down?" she asks after a while.

"You go."

"I don't mind waiting with you."

"I'd rather be on my own."

She's staring at me. I know if I turn to her I'll see the hurt etched into her face. She's never been good at hiding her emotions.

"Things are better than they were," she says, giving my hand a slight squeeze.

"I know."

She lowers herself down. The leaves whisper to one another as she descends.

Why am I being so unreasonable? She's only trying to help, to be a good friend. All I wanted – through all those weeks of torment – was to find her alive and bring her home again. So why isn't that now enough?

I spin the metal bracelet around my wrist. It's the one Aileen gave me on the day I married Lileas. I wondered that morning if Aileen felt jealous. Not of the fact

31

that I was being coupled with someone else – Aileen and I have never felt that way about each other – but because there was a stranger entering our lives who had the potential to change our relationship. The thought was laughable at the time; my friendship with Aileen was all that mattered to me, and I couldn't imagine anything ever coming between us. Now Lileas is dead and Aileen and I... Well, it's not the same.

The tree smells damp, of fresh rain and old earth. Above me, a spider is making a web between two branches. It scurries back and forth with intricate precision. How much simpler life would be if we could all create a new home that quickly, and whenever someone came along and destroyed it, we'd just move on and make another. I reach up towards the web, attracted by its fragility. I'm careful not to touch it; I don't want to undo the spider's work.

There was a time when everything felt great. When I saw my clan walk into the mountain chamber after the battle and realized that they were free – the elation I felt in that moment was real. And the whole journey back was a blur of happiness and celebration. It's since returning to Skye that the darkness has crept in, like something's not quite right, or like what we achieved wasn't enough.

But we're here, back on Skye. I succeeded. We succeeded, Agatha and I. Our clan is alive. Aileen is alive. Konge Grímr and the mountain deamhain were defeated. I should feel proud and full of joy, grateful for everything and everyone around me, yet I feel nothing. What's wrong with me?

It doesn't help that we can't return to our own enclave. We're in limbo here, unsettled and uncertain. After the traumas in the mountain, everyone's craving the stability that only our own walls can grant us. I see it in the eyes of my clan. No one's happy; we're all just pretending.

The spider has gone. I stare at the half-finished web, waiting for the spider to reappear, but it doesn't come back. I swipe up, tearing the weightless threads from their moorings. The destroyed web clings to my fingertips. I immediately regret doing it. I wipe the guilt away on my trousers and hurry down the tree before the spider returns and realizes what I've done.

It's a lot darker now, and quiet too; most people have already gone to bed. My stomach growls. The reduction in food portions has done nothing to improve tensions in the enclave. As I make my way to the communal bothan I now sleep in, I try not to jump at every shadow that moves. *The* sgàilean *are gone,* I remind myself. They're trapped in Nathara's necklace, lost somewhere in Norveg, far away. It doesn't stop them from haunting my dreams, though. Them, and the deamhain, and the wildwolves... There isn't a single night that I haven't woken up drenched in sweat.

A group of people emerge from behind a low-walled bothan. From the way they're stumbling and supporting one another, it's clear they've been drinking. People from Clann-na-Bruthaich drink a lot. Either their elders were more relaxed about it than ours, or they've started drinking more since returning.

"Hey, you're Jaime, right?" one of them says.

"Yes."

He plonks an arm on my shoulder. "Our *rescuer*. Our *hero*." He says the words too loud in my ear, accompanied by flecks of spit. "I've never thanked you... Thank you." He belches, smothering my face with the smell of sour fruit.

"I don't want your thanks," I say.

"Leave him alone," says a woman, tugging at his other arm.

"We've been talking about you." His tone sharpens, edging towards hostility.

"Have you?" I ask.

The woman gives up trying to pull him away. The rest of his friends loiter around us.

"Rumour has it the room was evenly split at the meeting this evening," says a different woman. "And that the only person who didn't speak up was you."

I can't deny that.

"So we're thinking your vote is going to be an important one," says the man. "Maybe *the most* important one." He lifts his arm and grips my shoulder, a little too hard. His drunkenness disappears, replaced by an intense clarity. "You need to vote against the attack." Is he threatening me? "We've been through enough. I'm sorry about what's happened to your enclave – we all are – and we're grateful to you for rescuing us, but our clan has been through enough. Stay here if you like, or don't, I don't care, but either way, we're not about to fight your battles for you. Whatever Kenrick might be promising, if it comes down to it, and you vote to fight those *meirlich* in your enclave, we won't be by your side. You hear me?" He looks me dead in the eye. "You and your clan are on your own."

SIGRID

Granpa Halvor turns over a piece of bark.

"Snow," he says, lookin at the picture on it. His hand hovers over the other barks what are laid out on the rug.

"Come on, Granpa," I say. "We just had that one."

The barks are facedown and cut square so they all look the same. He should know where the other snow is; I turned it over two turns ago. He chooses the bark next to it and flips it over.

"Mountain," he ses, shakin his head. He puts both squares back where they were.

"You gotta pay more attention, Granpa," I say. I turn over the two barks with snow on, then the two mountains cuz I know where they are and all. The next one I turn over is grass, and I find that match too. I add them all to my pile, which is hek towerin now. Granpa Halvor's only got two pairs, and even those ones I helped him with. It's always like this when we play. He

36

doesn't mind, though – he loves seein me do it, like he's impressed evry time. It's easy for me; if I see somethin once, I'll know it for always.

"I've been thinkin about what you said," I say as I flip over another couple of barks. "About havin choices and makin the right ones... What if I went north and joined Mal-Rakki's army?"

"Pah! Don't even joke. You'd be runnin to your death."

"You're the one who's always tellin me how great he is."

"And evry word of it is true, but you're too young to be joinin no rebel army. Until Mal-Rakki returns, all we can do is wait."

"But why hasn't he returned yet? How long we gotta wait?"

Granpa Halvor's convinced that Mal-Rakki – the White Fox – is still alive, but he's probly the only person in the whole country who's sure. Mal-Rakki was Konge Grímr's brother, but he disagreed with how the king was rulin, so Konge Grímr tried to kill him. Mal-Rakki managed to escape and he was forced into hidin. A few years back, Konge Grímr claimed he found him and had him executed, but Granpa ses he was only lyin to trick us all. I used to think that too, cuz no one ever saw no body, but if Mal-Rakki's still alive, where the skit is he? Now that Konge Grímr's gone, Mal-Rakki should've come out from wherever it is he's been hidin, with all the other rebels. No one's seen no peep of him, though.

"He's comin," Granpa Halvor ses. "Soon. And then we'll all be set free."

"What do you mean 'free'? We're not slaves."

Granpa scoffs, loud as a pigburp. "We may not be chained up or kept in prisons, but believe me, we're slaves all the same, and no mistakin. Workin hard day and night, then handin half or more of everythin we worked for over to the king. The fact that he's dead now's not gunna change nothin. What do you think's gunna happen next? Same thing I seen time and time again all my life: someone new'll take his place, take his power, and everythin'll stay exactly how it was. That's why we need Mal-Rakki, more than ever. If he was king, evrythin'd be diffrunt. He believes in a better life for all of us, not just for those in charge. *Evryone deserves the chance to live their greatest possible life;* that's what Mal-Rakki ses, and he's gunna make sure that happens. He's gunna come back and free us, and then evrythin'll be better. May the will of Øden assure it."

"Isn't it Øden's will for us to serve our king?" I ask it on purpose to make Granpa skapped.

"*Tush!* Course it isn't. I taught you better than that. You know as well as I do that's just the excuse they give to get evrythin they want. The king's just a man, same as you and me. Well, you're a girl, but you get my meanin. Those in power are always abusin Øden's name, tellin us what we gotta do because it's the *will of Øden.* Well, looks like Øden finally had enough of their lies. Sent that curse of shadows to wipe them clean out, didn't he?

Good riddance to them. They made a mockery of his name, of his values, of evrythin he holds true..."

Talkin about the king always gets Granpa fiery. He hates all the things what Konge Grímr used to do, pretendin it was for the sake of Øden: fightin bloodsplash wars, enslavin rottens from overseas, takin all our foods and our pennies... I gotta change the subject or he'll never stop yappin.

"It's your turn," I say.

He doesn't flip over no barks. He's still lookin at me. *"Evryone deserves the chance to live their greatest possible life,"* he ses. "That includes you, Sigrid. Especially you, and don't you forget it."

The door opens with a bang. I jump to my feet. It's Mamma. She crashes in and somethin breaks. Sure as the moon she's been drinkin today. I take a step back but she grabs my arm before I'm outta reach. Swear Øden she's got the strength of a growler when she's been neckin.

"Come on, girl. Time to go."

"Go where?" I'm tryin to pull my arm away even though I know there's no use.

"Wait, we're playin here," ses Granpa Halvor. He's standin up now too.

"We haven't got time for no games," ses my mother, and she kicks the barks on the rug to prove it. "I got someone hek important for you to meet."

"Who we meetin? Who's important?" I ask.

"You'll see," she ses. She has this look on her face

that's all pleased with herself and isn't just the drink talkin.

"Let go of her arm," Granpa Halvor ses. "You'll hurt her."

"You tellin me how to take care of my own daughter now?" my mother ses to him. She looks at him with stormfire eyes.

Granpa doesn't say nothin. I don't say nothin neither.

"Come on, then," my mother ses, and she takes me outta Granpa Halvor's shack.

Granpa tries to follow us, but he can't keep up cuz of the twist in his knee.

"I'll be fine, Granpa," I shout over my shoulder. "I'll come see you when we get back."

"I love you, Sigrid," he replies. His voice cracks a little when he ses it.

Mamma tuts and drags me down the hills. We walk for a hek long time. She doesn't let go of me for a blink, like she thinks I'm gunna try and run away or somethin. I'm not gunna run away; I haven't got nowhere to run to. Few times I stumble cuz she's pullin so fast.

"Keep up," she ses, and then she pulls even more and goes even faster. It's hurtin, but I'm used to that.

Once we're faraways from Granpa Halvor's shack, I start seein more people goin the same way we're headin. There's only one place I know in this direction: Sterkr Fjall – the hollow mountain, where the king used to live. It's small in the distance but gettin closer. All kinds of bad mess happened there. Granpa Halvor told me. People came from over the sea and brought death shadows with them, what killed the whole lot of them in the mountain: the king, dead; his guards, dead; evryone, dead.

So why we headin there?

There's been rumours of someone new already stepped into Konge Grímr's dead boots, but I don't know nothin about that. Like Granpa Halvor ses, it's not likely to be anyone good. Unless Mal-Rakki *has* come back, and that's who we're goin to meet? My heart skips a beat thinkin how hek *ríkka* that would be.

My mother stubs her toe on some skittin tree stump and swears loud to the high sky. She yanks my arm like it was my fault she did it.

"Maybe if we weren't goin so quick," I say.

"You shush up your mouth if you know what's good," she ses back.

I know what's good; I shush up my mouth.

When we arrive at the mountain, there's hek loads of people there. Mostly rotten folk like me and my mother – those with no pennies and no hopes. All of the children have their first ink, which means they're at least fourteen. I'm bettin they had theirs done proper, not like mine. I raise my hand to my face, the side with the ink. It's been a couple of weeks since it was done, so it's not as burnin like before. Whatever's happenin here, it's only for people who have their first ink. Must be the real reason why my mother paid all our money to that cheatin grotthief: so she could sneak me in here.

But sneak me into what? What the skit's happenin here?

We pass by the entrance of Sterkr Fjall. Granpa Halvor ses the mountain's empty now. Cursed by Øden. No one's been in since after the shadows killed evryone. It's just bats what live there now. We walk all the way around the mountain to another one what's behind it. The next mountain's got a tunnel you can go in too, and that's where all the rottens are leadin.

Inside it's hek dark, sept for blue fires here and there what light it up. I haven't never been inside a mountain before. It's hek skittin and smells harsk as hell. There's dirt all over, in big piles like whoever was diggin hasn't finished it yet. We walk around the dirt piles and then further in, until the tunnel opens into a big cave room. In the middle of the cave is a circle of blue fires. People in charge are takin all the kidlins and linin them up against the wall on the other side. I look at my mother. She smiles at me, though it's sorta drunken.

A man grips my arm and ses to my mother, "I'll take her from here." My mother lets me go and nods at me strange. Now the man's pullin me. I'm sick of evryone always pullin me. He leads me over to the wall with the others and tells me to stand between a boy with scraggin hair and a girl with a dirty face. They're both taller than I am, and they don't neither of them look too happy. The boy's first ink is a ship sailin on his cheekbone, which is for courage. The girl has a blade above her eyebrow, for cunnin. The boy is starin at my face, at my wreckmess raven with its broken neck.

"What you lookin at?" I say.

He turns away. More people come in. There's maybe thirty of us kidlins now, all against the wall around me. The adults wait on the other side. They're millin and itchin like they're nervous or somethin. Makes me get the jitters too.

"What's happenin?" I say to the girl next to me, the one with the blade ink. "Why we here?"

She flicks her eyes at me but doesn't answer. She looks scared. Evryone goes quiet then cuz there's new people comin in from deeper in the mountain. The tallest is an ugly man with a scar from his mouth to his ear. He stops in fronta the first boy and squeezes his chin in one of his thick skittin hams. Then he shoves the boy's face away and moves down the line, and he's proddin and pokin like he doesn't give two hells about nothin.

When he reaches me, he stops. He's lookin at me all close like. He's peerin at my new ink and the harsk dead raven on my face. I wonder if he knows it wasn't no proper *tatovmaðr* what did it. I look straight back at him. If he's starin at me, there isn't no reason I can't stare at him too. His scar is hek ugly. It goes across his face right through all his ink. One of his inks is a goat, and the scar cuts across its poor scraggin neck, makin it look sliced dead, same as my raven. Maybe that's what he's thinkin: our poor twin animals, both with their necks snapped, both stuck bein dead forever.

"She's a good girl. Well behaved, does what she's told." It's my mother sayin that, shoutin it from the other side of the cave. What's she shoutin that for? Some of the others mutter and one woman spits. The man with the scar tuts his teeth and moves on to the next kidlin in line – the girl with the dirty face and the blade ink. He doesn't look at her much. He grabs her arm and ses, "You'll do," and then he's pullin her away. She starts shoutin and tryin to grab her arm loose, but he's a giant of a man so she's foolin if she thinks she can break free.

"Stop making it so difficult," he ses, and with the back of his other arm he smacks her *thuk*! Right across the back of her head. Then he drags her some more and she's sobbin and her legs are scramblin to keep up.

"Let her go," I say, and I run at him and kick his leg as hard as I can. I don't know why I did that. It was a hek stupid thing to do. The man shouts out and lets go of the girl.

"You little *bikja*," he ses to me. He swings his arm at my face, but I duck out the way. Someone else grabs me from behind, and then more people are talkin and shoutin and it all goes batcrazy.

"Silence!"

The voice is loud and deep, but I can't see who said it.

"I ask you to do one simple job, and what do I get? This anarchy."

"Everything is under control, Your Supremacy."

What? *Your Supremacy* means the king, but the king is— Oh. Wait a cheatin moment. There's a man in the shadows. I can't see him too proper but now I'm lookin,

I can just about make out the antlers what grow out of the crown on his head.

Konge Grímr.

I thought he was dead. Evryone said he was dead.

"What happened?" he ses.

I don't know who he's talkin to. He sure as muck isn't talkin to me, but there's no one else replyin so I say, "This oafogre with the scar was hurtin on this girl here when he shouldn't of been, so I kicked him to make him stop."

Konge Grímr starts laughin. It's a deep laugh what sounds like the earth is breakin. "So you were bested by a little girl, were you, Bolverk?" he ses. He laughs more and other people start laughin too.

The giant man with the scar – Bolverk – is next to me, starin daggers. His nose is flarin like a wild horse and the veins in his neck are pumpin solid.

"The situation was under control," he ses.

Konge Grímr stops laughing. "Bring her to me," he ses. "I think we've found the one."

"You can't seriously be considering...?" ses Bolverk. "You don't want this one, Your Supremacy, she's nothing but trouble. And her first ink has been botched by some cheap fraud."

"Do not dare to tell me what I want," ses Konge Grímr. His voice echoes around us.

There's a silence, and then, "She's mine," ses my mother, and she's wavin her arm manic-like. She looks proud. My mother hasn't never looked proud of me before. Tears start comin to my eyes. I made her happy, even if I don't know why. She stumbles a bit from all the drink she necked earlier. "Where's my money?"

Wait. What money? What's she sayin about money for?

"You'll get paid," Konge Grímr ses.

I'm hek confused what's goin on now. This whole mornin's been confusin as hell and it sure isn't gettin no clearer.

"Come towards me, child," ses the king.

Whoever's holdin me lets go. I shake out my shoulders. Bolverk makes as if he's gunna push me, but I don't need him shovin. I go towards Konge Grímr on my own. "What you want me for?" I ask him.

He steps out of the shadows. A long fur hangs on his shoulders. In one hand he has a stick to help him balance, but mostly I'm just lookin at his eyes. Only, not his eyes, cuz he hasn't got none no more. Where they used to be is all dark and twisted with knots of skin. It's a hek mess of a face, like somethin ripped it all apart. Even though he can't see no more, he looks straight in my direction.

"You, my child," he ses, "are going to be my new eyes."

AGATHA

IT IS THE NIGHT-TIME AND IT'S DARK. I AM LYING ON my bed and I should be asleep but I'm not. I have a plan. I am the hero so I have to do it. The first part of the plan is that I need to wait. Everybody needs to be asleep for me to do the plan. I can hear from all the snoring that lots of people are asleep already but I wait some more just for being sure.

I don't like it in this bothan. It is not like the Hawk bothan in our enclave. There are people from all the different duties in it and even children. Also the bed is not comfortable. I want to go back to our enclave and live there again. The Raasay people need to leave and we need to make them leave. Maistreas Eilionoir says we can only do that if the Clann-na-Bruthaich people help us. Tomorrow is the vote and then we will know. I hope they say yes they will help.

It is enough of the middle of the night now. I get out

47

of my bed. I am already wearing my clothes and my boots which is very clever and no one knew. I walk to the door of the bothan and I am quiet. No one sees me go because they are all asleep. It is cold outside. I should have put my cloak on too. That was not the clever part. I will be quick so the blood does not freeze in my veins.

I know where Catriona's bothan is because I remembered. She is like an elder so she has a bothan that is only for her. It is next to the meeting bothan. I put my head down and I do the quickest running I can. I do not want the night Hawks to see me. I know where the night Hawks look and those are the places I don't go. All of the plan is clever because I thought about it a lot.

I stop outside Catriona's bothan. There is one window. I look in but it is too dark to see if she is inside. I think she is. It is the middle of the night so where else would she be? I open her door and no one stops me. It is very easy. I go inside.

I can see her now. She is asleep like I thought. Her bothan is small. It is only a bed and a chair and a chest. I mustn't wake her. That is the most important thing. She will hurt me if I do because I'm not supposed to be here. She is good at fighting. The best one. That is why Kenrick made her a leader person when we came back from Norveg even though she is younger. One of the other Hawks told me that. She does not look scary now. Her hair is a mess and not nice. It is the same colour as the straw coming out of her pillow. Her face is scrunchy like she is thinking bad things.

I cannot see the necklace. It is dark in this bothan so it's hard to see. The necklace is not on the chair and it's not on the chest. Maybe it's inside the chest. Or maybe she is wearing it still. Yes, that is what I think. That makes the plan harder but I can do it.

I walk to her bed. Her blanket is over her neck so I have to move it to see if the necklace is there. I shut my mouth because my breathing is too loud. I reach down and am going to move the blanket when all of her body moves. I step back and think I will scream but I don't. She is still asleep. I reach out for the blanket again and this time I move it. Only a little bit. Enough so I can see her neck and what is on it.

The necklace is there.

It's the first time I have seen it close because when the Nice Queen Nathara was wearing it I didn't see it close. The stone is big and black and shiny. I don't know how all of the shadow things fit inside. It is not big enough for them. I need to get the necklace and throw it in the sea so it will be gone forever. That is what Maistreas Eilionoir said we should do with it when we were in Norveg and she is right. If it is in the bottom of the sea, the shadow things cannot get out and hurt anyone or me. They are very bad things. I don't know why Catriona took it. It is not hers so she should not have done that. It is stealing and that is wrong. Also it is dangerous because what if the shadow things come out again? They tried to get me once and it was bad very bad. After I throw it in the sea, Maistreas Eilionoir will say that I am the hero again and so will everyone else because I did protecting my clan and am clever.

There is a twist part on the chain that is how you get it off. I move that part away from Catriona's neck and try to click it so the chain comes open. It is hard to do with my fingers. There is wet in my eyes that is sweat. I wipe it away with my hand but some more comes. The part on the chain won't come apart and I can't do it. Catriona moves again in the bed and I think she is going to wake up soon. I have to be so so quick. I cannot do the small twist part on the chain so I have to do a different way. Maybe if I pull really hard and it breaks. Then I will have it. That is the new plan.

I pick up the necklace stone and hold it in my hand. It is warm a bit. My hand is warm too with the sweating. I am strong and I can do it.

I pull as hard as I can.

Catriona's neck lifts off the pillow and her eyes open. The chain does not break. I pull again. It's still not broken. Catriona is awake and she is looking at me. She is all confused on her face and then she is angry. She grabs the necklace with her hand to stop me taking it. I pull once more my biggest yet and this time the chain breaks. It goes through Catriona's hand and I fall backwards onto the floor on my bottom. It hurts a bit but I have got the necklace in my hand and now I need to get out.

I go for the door but Catriona is there already and she is standing in front of it so I can't get out. I step back so she doesn't reach me. There is the window but it is too small to go out through there. I am trapped.

"What the hell do you think you're doing?" says Catriona. Her eyes are big and her mouth is a tight one. "Give it back."

"No!" I say.

"You're going to be in so much trouble for this. I'll have you whipped to within an inch of your life."

"It's not y– y– yours," I say.

"Give it back or I will take it back."

She is going to hurt me. She wants to hurt me. I step onto the bed to be further away from her.

"Fine, then we do it the hard way," she says.

She comes towards me slow slow and then very very fast. I fall onto the bed. I am screaming and she's on top of me. I try to kick her with my legs so she goes away. I'm holding the necklace with both my hands so I can't use them for helping me. Catriona is digging into my fingers to get them apart. I try to bite on her knuckles. She pushes hard at my head. It goes backwards and hits against the wall and hurts a very lot. She has a hold on the chain now. I still have the stone part and I fall down off the bed to get away but she keeps pulling the chain harder and is tugging it.

Something breaks on the necklace and I don't know what but when it happens my hand flies quick in the air and I let go of the black stone. It hits the wall and falls on the floor.

I don't move and neither does Catriona. We are both

looking at the black stone. It is making a hiss sound.

"What have you done?" says Catriona.

Something black is running out of the stone like water. It goes up the walls and all around. The sound gets louder and more horrible which is when I know it.

I have done a very bad thing. The necklace is open and the shadows are coming out.

JAIME

THE SCREAMING WAKES ME UP. SOMEONE'S IN PAIN. It's a distant cry, from the other side of the enclave, accompanied by more distressed shouts and muffled clamour. Other people are already getting out of their beds and hurrying towards the door. I leap up and join them, slipping on my boots and throwing a cloak around me as I do so. It's still dark outside, the sky so sharp it might shatter.

The yells intensify, hiding a different noise that I can't quite place. My mind is dragged back to when the deamhain stormed our enclave, to when I stood looking over the wall, watching it all happen, unable to move or do anything about it. I shake my head as my heart starts to race. *No, no, no, no, no.*

"We're under attack. Seize your weapons!" someone shouts.

There's an outbreak of movement and chaos.

How is this happening? We're supposed to be safe here. Is it the deamhain? It can't be. Or the traitors from Raasay? I can't go through this again. It's supposed to be over.

I'm breathing too fast, but it's out of my control. The ends of my fingers are so numb they hurt. I slump to the floor and pull my legs into my chest. Not again. Not now. I scrunch my eyes closed. Blood rushes to my head, making my eyes pound against my eyelids.

"Jaime!"

Aileen pounces on me with worried hands. She's shaking me, trying to lift my head. "Jaime, are you hurt?" I don't open my eyes. My breathing is getting worse.

That's when I hear it. It's so clear, it's hard to believe I didn't recognize it before. I stop breathing altogether. Underneath all the other commotion is the unmistakable, hideous whispering that can only mean one thing.

Sgàilean.

How can they be here? And why are they attacking? Our blood is supposed to protect us. It's clear from the cries that, for some reason, it no longer does.

The realization sucks away my panic and replaces it with a much deeper fear. I'd always been taught that Clann-a-Tuath doesn't feel fear, but I learned in Scotia that that wasn't true. Fear is a warning, forcing us to act. I stand up, shaking off Aileen's hands.

"Fire." My throat is still tight, my legs shaky. "We need fire."

"Fire? Why?"

"It's the shadows. *Sgàilean*. They're afraid of light, especially fire."

I run back to the bothan, Aileen following close behind. There are two lanterns hanging in the doorway. I unhook them both, hand one to Aileen, and hold the second close to my chest. "Don't let go of it," I say to her.

"Okay." Aileen's eyes are wide and fierce; the reflection of the lantern's flame shakes within them. "We need to warn everyone else. I'll head west; you tell the people here. I'll circle around and meet you at the loch."

The loch. Yes. "*Sgàilean* also dislike water – they can't move through it or over it. Tell everyone to go to the loch; they'll be safe as long as they're standing in the water."

Aileen nods and bolts. It's only after she's gone that I realize I don't know how to get to the loch from here. I'll worry about that later. I go the opposite way to her, shouting at everyone I pass to find lanterns and head for the water, but people aren't listening to me; they're too caught up in their own hysteria. The whispers are drawing nearer. My heart is rampaging. Every shadow is a potential threat. I should be trying harder to warn everyone, but the darkness is too much.

I run. I don't know where, I'm just running, anywhere, away.

I raise the lantern above my head so that its light fully covers me. It bounces around with every stride. The wind slips in, ambushing the flame and almost putting it out. I lower the lantern for as long as I dare, holding it close to my body until the flame regains its strength; it's all that's keeping me alive.

I thought I was heading in the direction of the loch, but nothing looks familiar. People are still shouting throughout the enclave, but there's nobody nearby. I'm lost.

Something snags my ankle, causing me to trip. The lantern falls out of my hands. *Don't go out, don't go out.* I scramble to retrieve it. The light is dim, but it's still there. I keep running, aware now that there are *sgàilean* all around me, keeping pace, slinking through the grass just outside the lantern's glow. Their whispering is even wilder than I remember, like a hungry tide devouring sand.

I'm so distracted that I almost run straight into a tree. It's the meeting tree, which Aileen and I were in yesterday evening. It's nowhere near the loch, so I've come in completely the wrong direction. Can *sgàilean* climb trees? Of course they can: they're able to slide across any solid surface. All the same, I start to climb. A few steps up, my foot slips, and I'm back at the bottom. The whispers circle me, the sound unbearable. I scream and shout for help, but I know no one's coming.

The glow from the lantern is getting smaller. It's running out of oil. It's no longer bright enough to cover the whole of my body. I press my back into the trunk of the tree and move the lamp in erratic circles in front of me. The bark digs into my shoulder blades. Wafts of burnt metal drift through the air. The *sgàilean* are poised on all sides, waiting for the flame to burn itself out. Every now and then, one of them makes a snatch for one of my limbs, deterred at the last moment by a quick flick of the lamp. I bite my lip so hard it bleeds.

Then one of the *sgàilean* gets me. It grabs hold of my left elbow and digs in with the pain of a thousand needles. I swing the lantern at it, except I can't tell where its body is, so I'm swinging blind. The lantern slams into the tree trunk and shatters the moment it hits. I sense the *sgàilean* freeze, as if holding a collective breath. But the fire hasn't gone out. The little oil that was left spreads onto the tree trunk, and the fire leaps across with it, gorging on its newfound fuel. Within moments, the whole tree is ablaze.

The *sgàilean* disperse at once. I take a couple of steps away from the fire and collapse onto the grass. I'm safe; they've gone. For now.

The tree is so large that the fire is visible from the whole enclave. People flock to it, attracted by the safety of its flames. The first to arrive praise me for my quick thinking. I nod without smiling. I have no intention of admitting that I started the fire by accident. Others from Clann-na-Bruthaich lament the destruction of the tree in unnecessarily loud voices, discussing what it means for the future of their people. Someone even has the kindness to tell me that Kenrick will almost certainly punish me for my vandalism. I don't really care – I'm just glad to be alive.

There's lots of speculation about how the *sgàilean* could have arrived on Skye and why they're attacking us now, when they didn't in Norveg. A couple of people ask my opinion, but I don't have any answers for them.

Despite the heat raging from the tree, we huddle beneath it, waiting out the long night until the sun starts to rise.

Dawn is sticky, like cold oats. I ask if someone will take me to the loch, but there are no volunteers, even though I insist the *sgàilean* will have retreated now that the sun has risen. In the end, we compromise, and two women agree to take me, under the protection of some flaming branches. In truth, I'm happier that we have fire with us too.

It's a misty morning, making everything in the enclave seem less real. We pass abandoned weapons and broken lanterns – items that were discarded during the struggle. I'm grateful to the mist for hiding the majority of what occurred.

Dew from the grass brushes over my boots and by the time we reach the loch, my ankles are sodden. I'm heartened, however, by the number of people standing in the shallows. Aileen must have spread the word fast enough to save the majority of our clan. I strain to check and, yes, she's there, along with Agatha and Maistreas Eilionoir. They're shivering, but alive.

Catriona wades towards me as I approach.

"Someone burned our tree," she says.

I drop the branch I'm holding into the loch. The flames wither away with a sharp hiss.

"Yes," I say, unable to look her in the face. "That was me..."

"We'll deal with your destruction later. Right now, I need to hear everything you know about these shadows."

She's standing too close to me, her jaw tight.

"Where's Kenrick?" I ask.

She doesn't answer my question. "Come with me," she says. I do as I'm told and follow her away from the loch.

An emergency meeting is set up in the bothan we used yesterday, with the same people in attendance. All except Kenrick. Agatha sits on her own and refuses to speak to me when I ask if she's okay. It doesn't take me long to discover why.

"Kenrick is dead," Catriona starts. "The shadows took him. I watched them drag away his broken body with my own eyes. He is not the only casualty from last night, and the girl who caused it all to happen is sitting right here among us. If you're looking for someone to blame, there she is." She points at Agatha with a rigid arm.

Agatha nearly falls over in her haste to stand up. "It's not my fault, it's y– yours!" she says. "You shouldn't have— taken the necklace in the— first place. It wasn't yours and you sh– shouldn't have taken it."

All eyes are on Catriona now. She addresses everyone.

"It's true I took the amulet from the Scotian

queen – I slipped it from her neck while we were still in Norveg. I have no shame in my actions; it contained the greatest weapon we have ever known. Yet this woman," – she gestures to Maistreas Eilionoir – "was planning to throw it in the ocean. Another example of weak leadership."

"It is riddled with the darkest blood magic," says Maistreas Eilionoir. "I should not need to remind you that magic is not *dùth*. That necklace has no place on this island."

"It was our protection," spits Catriona, "in case the deamhain should return. Have you forgotten so soon the threat they represent? Their attack on our enclave is scoured into every fibre of my being: the people we lost that day, the amount we have suffered since... There was no way I was going to leave us vulnerable to another in-vasion. The necklace was our insurance against that. A true leader would have recognized its necessity."

"A *true* leader would not have been so reckless," says Maistreas Eilionoir.

"It would have been safe under my protection had that *retarch* not tried to steal it."

"You will not speak to her like that." Maistreas Eilionoir's voice booms. She stands up to add extra weight to her words. "Do I really have to keep remind-ing you that if it weren't for Agatha, you would all still be locked away in the bowels of a mountain."

"Do *I* have to keep reminding *you* that this is *our* home? Do not outstay your welcome."

The two women stare at each other for an uncomfortable amount of time. It is Lenox who breaks the silence.

"We are not here to lay blame," he says. "Rather, to decide what must be done. Come nightfall, the *sgàilean* will return, and we need to be prepared."

"Correct," says Catriona, still staring at Maistreas Eilionoir. "Jaime, you know more about these entities than anyone. Why did they attack us now, when they didn't in the mountain? I was told they only hurt people with foreign blood."

My cheeks flush as everyone turns their heads towards me.

"I ... I don't know," I say. My throat feels like it's full of thistles, making it difficult to get the words out. "They've changed somehow. Maybe because of Queen Nathara? Because she died, I mean." Catriona is still staring at me, so I carry on talking. "The *sgàilean* were made to serve the royal family, and Nathara was the last one alive. The shadows stayed at Dunnottar Castle – even after the plague killed everyone else in Scotia – because of her; the magic that created them tethered them to her somehow. But now that she's gone, they don't have anyone to serve. Maybe the rules that bound them died when Nathara did." I raise my shoulders to my ears. "That's only a guess, though."

"How do we destroy them?" Catriona asks.

"I don't know," I say.

"Then how do we get them back in the amulet?"

"I don't know that, either... Nathara had a special

phrase she used to say, but I ... can't remember what it was. And I'm not sure they'd listen to anyone but her."

Catriona exhales sharply through her nose. "Some use you are," she says.

Hot beads of sweat gather around the base of my neck. "Well. There is one person ... who might be able to help."

"Oh?"

"Um. I don't know but... There was a man. He called himself the Badhbh."

"The Badhbh? What sort of a name is that? Who is he?"

"He's the one who made the *sgàilean*, with King Balfour. I found his diary in Dunnottar Castle. He's one of the few people to survive the plague, so he could still be alive. If he is, he might know how to stop them."

"How do we find him?" All of Catriona's questions come out as a bark.

"I..." I hate myself for having to give the same answer yet again. "I don't know."

Catriona looks like she might spit at my feet. Or on my face.

"His last diary entry said he was going to travel west," I say. "So maybe he's somewhere ... west?"

"The whole of Scotia is west of Dunnottar," she says. "That doesn't help us in the slightest. He could be anywhere. If he's even still alive. The plague was over forty years ago; anything could have happened to him since then. Anyone have any *useful* suggestions?"

I shrink into my chair as another wave of heat rushes to my cheeks.

"We should send runners to the other Skye clans without delay," says Maistreas Eilionoir. "They need as much warning as possible in order to prepare their defences for tonight. As for here, we should erect fires around the entire enclave with enough wood to burn through the night. The fire will protect us until we discover how to make the *sgàilean* return to the necklace."

Catriona sucks in her hollow cheeks. "Wait," she says. "We can use the *sgàilean* to our advantage. We know about their existence and we know how to protect ourselves from them. Once we share this information with our allies – the other clans on Skye – then the shadows will have no one left to attack except the Raasay islanders. The *sgàilean* will clear out your enclave for you, leaving you free to return."

There's a moment of silence, then Maistreas Eilionoir replies, "What you're suggesting is mass murder."

"Is it really any different to what you suggested yesterday: storming the enclave and killing everyone yourself?"

"That is not what I was suggesting. I proposed a show of force to convince them to surrender. That's completely different. And if our advance did lead to battle, we would kill only their leaders and anyone who tried to stop us. All other lives would be spared."

"Do you want your home back or not?" Catriona scowls. "This is the perfect solution."

"There are children in that enclave. Innocent lives," says Lenox.

He's right. It'll be full of children just like Lileas, the girl from Raasay who I was forced to marry. The girl I failed. I imagine a whole group of children playing, and every one of them has her face.

"Also there is H– Hector and— and Edme," says Agatha. "They are Lileas's parents and they are nice people and kind. Lileas told me."

Catriona acts as if Agatha hasn't spoken. "These people chose their fate the moment they took over your enclave. Do you think they cared about *your* children? Or what the deamhain would do to them? Of course they didn't. So I don't know why you're so keen to offer them your mercy. This is exactly the kind of strong leadership I have been talking about – the difficult decisions that must be made." She sweeps her hair back from her forehead. "We have no time to vote with stones, so let's see a show of hands. All those in favour of not warning the Raasay islanders about the *sgàilean*, vote now."

One by one, hands start to rise throughout the room, all of them belonging to people from Clann-na-Bruthaich. A few shoot up with confidence. Others drift up after some intense staring from Catriona. It's incredible to witness the power she has over them; in their fragile state, they're easily swayed.

My hand stays pressed against my leg. I've seen what *sgàilean* do to people. Every time I close my eyes, the memories are there. It was my idea to take the shadows

64

to Norveg, and while I don't regret that decision as such, I can't vote to inflict that fate upon anyone else. The chiefs of Raasay are our enemies, but not everyone there is.

"And all those against?" Catriona sounds bored with the formality.

I am the first person to put my hand up, closely followed by Agatha. Maistreas Eilionoir, Lenox and a few people from Clann-na-Bruthaich also raise their hands.

"You don't get to vote," Catriona snaps at Agatha. "Not that it makes any difference. With only seven votes against, it is agreed: the people of Raasay are not to be warned about the *sgàilean*."

"No!" shouts Agatha. Her chair clatters to the floor as she leaps from her seat. "You are wrong. You can't d– do this."

I agree with her – of course I do – yet I remain in my seat, staring at the floor. My whole body has shut down, my thoughts turned to nothing.

"We *can* do this, and we will," Catriona says. "And don't forget: the *sgàilean* are only a threat because of *your* stupidity."

"It's you who is— stupid!" Agatha's fists are two tight balls. She roars in frustration and kicks her chair, then marches out of the bothan. Catriona watches her go with a flicker of a smirk on her face. Just when I thought I couldn't despise her any more.

"As I was saying," says Catriona, "the consensus is

65

clear: we will not seek to contain the *sgàilean* until the Raasay islanders have been destroyed. *Leig leis.*"

"*Leig leis,*" echo most of the people in the room.

"Let's hope they do it soon," says Catriona, once again looking at Maistreas Eilionoir. "The sooner you leave our enclave, the better."

SIGRID

"THERE'S NOTHING QUITE LIKE THE SMELL OF THE open sea," ses Konge Grímr. He's talkin more to himself than to me. "Tell me what it looks like."

He made me describe it to him yesterday and all, and the day before that, and it hasn't changed none since then.

"There's loadsa water," I say. "Evrywhere … Your Supremacy." I gotta call him that, even though it's hek skap.

"I need more than that," he ses. He always wants more. I'm not good at describin.

"I can't see nothin but water. I don't know what else you want me to say. It's all movin about up and down. And it's blue."

"What kind of blue?" he says.

"Miserable blue," I say.

His mouth twitches a little at that. "Better," he ses.

It was the bats what ripped out his eyes – the white bats what live in Sterkr Fjall. They got him durin the fight with the people from overseas. He's hek fiery about it and all, talks about it all the time and I haven't got no choice but to listen.

He starts walkin towards the front of the boat. *Wind Serpent*. That's the boat's name. He uses the sides to guide him, and I've gotta follow cuz of the skap trappin chain what's tied on my wrist. The other end is tied to the king's so evrywhere he goes, I go too. Sept when he's washin or wastin, of course. When he's doin that, I'm left chained outside, but I still gotta hear it and smell it and all.

I've been chained to him for a week now. Ever since the mountain. Ever since my mother – my own mother…

I never want to see her again. She's nothin to me now. How could she do it? Send me away, chained to this grotfiend? I bet she's already necked the money they paid her. She'd better hope I never see her again, cuz if I do there isn't no sayin what I'd do.

They never let me say goodbye to Granpa Halvor; that's what makes me most fiery. What if my mother doesn't tell him the truth about where I'm gone and he never knows what happened to me? Right now, I don't know if I'll ever go home again. All I know is we're goin to Ingland, which is a diffrunt country a long ways over the sea. I don't know why we're goin there. I hear a lot of things bein chained to the king all the day, but he hasn't never mentioned why we're goin where we're goin.

This is my life now, and it's a hek wreckmess of a one. I tried breakin out of the chain. Course I did. But it's stuck hek tight, and Konge Grímr is dirty clever and always hides the keys too far away for reachin.

He stops in a sudden and I'm so busy thinkin about my mess of a life that I nearly crash into him. We're close to the front of the boat now, on the platform above the open deck. Most of evryone else is rowin beneath us. It's cold. It's not spewin no more, but it looks like it might start again soon. I don't like bein on the boat. My stomach feels like dead fish the whole time. Three days we've been on the sea and it's not gettin no better.

"*Róhh! Róhh! Róhh!*" shouts the man at the front. He's keepin evryone rowin in time.

Konge Grímr reaches out with his hand to find my head. His rank scraggin fingers poke about until they locate my ear and then he leans in and whispers, "Look at all the people below. Is anyone rowing out of time? Who's not exerting themselves as much as the others? Tell me what you see."

I look at the hundred or more men and women rowin together as one. They're sweatin and strainin their nashers. When they see me lookin, they start rowin even harder, like they know what the king asked me, like they know I'm spyin for him.

"*Róhh! Róhh! Róhh!*" the man keeps shoutin.

"Evryone's rowin good," I say.

"Very well," ses Konge Grímr. "As it should be."

69

"They're sweatin rivers cuz they know I'm watchin," I say. "They're scared of you."

"No," Konge Grímr ses. "They're scared of *you*. They know you'll tell me the truth." He twists his back, makin his spine go click. "Why do you think, out of everyone in that room, I chose you to be my eyes? A meeker, more placid child would have been much easier to control, less likely to cause trouble... But I needed my people to know that my new eyes were ruthless, that they would not hold back, that they would not be scared to speak up if they witnessed someone trying to deceive me. That little display you gave in the mountain was a perfect demonstration. You're more like me than you realize." Well, that isn't no compliment, that's for hek sure. I'm not nothin like this grotweasel. "It *was* the right decision to choose you ... wasn't it?" he asks me.

"Yes," I say, cuz what else am I sposed to say to that?

"Good," ses Konge Grímr. "Because if you ever betray me, I will crush you with my own bare hands. Don't ever forget that."

I swallow nothin and turn out front, facin the water. There's a grizzlin wind what's splashin my face with seadrops. In front of me, a bulkin great sea dragon looms up outta the front of the boat, with flowers and swirlins carved in its neck. It's sposed to stop monsters from attackin. Granpa Halvor must've told me that. Can't see what no hunk of wood's gunna do to save us – carved up all pretty or not – but there you go.

70

"I've had enough air. Take me back to the cabin," ses Konge Grímr.

The cabin is the inside part where the king sleeps. I hold his elbow like how he taught me and lead him to it. On the way, we walk past the ugly giant man with the scar, Bolverk. He's not rowin; he's the leader of Konge Grímr's invasion force, so he doesn't have to. He's the king's favourite, I reckon. He stands there watchin me with a mad-fox snarl. I haven't never felt so hated by one person before. He's still skapped I kicked his leg when we were in the mountain, specially cuz it made evryone else laugh. He points at me and then puts his finger across his neck like he's sayin he's gunna kill me. I spit at his feet to show I'm not scared.

"Who spat?" ses Konge Grímr.

I shouldn't of done that. The king's askin me, but Bolverk answers. "It was me, Your Supremacy. Forgive me. I didn't see you walking past."

"I'm the one with no eyes," ses Konge Grímr. "I suggest you use yours better in future."

"Of course, Your Supremacy."

Why'd Bolverk lie about the spittin? Does he think I owe him somethin now or what? I don't owe him nothin.

Konge Grímr hits my shoulder, impatient to keep walkin. Bolverk doesn't stop lookin at me for one blink as we go past.

*　*　*

At night, Konge Grímr makes me sleep next to him, on the floor. It's hek freezin. I don't even have no blanket or nothin. Even when we're sleepin, I'm still chained to him, so evry time he moves he's pullin on my arm and jostlin, which isn't no way to get a good night's nappin. I haven't slept proply in days. Not since my own mother let them take me away to the end of the world on this harsk skittin boat.

There's a tear snakin down my face, but I'm not cryin. I wanna visit Granpa Halvor. I want him to make me sweetmilk and tell me tales of Mal-Rakki, and promise evrythin's gunna be okay. But it's not. His shack is a long ways away now. A hek long ways. I slide my hand into my pocket and touch the stone what's in there. It's the one from the plum what Granpa Halvor gave me. I've still got it. I'm never throwin it away. I hold it tight in my hand and pray to Øden for sleep to come.

Somethin wakes me. I musta dozed off. First I'm thinkin Konge Grímr was pullin on the chain in his sleep again, but he's still on his side and the chain's hangin slack. Musta been somethin else. It's dark in the cabin so I can't see almost nothin. I squint into the blackness. Was that somethin movin? A shadow by the window? Maybe a death shadow, like the ones what killed evryone in the mountain? Well, not evryone, cuz the king's not dead, is he? More's poor to me. I keep thinkin about the shadows ever since Granpa Halvor told me about them. No one knows what happened to them after the fight. They could of left the mountain and hid on this boat. They could be in the walls right now.

Somethin moves again. There's definitely somethin in the cabin with us. I sit up, careful not to make the chain rattle. Maybe I should wake Konge Grímr? I'm sposed to be his eyes, after all. What if whatever's in the room's plannin on killin him dead?

Too late. The shadow leaps forwards and there's a great smackin *pwok!* right over my mouth. Somethin's holdin me around my waist, tight as a thunderclap. I'm strugglin but there isn't no way I'm gettin free.

"Where are the keys?" someone whispers. Not shadows, then. Someone who wants to take me away, but why do they wanna do that?

"Check above the bed," ses a diffrunt voice. Two people, one man one woman.

"Got it."

There's a rattle of the keys and then they start unlockin the chain. They're tryin to be quiet, but they're doin a bad job of it. If Konge Grímr wakes up they're gunna be in hek trouble. I dunno if I want him to wake or not. Am I safer chained to him or in the hands of these strangers? The skittin handslap is still tight over my mouth, so there isn't nothin I can do to wake the king even if I wanted to. The chain falls off of my wrist. The disappearin weight is a straightaways relief. Underneath, the skin on my wrist stings raw. The people drag me out in a stumble sorta way.

73

Once we're outside, the wind hits me bamsmack in my eyes and it's hek chills. I'm dragged around to the back of the boat, where there's a group of four or five people.

"We got her," ses the man who's holdin me. His voice is drunken. I got lots of experience in tellin when someone's been neckin. There's a cheer. They've all been neckin.

"What should we do with her?" ses the woman what took me.

A man steps forward. Bolverk. I shoulda guessed it would be him. It was hek stupid antagonizin him like I did. I was thinkin as long as I was tied to the king he wouldn't be able to do nothin to me, but I hadn't thought on him stealin me away like this.

"Hello, little raven," he ses to me. It's not the first time he's called me that. I hate it. He only ses it to mock my messed-up face. He leans in. His blue-inked lips peel back to show a mouthful of harsk yellow teeth. "Still think it was clever spitting at me earlier?" So that's why he took the blame: he wanted to punish me himself. I don't say nothin. I'm not apologizin. "I'm not sure if you've noticed, but you're not very popular on this boat. People think you're spying on them. And they're right, aren't they? The king's eyes, the king's spy, constantly whispering in his ear, telling him what you see, and maybe a few things that you don't. You could be telling him anything, turning him against us. I don't trust you. None of us do. Konge Grímr is a great man, but he made a poor decision choosing you. Who knows what filth you're filling his head with?"

"I haven't told him nothin but what I've seen," I say.

"Well, you won't be telling him anything any more. Throw her overboard."

"Wait! No—" But before I can say another crumb, that heavy, fat slap is over my mouth again.

They can't throw me overboard. I can't swim. If I go over, I'll drown.

The one who's holdin me is pullin me to the side. I'm strugglin to break free but there isn't no room for movin. We're at the edge now and I can see the water below. It's black, tipped with shinin glints like fish scales. I'm lifted off the deck and my head's tilted back. For a moment all I see is stars, a hundred thousand stars or more. So many stars that the sky is more star than sky. It's the most beautiful thing I've ever seen.

"Goodbye, little raven," ses Bolverk, jerkin my attention back to what's about to happen.

The man holdin me shoves me over the edge. The stars are a swirlin blur as I fall into the water.

AGATHA

It is not my fault. I was trying to do the good thing. Catriona is the bad one. She shouldn't have taken the Nice Queen Nathara's necklace and she shouldn't have worn it and if it wasn't for her none of this would have happened.

Now the shadow things are on the island and we can't stop them. Also Catriona does not want to stop them. It is her plan to let them go to our enclave and kill the people there. Some of the Raasay people are bad ones and it is right that the shadow things should get them but some of the Raasay people are good ones so it is sad.

I am outside Maistreas Eilionoir's bothan which is where I was walking. She summoned me which means she wants to see me. I think she is going to tell me off for making the shadow things come out or maybe punish me. I do not want to be punished. I knock on the door

76

and she says "enter" so I go in. She is sat on the floor with her legs crossed.

"Hello, Maistreas Eilionoir," I say.

"Agatha," she says. "Sit." She does not look happy.

I sit.

"What you did last night was beyond foolish. You put the lives of every single person in this enclave at risk."

"I—" I try to say more, but she does not let me.

"You made terrible decisions, acted impulsively and did not think through the consequences." My head is sad. I do not like Maistreas Eilionoir to say what she is saying. "As punishment, you are forbidden on the wall until further notice."

"That's not fair!"

"Silence! Instead, you are to walk around the outside of the enclave and count how many paces it is in its entirety."

"No," I say. "I don't want to do that and I won't d– do it." It sounds like a boring job and a not important one.

"Yes, you will. Because I am your elder and I am telling you that's what you must do. To determine how best to defend ourselves from the *sgàilean* we need to know the exact size of the enclave. So you will go outside and count the paces. Understood?" I do understand but I do not tell her yes. "The *sgàilean* are a risk to all of us now, not just you."

What does she mean not just me? Maybe she's talking about what Knútr the nasty deamhan said when the shadow things tried to get me on the ship. He said I am a foreign person like him but he was wrong.

"I am not a f– foreign person," I say.

Maistreas Eilionoir's forehead is crinkles. "Why do you say that?"

"I am from Clann-a-Tuath and from Skye."

"Of course you are."

I do not want to ask it because what if the answer is bad? I have to ask it. "Knútr the nasty deamhan said I am a foreign person. Why did he say that? He said it's why the shadow things tried to g– get me on the— boat."

Maistreas Eilionoir is still for a long time so I think that maybe she has fallen asleep with her eyes open or is dead. But then I know she is not dead because she says, "You are Clann-a-Tuath. You always have been and you always will be. However, there is a small grain of truth in his words. As you know, it is *toirmisgte* to speak of who your birth parents are, but perhaps – given the current threat we are under – it is necessary to say this much: your birth mother is a member of our clan, but she fell in love with the wrong man – a foreigner. Their affair was brief, and you are the result of it. No one else is aware of what occurred between the two of them, and I suggest you keep it that way."

My eyes are popping out big big. "But what—? Who was—? I am still Clann-a-Tuath. You said it. It doesn't mean I'm a— a f– foreign person. Who was the foreigner man? Where was he— from?" I have lots of questions and they are all whirry in my head.

"Enough," says Maistreas Eilionoir. "You know very well it is forbidden to ask such questions. Every woman in this clan is your mother, and every man is your father. You should think no more about it. I mentioned your parentage only because not knowing it almost got you killed once before, and I wouldn't want that to happen again. But right now, the *sgàilean* appear to be attacking us all, regardless of our blood, so what I need from you is to go outside and do as I have instructed. You are to ask no more on the subject, nor speak about it to anyone else. Understand? Not now, and not ever."

I am trying to count the paces but it is hard to keep the numbers in my head because I am too much confused about what Maistreas Eilionoir said. I am not supposed to think those things like who my birth parents are. It is not *dùth*. But also it is hard not to think of it. My father is a foreigner man. I wonder what he looks like. I try to picture him in my head but there is nothing there.

Lileas knew who her parents were, but now the shadow things are going to get them. Lileas was my friend. She helped me to do swimming when our boat sunk and she told me funny things to make me laugh. She told me about her parents too. They are called Edme and Hector. They are her real birth ones. In their clan it is different and strange because they tell their children who is their mother and father even though it is wrong to know that. Lileas told me that her father catches the fish and laughs and her mother is kind.

If they were my parents I would go and warn them. Lileas cannot warn them because she is dead. The nasty deamhan Knútr killed her. He is my worst person.

Maybe I could warn Lileas's parents instead. Yes, I could do that. I am outside of the enclave so it will be easy for me to go there. I stop walking and look at the island that is Skye. It is lots of grass which is green but also grey rocks in some places and purple which is the heather. There are bigger hills and mountains further away. It will be a long way to walk I think, but Skye island is smaller than the mainland and I walked there before so I can do it. I will do it. I will warn Lileas's parents about the shadow things. I will do it for Lileas my friend.

The plan is coming in my head. Clann-a-Tuath means the clan from the north which is the name of my clan. I know where is north because there is the North Wall on Clann-na-Bruthaich's enclave and that's where I am now so it must be this way. That is called using your brain and good thinking.

The most important thing is that the Hawks don't see me leave. They know I am allowed to be walking around the wall because Maistreas Eilionoir told them but if they see me leave they will shout and chase me. I walk a bit more until I am near where there is some trees. The Hawks think I'm still doing the counting but I am only pretending now so I tricked them. If I am in the trees they won't see me or know that I am gone. Two Hawks are talking and they are not looking where

I am. That is being a bad Hawk. I run into the trees and I keep running more and more until I am too tired and then I do walking. I don't look back until I am out of the trees on the other side. I am too far away for the Hawks to see me now. I did it!

After I have been walking some more I remember that I do not like walking. I had to do lots of walking when we were in Scotia and it is boring and hard for me. I am tired on my legs. I sit down on a stone. The grass is tall here and tickles my ears. Milkwort comes out and sits on my shoulder. I tell him he is lucky because he only has to sit in my pocket and doesn't have to do the walking. I do not want to do more walking, but then I remember that the shadow things are going to get Lileas's parents and I have to be fast so I do walking again. I have to get there before it gets night-time and I don't know how far it is. I think it is a far way. Lucky it is the morning so I have lots of time still. The only bad thing is that I cannot see Clann-na-Bruthaich's enclave any more so I don't know where north is now. I went only straight but then there was a big hill and more hills and now it is more harder to know. Also when I sat down and stopped that made it more confusing. I will walk this way. I think it is the right way.

It is cold in my ears but also I am hot because of so much walking. I wish I had a bull for riding like Duilleag who is Mór's bull or Bras who is Crayton's bull. When we were in Scotia I went riding on both of them and it was fun. The bull people are nice and my friends. They helped us cross the whole of Scotia so we could get the boat and rescue our clan. If Bras was here then Crayton would be here too and that would be the best. Crayton is my favourite, even though Jaime told me he likes to kiss boys and not girls. That is not right because it is not *dùth*. Only girls should kiss boys. I don't mind, though. I kissed Crayton once and he liked it.

I can see the sea but it is in the wrong place. It is in front of me but that's wrong. If it was right I should be at our enclave already. That means our enclave isn't there any more. Or I went the wrong way. It was hard with all the hills. Now where do I go? Also I am hungry and I don't have any food. I should have brought some food.

There is a rabbit hopping in the grass near where I am.

Hello, rabbit, I say to it in my head. *Do you know where is our enclave please?*

All I can hear in my head is confused noises, then the rabbit hops away. I think it did not know where the enclave is but also it was rude not to talk to me because I was very nice and said please.

I start to walk quicker and then I start to run. I don't run towards the sea and I don't run where I was before. It is another way which I hope is the right one. If it gets dark and I do not find our enclave, the shadow things will come and they will get me. I remember when they did it on the ship and in the mountain room. They are bad bad bad. I am thinking about them too much so I don't see the big branch on the ground and I trip on it and bang my knee.

"Ow!" I shout.

"Hey, are you okay?" someone says.

Who is it? I stand up. Oh, it's her. "Why are y– you here?" I ask.

"I could ask you the same question," says Aileen. "We're a long way from Clann-na-Bruthaich's enclave, you know? Where are you going?"

I don't want to tell her. How did she know I was here?

"I can't tell you," I say. She'll make me go back. I walk away from her. She catches up and walks next to me.

"If you tell me, maybe I can point you in the right direction? You look a little lost."

Aileen stops and I stop too. She is right. I am lost. Maybe if I tell her she will go away.

"I'm going to our— enclave," I say. "I have to tell the R– Raasay people about the— shadow things. It is not right that they all die."

Aileen chews on her lip. "I agree," she says, "but it's too far to walk. You won't make it before nightfall. We should head back."

"No," I say. "I'm not going back."

"It's dangerous out here, Agatha. You'll get lost on your own. And as soon as it's dark..."

"I know what will happen!" I say. "But I'm not going back." I walk away from her to show her it is true.

She catches up with me. "Okay, fine, but it's this way," she says. "And we'll have to be fast if we're going to make it in time."

* * *

I don't like Aileen and I don't want her to come with me. I am the hero, not her. Also she always says she is Jaime's best friend but I am his best friend too. I want her to go away. But also I do not know where the north is so I need her to show me.

She has a bag on her back and there is water in it and also food. She gives me some which is kind. I am still hungry after I eat it but it is better. We walk a long far way. Aileen is always saying we need to be faster otherwise we won't get there before it is dark but I can't go faster. It is raining now which makes it more worse and harder. The ground smells of soggy and mud. Milkwort goes back into my pocket because he doesn't want to be wet.

"How did you know I was— here?" I ask to Aileen. It is what I am wondering.

"What do you mean?"

"When you were here and you— found me..." I say. "Why were you h– here?"

"Uh ... I overheard one of the Hawks saying they saw you run away," she says. "I was worried about you, so I left the enclave to find you. After I caught up with your trail, I started following you. Sorry, I know it's not nice to be followed, but I wanted to find out where you were going."

"Why did the— the Moths let you— out?"

"They didn't. I slipped past them when they weren't looking."

That's not true. Moths are good at stopping people

from coming in and going out. They would have seen her and they would have stopped her. She is lying. Also the Hawks on the wall didn't see me running. She is lying about that too.

"Why are you— lying?" I say.

"I'm not lying," she says.

I don't ask her again. I know it is a lie.

Her hair is wet on her face now. So is mine wet. Her hair is dark red colour and curls. Mine is nicer.

"How much m– more do we have to walk?" I say. I am too tired for more walking.

"Not too much further. We just have to keep up this pace."

She is walking faster now and it is the hardest ever. I know why she is going faster. It is starting to get dark. She is worried that we will not get there in time and then the shadow things will come and get us and we cannot stop them. We can't even make a fire because of the raining. The shadows things do not like the rain, but if the rain stops when it is dark it will mean bad trouble. That is why I am trying to go fast too. Sometimes I have to run a bit which makes me more tired. Soon I will be all out of puffs.

"There it is," says Aileen.

I look and she is right.

Our enclave! It's our home and we are nearly there. I want to be living in it really much, the same as we were before.

There are people on the wall. They are only small

because they are far away, I know that. They are the bad Raasay people and our enemy. They ring the chimes which means they have seen us. We don't stop walking. We keep looking up and walk straight towards them.

SIGRID

THE MOMENT I HIT THE WATER, MY HEAD EXPLODES with the cold. I'm kickin and scramblin and it's splashin all over. Somehow my flappin gets my head back above the surface, and I slurp in great gulpfuls of air what are so cold they burn my throat. The boat's there, close, ridin up and down on the waves. I gotta get back to it. That sickweasel mighta thrown me over, but he didn't throw me far. The water tastes like herring mould and makes my eyes sting. A bulkin wave pushes my head back under. I slap in the direction of the boat and my nails scrape wood. They scrape it again. *Come on, grab somethin.* It's hard with all the movin. I dig in. Skin tears on my fingers. I've got it. I'm holdin on. I pull my head outta the water. I'm not drowned yet.

If I thought I was cold in Konge Grímr's cabin, I didn't know nothin about what it meant to be cold. The water is a million times more freezin than it was bein on the boat. My teeth are gnashin and I'm shiverin like a crazy goose. If I don't get out of the water quick-spit, I'm gunna be dead and no mistakin.

Above me I can hear laughin. They must think I'm dead already. The underside of the boat is hidden in darkness so praps they can't see. I start makin my way along the hull of the boat, always stayin in the shadows, lookin for somewhere to climb back up without them seein. The waves keep pullin down, down, turnin my legs to iron, but I'm not lettin go. I'm not finished with this world yet. Not by a long way.

Halfways along the side there's some notches in the wood what I can climb up. I don't know if that's why they're there, but it's what I'm gunna use them for – if I've got the strength, which I'm not sure I have. It should be easy, but the cold of the water has sucked me dry. Even liftin my arm is hek effort. I hang there shud-derin, ice from my own breath smokin in my face. I'm startin to feel sapped, which sure isn't good. I smack my head into the side of the boat to wake me up, then start heavin with evrythin I got. One notch at a time, up and up until my feet are out of the water and I can use my knees and my feet and my legs and all. When I finally make it to the top, I flip over the edge on my belly and fall back in the boat.

Too loud.

The grotcreeps what threw me over stop talkin in a sudden. They must've heard me from where they're standin at the back of the ship. I gotta hide, but I haven't got no more energy left for runnin. They're comin towards me. I pick myself up and I'm half runnin, half crawlin in any direction what's away from them. It's a hek bulk boat, but it's not nearly big enough to hide when you got a whole group of wreckers chasin you and you're halfdead from nearly dyin.

"She's down the front – quick, get her. How the hell did she...?" is what they're sayin in their too-loud drunken whisperin. I haven't got no idea where I'm goin. I'm just stumblin around like some snap-legged goat with no sense of nowhere or nothin.

I trip. *Jarg!* Sure as muck they got me now. I slip down to the lower part of the deck where evryone else is sleepin and crash straight into who knows who. The ones I slammed into are wakin up and so are others and they're shoutin like they're under attack and about to start warrin. Who knew me trippin could cause such a clutterflap?

"It's the girl; she escaped," someone ses, twistin me hard by my shoulders.

"Get you're skittin hams off me," I say. "I'm not goin nowhere."

"Someone wake the king."

"The king is already awake," ses Konge Grímr. He's standin by the entrance of his cabin, at the top of the steps that lead down to where evryone else is. He must've just woke up, but he looks mighty in his long furs and antler crown. The chain what I'm sposed to be attached to hangs limp at his side. "Come here, girl."

87

I tread up the steps towards him. Evryone is awake now and they're all of them watchin me. When I reach Konge Grímr, I pick up the chain and hold it in my hands. I can't put it back on cuz I don't have the keys. Konge Grímr feels his hands across the chain until he reaches me. He squeezes my arm and feels my wet hair. I'm shiverin so much I think I might fall over.

"You're wet," he ses.

"I went for a swim," I say. I don't know why I'm thinkin it's a good time to be funny.

"What happened?" He grips my head just a little bit tighter, threatenin me not to lie.

"She broke free," ses someone from the crowd. "She jumped overboard and tried to escape."

"That's not true," I say. "They took me. They took me and they threw me."

"Who took you?" Konge Grímr asks.

Bolverk looks at me with death eyes. I know it was him what planned it all, but if I say it was him, he'll make my life worse than hell bad. I don't know what to say; if I say no one, it looks like I'm lyin.

"I didn't see his face, but I know the ink on his hams," I say, speakin of the man who did the chuckin. "He's got cloudberries on his knuckles and thorns round his fingers, sept for the middle what's got a water snake. His other hand's got a mink's head, a *snekkja* ship and a white-throated dipper bird what looks like it's only got one leg."

Evryone turns and stares at a man. He's not as bulk as Bolverk, but he's not far smaller. His nose is flat like it got bust one time too many. He's hidin his hams behind his back, but I know they're exactly what I described. He's shakin his head no.

"How could she know all that?" he ses.

"I gotta good memory," I say.

"Bring him to me," ses the king.

Four people grab him, two on each side.

"She's lying," the man ses. "You can't believe that filthy rotten over me!" He gets dragged up the steps until he's right in front of us. He's sweatin now, all wet on his forehead. The ink on his bent nose is a spruce tree, what's sposed to mean honesty. He's already proven he doesn't deserve that one. "You can't trust her. She's lying. I never touched her."

"I'm not no lier," I say. "I may not be much, but I'm tellin you for nothin I'm not no lier. He's the one what threw me over."

"I've always considered myself an excellent judge of character," Konge Grímr ses to me. His hand is still on my head, which helps stop the shiverin. "I used to be able to look into a person's eyes and know immediately if they were lying. Obviously, that is a skill I no longer possess. But as one sense fails us, another takes its place. Right now, I can *hear* that you're lying."

"I'm not!" I say. "Swear Øden I'm not."

Somethin flashes forward from Konge Grímr's robes. A knife. It goes in so quick and then out again.

The man in fronta us looks down at where he's just been stabbed.

91

"I wasn't talking to you," ses Konge Grímr, givin my head another squeeze. "Throw him overboard," he ses to the ones holdin the man.

The man doesn't even struggle. He's been stabbed real bad. The splash when he hits the water sounds like it's swallowin him up.

"Now someone find the keys for this chain," ses the king. "I'm lost without my eyes."

JAIME

THE OTHERS ARE LAUGHING AT ME, I'M SURE OF IT. It makes me swing the axe even harder. Or maybe they're not laughing; maybe it's pity. I swing the axe again. The impact makes my arms judder and my teeth sting.

Since we came back, the number of people in each duty has been imbalanced because of all the clan members who were killed when the deamhain first attacked, but the decision was made almost straight away that the duties would be respected. It's one of the few things Maistreas Eilionoir and Catriona have agreed upon. "When you are initiated into a duty, you commit to it for life. In these unstable times, it is exactly the sort of stability we need," was Maistreas Eilionoir's argument. It doesn't make sense to me. We need more Hawks to patrol the wall and more Moths to guard the gates, and the Reapers are practically redundant, since there's nothing for them to harvest. I haven't mentioned it, though, since I appear to be the exception; there's been no talk of me resuming my duty as an Angler. Perhaps Maistreas Eilionoir has kept quiet about it as a way of rewarding me for the role I played in rescuing everyone. As a result, I'm in a strange sort of limbo, where I'm invited to meetings, but I'm not an elder, I help out in the kitchens, but I'm not a Stewer, and I spend a lot of time with the Wasps, even though I'll never be one. I don't really know what I am.

It also means that when there's a job that requires extra people, I'm the first person to be asked.

Hence cutting down trees.

There was a time when I thought being an Angler was the job I was least suited to in the world, but maybe I was wrong. Maybe it's cutting down trees.

After this morning's meeting, runners were sent to warn the other Skye clans about the *sgàilean*, like Maistreas Eilionoir suggested, and the Scavengers were sent out to collect as much firewood as possible. The plan is to make numerous fires around the entire enclave, including ones in every bothan, because no one wants to spend another night standing in a freezing loch. It's a short-term solution, though; we can't keep fires burning forever. And what if the *sgàilean* find a way to put them out? It's not safe for us here any more.

I lean the axe against my leg and shake out my aching arms. Sweat is pouring down my back despite the cold. The Scavengers around me have all perfected the technique and make it look so easy. I lift the axe above my shoulder and focus on the pathetic dent in the tree I've been chipping away at. I tighten my grip on the handle and swing with all the strength I can muster. Just before it hits, I shut my eyes. The impact doesn't come. I miss the spot I was aiming for, spin in a full circle and the axe ends up lodged in a completely different trunk.

I attempt to yank it out, but it's stuck tight. I give up and slump onto the ground, filled with an overwhelming desire to do nothing at all.

"Need a hand?" says one of the Scavs, a hulking boy not much older than I am. I quickly stand back up. He reaches behind me and pulls the axe from the tree with minimal effort.

"Thanks," I say. He doesn't give the axe back to me.

"There's lots of fallen branches a bit further in. Why don't you pick up a load of those? That'd be just as useful."

I'm on the verge of protesting, torn between struggling on with a task I'm clearly no good at, and the humiliating demotion to picking up twigs. I don't *want* to chop down trees, but I want to be *able* to chop down trees. Who'd have thought I'd find it easier to cut off a person's hand than cut down a tree? That particular memory – of the deamhan I struck when the fight first broke out in the mountain – unfurls in my brain like a poisoned flower. A sour taste rushes into my throat. I look at the axe, which the Scav is still holding.

"Fine," I say, turning my back on him.

I keep my eyes down as I go about my work. Every

now and then there's a yell of "Falling!" and everyone stops to watch as a defeated tree creaks to the forest floor.

Once I have as much wood in my arms as I can carry, I make my way back to the enclave, struggling not to drop pieces as I go. Despite my best efforts, a twig falls out here and a branch slides off there so that by the time I reach the gate, my load is pretty pathetic. Why did I even bother?

The Moth keeping guard watches me approach. He's Clann-na-Bruthaich, an older man with long wisps of white hair which the wind spreads across his face like grass under water.

"You dropped a few," he says, pointing behind me. He means it as a joke, but it hits a nerve. I walk past him without saying anything.

As soon as I'm inside, a young boy runs up to me.

"I was sent to find you," he says, bouncing on the balls of his feet.

"Me?" I ask. "Why?"

"Catriona wants to speak to you. Come with me."

He scampers off, stopping every few yards to check that I'm still following. Why would Catriona want to speak to me? It must be about burning down the meeting tree. The boy leads me to a small bothan with a tatty thatch roof.

"Is she inside?" I ask.

He nods, digging his buck teeth into his bottom lip, then sprints off on flat feet.

I'm still carrying the bundle of branches, more of which fell during the jog across the enclave. I ditch the remaining few on the ground and knock on the bothan door. No one answers. I knock again and strain my ears for a response. It's hard to hear through the stone walls and thick wooden door, especially with the wind wheezing all over the place like it is. I knock for a third time, then clunk the latch and open the door. It's dark inside, so it takes me a moment to register who all the staring eyes belong to. Catriona is the first to come into focus, standing near the centre of the room with her hands on the back of a chair. Leaning against the far wall are a man and a woman. I've never seen the woman before; she's slim, with a long, oval face and prominent eyes. The man is Donal, the Wasp who showed me how to make an Angler boat in the days after Agatha accidentally set one of them on fire. He smiles at me through his dense ginger beard, and I give him a little mouth twitch in return. The final person in the room is Maistreas Eilionoir. She's sitting in the opposite corner, so hidden in shadow that I almost didn't see her. She blows into the steaming mug in her hands.

"Come in," says Catriona, and indicates that I should sit down on the chair in front of her.

I walk over to the chair with slow steps. "I really am sorry," I say, "… about the meeting tree … I didn't mean to—"

"This isn't about the meeting tree," Catriona says, cuting me off.

"We've been thinking more about this 'Badhbh' of yours," says Maistreas Eilionoir. "We may have been too hasty earlier, when we dismissed the possibility of him still being alive." She looks pointedly at Catriona.

"You'll be chasing ghosts," Catriona says to me, "but if you're that desperate to go..."

"Oh," I say. "No, I didn't mean—"

"I believe you are already acquainted with Donal?" says Maistreas Eilionoir. "He's an exceptional Wasp, incredibly resourceful in every way. And this is Violet from Clann-na-Bruthaich. She's the best tracker they have." The woman nods at me with a kind smile. "I'm sure you will make a fine team."

My head is shaking fast, a repeated tremor.

"Yes," says Maistreas Eilionoir. "You will be joining them. We want you to go back to Scotia."

They can't be serious. The last time I was there I nearly died, many times. It's where the wildwolves live, and who knows what other terrors. It's where I watched as Lileas was—

No. I can't.

"I understand that it will be difficult for you," Maistreas Eilionoir continues, "but you are the only person to have been to Scotia before. Other than Agatha, of course, but she is preoccupied with a different task. You were the one who read this Badhbh's diary. If he is alive, he may be the only person who can stop the *sgàilean*, and you are our best hope of finding him."

"But Scotia is huge and his plans were so vague... He wrote all that forty years ago; he could be anywhere by now. If he's even still alive, like you say."

"I know, it's not going to be easy," says Maistreas Eilionoir, "but you've seen what the *sgàilean* are capable of. We must find a way to return them to the necklace, and the only person we know who is capable of such a feat is the Badhbh. So we have to try. *You* have to try."

It's hopeless; there's no way I'll be able to find him. I wouldn't even know where to start. The only clues as to his whereabouts were in his diary, and I don't even have that any more; before leaving for Norveg, I left it with Cray.

A strange feeling jolts my stomach. Cray took the diary to show it to the other Bó Riders, so he should still have it. If I return to Scotia, maybe I'll get to see him again. That would be one positive, at least. I've thought about him quite a lot since we got back, about how safe I felt when I was with him. I've missed him, and the other Bó Riders too.

It's the thought of seeing them again, and no other, that causes me to open my mouth and ask, "When would we have to leave?"

"Straight away," says Catriona. "You'll want to reach land before it gets dark. A boat is being loaded up with supplies as we speak."

I'm not given much choice. I'm bustled out of the bothan and Donal is ruffling my hair and Maistreas Eilionoir is telling me again that she knows I will do what's best for the clan. Catriona and Violet follow close behind.

I don't protest. I let them lead me through the enclave, out of the gate and around the perimeter wall. I feel numb. Sailing to Scotia is the last thing I want to do, but nothing feels right here either. Perhaps going back will help lift the darkness that's been clinging to me ever since we returned.

We follow the curve of the wall, and the sea peers out at us. Clann-na-Bruthaich's enclave is a short distance from the water. A solitary boat rests on the beach, which we heave into the surf at Catriona's instruction. As we're checking through the supplies, the same messenger boy from earlier runs up to us. "I can't find either of them," he says. He's talking about Agatha and Aileen. My only request was that I could say goodbye to them before I left. "No one's seen them all day."

A niggling worry worms into my brain. They were both at the loch this morning, so their disappearance can't be anything to do with the *sgàilean*. They should both be in the enclave. Aileen is supposed to be fishing in the loch, and Agatha is almost always patrolling the wall.

My right hand drifts towards my left wrist and I give the bracelet there a gentle squeeze. The strips of metal are hard and cold.

"You haven't got time to wait for them," says Catriona. "Get in the boat."

I clamp my mouth closed to stop myself from saying something I'll regret. I was planning on apologizing to Aileen for the way I spoke to her in the tree last night. With all that's happened, we haven't talked properly since. It doesn't look like I'm going to have the chance now. I want her to know that, despite how I've been behaving recently, I still care about her more than anything in the world.

Before getting into the boat, I look across the water and see Scotia – a haunting mass in the distance. My legs start to shudder, a violent tremble that spreads up into my chest and down my arms. I try to resist it, but my body refuses.

Maistreas Eilionoir turns me towards her and embraces me in a tight hug. The shaking slows and while I'm enfolded in her arms, she whispers something in my ear. "Pardon?" I say, unsure I heard her right. She doesn't repeat it. She breaks away and, holding me at arm's length, gives both my shoulders a squeeze. I think she said the same words she whispered in the mountain room on the morning after the battle with the deamhain: *You truly are the bravest of us all.* It gives me the courage I need to step into the boat.

My history on water is not great. Three out of the last four boats I've travelled in have ended up destroyed: the first was set on fire by Agatha, another was damaged by rocks and sank off the shore of Scotia, and the third shattered when we crashed into the Norvegian coastline. At least the journey today won't be as far as the other ones were, and Donal looks like he's strong enough to row for four.

There are no long, drawn-out goodbyes. Violet says nothing at all. Donal gives a few cheerful waves, and that's it. We're on the sea, and I'm at the mercy of the water once again.

Scotia creeps up on us far too quickly. All of the horrors I'd heard about the mainland did not prepare me for the reality of it. It was much worse, in every way, and very soon I'm going to be back there.

AGATHA

THE CHIMES ON THE WALL OF OUR ENCLAVE MAKE clatter noise. The Raasay people should be hitting the First twice at the top which is meaning they can see people they don't know, but they are not. They are hitting all of them. They do not know how to do the chimes properly.

My heart is bum bum bum bum booming because the chiefs of Raasay are inside and they are bad ones. I hate them the most in all the world. If the shadow things get them I don't even care. More people come on the wall when they hear the chimes. They are looking down at us too.

"Hold up your hands to show you're not armed," Aileen says to me. "And let me do the talking."

I do what she says the holding up my hands.

"No further!" shouts a man from the wall. It is hard to see his face but I think it is a scowl one. "Who are you and what do you want?"

"We are Clann-a-Tuath," I shout. This is our enclave and you sh– shouldn't be here."

Aileen looks at me and shakes her head. She doesn't want me to do the talking but it was my plan to come here, not hers.

"Turn around and walk away," says the Raasay man on the wall.

"We're here to warn you," says Aileen, but I shout louder.

"I want to see Lileas's parents! They are called Hector and E– Edme. I need to— speak with them."

"Leave now or we will be forced to fire."

"But the shadow things are coming to get you!" I say. "You need to— listen to us." It is not raining here which means the shadow things can come even sooner.

"We do not listen to our enemy," says the man.

"Then you are— stupid!"

"Agatha!" says Aileen.

An arrow fires then. It lands in the ground close to me and I yelp and step away from it.

"That was a warning," says the man. "The next one will not hit the ground." That means it won't hit the ground because it will hit me instead.

"We've walked all the way from the south," says Aileen. "We may be your enemy, but we value the lives of your children. If you don't open your gates and listen to what we have to say, come nightfall you will all be dead."

The people on the wall are talking to each other.

I cannot hear them. They are too far away and too quiet. One of them whistles and then the gate opens. They are letting us in, I think. It means we can put our hands down now which is good because my arms were big aches. I do not like it that the people listened to Aileen and not to me. It makes me not like her more.

Inside it is strange because it is our enclave and everything is the same but also some things are different. Some of the bothans are not there any more and there are new smaller ones. Also the people are all wrong. They are Raasay people and not Clann-a-Tuath people. There are six of them near to us. I know it is six because I counted them. I think they are the ones from the wall. One of them is a woman with a long nose who comes to us. She doesn't say anything. She takes Aileen's bag without asking first which is snatching. She throws it to a man. Then she touches Aileen all over her body. When she is finished she comes to do the same thing to me.

"Don't touch me," I say. I do not want her to touch me. I move my arm away from her.

"It's okay, Agatha. She's just checking you don't have any weapons," says Aileen.

"But I don't have any— weapons," I say.

"I know that, but she doesn't," says Aileen.

"She should believe me when I say it," I say.

"Just let her do it, okay?" says Aileen.

I do not want her to do it. She does it anyway and is rough. She doesn't find any weapons because I don't have any which is what I said.

"I told you I didn't— have any," I say to her. "You should have believed me when I said it."

"What's wrong with your face?" she asks me, and she stares which is rude.

"Nothing's wrong with my— face," I say. "I am very pretty. Much prettier than y– you." She doesn't say anything to that because she knows it is true.

The man empties all of the things from Aileen's bag onto the mud. They are dirty now so that is mean. He moves some of them with his foot. Then he looks up and is looking at us and says, "What was it you wanted to tell us?"

"I want to say it!" I say before Aileen can. She shrugs a little one at me. "You need to make a big one. A fire. A– a qu– quick— I have to tell it to Hector and Edme. Soon it will be— soon it will be night and if you d– don't have the fire the shadow things will— g– get you."

"What do you mean 'shadow things'?" says the woman.

Doesn't she know? Oh, I remember Lileas didn't know about the shadow things either. They do not know about them on the Raasay Island.

"They are dark entities made through blood magic," says Aileen. I let her say it this time. "They've been released on the island. There's every chance they're all around us right now, waiting. As soon as the sun goes down they will attack, unless you are prepared. That's why you need the fire: its light will offer you protection."

"That may well be the most ridiculous lie I have ever heard," says a new man. He came over when Aileen was talking. Now I can see him more properly and I know who he is. He is one of the chiefs of Raasay. I remember what he looked like. He was on the wall when the deamhain were taking my clan away. It is him who opened our gates and let the deamhain in. I am all hot inside with the angry. I am better at stopping the angry when it comes because Maistreas Eilionoir taught me how, but I do not want to stop it now.

I run at the man and I hit him in his face with my hand that is a fist. Ouch! It hurts a very lot to do it but I think it hurts the chief of Raasay man more. He is holding his face near his nose and it is bleeding.

"Agatha, stop it!" says Aileen, but I can't and I won't.

I kick to his legs but it doesn't get them. Someone is grabbing and holding me then and I am pulled away.

"I h– hate you!" I shout at him. "You made the deamhain come. You made them k– kill all the elders."

The chief of Raasay man spits a blood spit on the ground.

"You stupid girl. Have you ever stopped to think *why* we did what we did? Of course you haven't. Do you even know the truth? This island was *ours*, girl, long before it was yours. That's right, your ancestors came from the mainland and took it from us, forcing us into exile. My people lost everything that day – their homes, their way of life, their hope. This island has always been ours; all we have done is reclaim it."

"It's not true," I say. "You're horrible and you're— lying."

"Believe me or not, I really don't care, but it is the truth," says the chief of Raasay man. "The history of your people is stained with the suffering of others." He presses his fingers on his nostrils where blood is then says to the people around us, "Lock them away until we decide what to do with them. And the rest of you, get back to your posts in case this is some sort of diversion."

"Wait!" says Aileen. "You have to believe us; the *sgàilean* are coming – tonight!"

"I want Lileas's parents!" I shout while they are taking me away. "Hector! Edme! Where are they? They are the nice ones."

No one answers me or speaks to me except for the one that is holding me who says, "Get inside, you good-for-nothing rat-flea," when he pushes me into a bothan. Aileen is pushed in too and then the door closes and we are alone.

It is a very small bothan with nothing in it and the window has bars. It is a prison one. I bang the door and shake it but it is locked. I shake on the window bars as well but they are stuck and won't come out. I am tired from doing it and my jaw is sore on both sides from all the shaking. I sit down on the floor.

"Well, that could have gone better," says Aileen. She turns her head to look at me. "Remember the part where I said I should do the talking?"

"Yes, I remember that," I say. I do not know why she

wants me to remember that. I do not want to be in here and I am cold. I put my head in my hands. I am angry and I am sad. "They should have said thank you to us for telling them about the shadow things," I say. "Not put us in the prison and locked it."

"Maybe they forgot their manners when you called them stupid?" says Aileen. "Or when you punched their chief in the face?"

That is maybe true. "He is a bad man and I'm glad that I did it," I say.

I think Aileen will be cross but she smiles at me instead.

"You landed a good blow," she says. "And he definitely deserved it." She sits next to me and puts her arm around me. I do not make her move because she is being nice.

"It was b– bad to come here—   wasn't it?" I say to Aileen.

"No, it was very brave," she says.

"I am brave," I say.

I take Milkwort out and he runs around the room. He will only need a small hole to escape but I will need a big one or a door.

"It's not true, is it? What the chief of Raasay man said about them l– living on this—   island?" I ask to Aileen.

"It would have been a very long time ago if they did," says Aileen. "It's true our ancestors came from the mainland, but I always assumed the island was uninhabited when they arrived. Either way, it doesn't excuse the fact that the chiefs of Raasay allowed our people to be murdered and enslaved."

That is true but also I don't know how to think about it all and I don't know. Aileen picks up a small stone and flicks it at the window. It hits one of the bars with a ting noise and then it goes out.

"You were right, by the way," says Aileen. "Earlier, when you said I was lying. I was."

"What?" I say.

"I was lying about the Hawk seeing you and about slipping past the Moth."

I knew she was lying. "I knew you were," I say.

"The Moth let me past at Maistreas Eilionoir's request. After the meeting this morning she took me to one side and asked me to keep an eye on you."

"You were s– spying on me?" Spying is what you do to enemy people, not to hero people.

"Not spying exactly. Just watching over. It's because she cares about you. She could see you were upset about what happened with the *sgàilean*."

"It wasn't my— fault!" I say.

"I know it wasn't."

Neither of us says anything after that. Milkwort comes back to me. He doesn't like the prison room either. He crawls into my pocket where it is warm.

Aileen gets up and goes to the window. "Why won't these bloody *meirlich* listen to us? Hello! Hello! Is anyone there? You have to believe us: *sgàilean* are coming. They're going to attack you. We came here to warn you!" She shouts again and more for a long time until she has an old-lady voice from too much shouting.

No one comes. She sits on the floor again. It's getting darker. The shadow things will be here soon. It is so cold and I am shivering. All my clothes are wet from the rain and so is my hair. I move closer to Aileen and give her a hug. She hugs me too. Hugs are nice when you are sad and wet with rain.

I think again about what Maistreas Eilionoir said that my birth father is a foreigner man. It keeps remembering me. I want to say to Aileen about it but it is not *dùth* to do that so it stays in my head.

"Hello?" says a person in a whisper voice.

I stand up quick. So does Aileen. There is someone at the window with the bars. Two people.

"Who— who are you?" I ask.

"We shouldn't be here," says the lady one.

"We heard you were asking for us," says the man one.

I know who they are then. "Hector!" I say. "And— and Edme?"

"Yes," says the lady one who is Lileas's mother who is Edme. "Please, how is our daughter? Is she okay?"

Oh. They do not know. I didn't think that they wouldn't know. I don't want to tell them. I shake my head fast because I cannot speak it.

"What? What is it? Please tell us," says Hector who is Lileas's father.

"We're really sorry..." says Aileen.

"No ... no..." says Lileas's mother Edme. She is the one shaking her head now.

"It was the nasty d– deamhan man. I tried to— I tried to stop him. Lileas was my friend. I tried to stop him but he k- killed her. It wasn't— it wasn't my— fault," I say.

Lileas's mother Edme makes a loud sound that is wailing. I have never seen big crying like that. Lileas's father Hector puts his arm around her and she cries into his chest. She should not cry. It is not *dùth*. Doesn't she know that? It is because she is sad and I am sad too but I do not cry.

"They promised us she wouldn't get hurt," Lileas's father Hector says in a small voice. "The chiefs *promised* us."

He isn't talking to me. I don't know who he is talking to. Lileas's mother Edme slides down onto the ground so it is harder to see her. She is still crying.

Lileas's father Hector wipes his eyes with his fingers. "I... I don't know what to... My precious little girl..." He wipes his eyes again and then squeezes the top of his nose. He makes a "huh" sound and does a big swallow. "We have been wronged," he says, "and so have you. This is all so, so wrong. We should never have... Believe me when I say we are truly sorry for what happened to your people. We knew nothing of what the chiefs had planned, about the deal they'd made with the deamhain. The way this place was taken from you was wrong, and we are not the only ones who feel that way."

"Then can you help us? We need to get out of here before it gets dark," says Aileen.

Lileas's father Hector shakes his head. "It's impossible. There's only one key and no way for us to obtain it. And if they found out we'd helped you escape... Even talking to you is putting our lives in danger."

"We need to go," says Lileas's mother Edme. The words are crying ones.

"Wait," says Aileen. "We're here to warn you. There's something coming, something dangerous." She tells them about the shadow things and that they need to make the fire.

"Have you told the chiefs?" asks Lileas's father Hector.

"They won't listen to us," says Aileen.

"They are— stupid," I say.

Lileas's mother Edme sniffs in some tears and stands back up. "You came all this way to warn us?" she says. "After what our people did to you? Why?"

"It was Agatha's idea," says Aileen.

"Lileas t– told me about you," I say. "She said you were kind so I didn't— I didn't want you to be— hurt."

"You have a good soul, Agatha," says Lileas's father Hector. "Just like our daughter. I am so sorry we cannot help you further."

"Someone's coming," says Lileas's mother Edme. She pulls Lileas's father Hector away from the window. "I'm so sorry."

"Wait! Wait!" says Aileen. She presses her head into

the bars in the window. "There must be a way. We'll die in here."

Lileas's parents are gone. Aileen shouts and bangs her fists on the bars but it won't break them.

"So that's it? They're just going to leave us here?" says Aileen.

I don't know if it is a question for me or not so I nod my head and shake my head a little bit at the same time.

Aileen goes next to the door. She touches it all over and bangs parts with her hand and her elbow. It is dark in the prison room now. I think it is nearly night-time.

"Are we going to die in here?" I ask Aileen. I want to know it but I am not afraid.

"No," she says. "We'll find a way out. Maybe the *sgàilean* won't have travelled this far north yet. It was a long way, after all. Maybe they stayed around Clann-na-Bruthaich's enclave. Tomorrow we can talk to the Raasay chiefs again. We'll explain and figure this out—"

Aileen stops hitting with her elbow. Her head tips up which is listening. She has heard something. Then I hear it too. The horrible noise. It's the same one I heard on the ship and in the mountain room and when the necklace opened in Catriona's bothan.

It's the shadow things. They're here.

SIGRID

We're here.

Ingland.

It's hek diffrunt to Norveg from what I've seen so far. The sea turned into a river and before long, shacks and buildins started tumblin over one another on the bankside. Lots of buildins, lots of people. Smells diffrunt and all, like fishrot and goatpuke.

We reach a long wooden dock with lots of boats comin in and out and around it. Men on the dock pull our boat in and secure it. Evryone's told they have to leave their weapons onboard. There's some grumblin at that, and no one's happy, but Konge Grímr ses it's fine and they all gotta do it. He's the first to take out his dagger and put it on the floor of the boat. Evryone does the same, puttin their weapons down too.

I take Konge Grímr's arm to guide him up the steps from the water to the street. When we're at the top, there are men waitin for us who are all wearin the same clothes. They pat us all over to make sure we haven't got no more weapons. The one pattin the king is all "Your Majesty" this and "Your Majesty" that and "Welcome to Ingland," and "accept my apologies," and on and on. Then he ses, "I'm so sorry about your eyes," and straightaways Konge Grímr headsmashes him with a rock-crackin smack. The man falls to the ground, cradling his battered head.

Konge Grímr straightens his antler crown. "Do not mention my eyes," he ses in the foreign tongue.

"Forgive me, Your Majesty. Never again, Your Majesty," ses the man from the ground.

Konge Grímr asks me if I can understand what the man's sayin. I tell him no. I don't know why I lie. Truth is I understand him just fine. One of the books Granpa Halvor lent me had all the foreign tongue words in it alongside what the words meant in our language. He taught me the sounds of the letters and all. I read the book from front to back, so now I know all the words. Granpa was hek surprised afterwards that I could re-member evrythin. He opened the book at random and tested me again and again, and whatever word he said, I could tell him what it meant. He ses it's not normal to see somethin only once and then remember it forever, but it's normal to me.

We follow the guards away from the river and Konge Grímr squeezes my head as we're walkin, which means he wants me to describe it to him. He hasn't been to Ingland before neither.

"It's the most skit awful place I ever saw," I say.

He huffs a quick laugh when I say that. "I guessed as much from the smell. Tell me more."

"Evryone's grubby, there's crapmuck smearin the houses, mangy dogs are lyin dead or dyin... The people look strange. No one's got any ink. They're all starin at us. Well, mainly at you, I think."

"How do they look when they see me?"

"I dunno. A little bit scared, a little bit awe."

There's a broken cart lyin slumped in our way. I pull Konge Grímr towards me so he doesn't trip on it, then weave in and between the mud puddles. Bein honest, I don't think it's mud at all. Smells like somethin a lot worse than that...

Bolverk walks on the other side of Konge Grímr, listenin to evry word I'm sayin. He's always hangin close by, like he's jealous if I'm closer to the king than he is. He doesn't trust me none – I can tell from how he looks at me. Also, he told me as much, straight from his yapper, let's not forget that. That's fine; I don't trust him neither. Not as far as I could spit him. I wonder what would've happened if I'd told the king it was him who took me from the cabin instead of the spruce-tree man. Would Konge Grímr have killed Bolverk instead? Probly not. He trusts him more than anyone. If I'd said it was Bolverk, maybe it would've been me gettin stabbed.

"King Edmund's palace is just up ahead," ses one of the guards, so I guess that's where we're goin. King

117

Edmund is the king of Ingland, so it makes sense that's who Konge Grímr's here to visit, I spose.

I see the palace long before we reach it. It's hard to miss. It's the most bulkin buildin I ever saw, goin right up into the sky. All the buildins around it are skittin with muckgrime, but the palace is clean as if it's lookin down on evryone else all superior like. There are guards evrywhere, dressed smart like the ones what brought us from the boat. Their hair's cut short and they're all of them men. I don't know why the Inglish king hasn't got no women guards. None of them have ink, but they've all got the same silver lynx pattern stitched on their clothes. Outside the palace, there's pieces of material flappin on poles, and they've all got the lynx on them too. A silver lynx with red eyes. When it's done in ink, the lynx means bringer of death. I wonder if they know that.

Konge Grímr is squeezin my head again and again, so I keep on sayin evrythin I see like I'm sposed to, but he's still squeezin evry two blinks. It's hek skap when he does that. What more does he want me to say?

The new guards check us for weapons again and there's more pattin. The one pattin me even makes me stick out my tongue and looks in my ears. How big does he think my skittin ears are? Finally they nod their heads and let us through. I thought the outside of the palace was bulkin, but the inside's even mightier.

"We're in a huge room with a hek high ceilin," I say when Konge Grímr squeezes my kog for the skap thousandth time, "and lots of other rooms goin off it. There's soft on the floor what's coloured red and high up there's a chain with candles in a circle to make light." I try and say evrythin I see, even though there's so gawkin much of it.

"If it would please you to proceed to the Feast Hall, His Majesty King Edmund will join presently," some man in tight clothin says to Konge Grímr, all the whiles bowin low to the floor, which is a waste since he can't see none anyways.

"Of course," ses Konge Grímr.

We go through to another room what's even bigger than the first one. I never knew a room could be this big. There are hek loads of tables set out in six long lines, with fancy bowls and cups and other things on them, which I'm guessin are for eatin. I lead Konge Grímr to the chair which the man shows me is where he's sposed to sit, right in the centre of the table in the middle. The chair is the largest I ever saw, with lynxes carved in its top. The wood smells like it's fresh chopped. I say to Konge Grímr about the tables and the chair and the room. Bolverk sits in the chair next to him. I know sure as the moon that they're not gunna let me sit on no chair, so I sit on the floor instead. All of the wreckers from our boat come in and so do lots of Inglish people. All of the Inglish people are men, though, makin me wonder where the Inglish women are. The Inglish men look at the female wreckers sittin at the tables like it's hek strange them bein there.

Soon there's someone sittin in evry seat sept for the two on the right of Konge Grímr.

"Please be upstanding for His Majesty King Edmund, and Her Royal Modesty the Lady Beatrice."

Evryone stands up. As Konge Grímr stands, he yanks on my chain, makin sure I'm standin too. I was gunna stand; he didn't need to do no yankin.

Comin through the door – and I can't hardly believe it as I see it – is a bed, carried by eight of the men guards. It's not no ordinary bed, though; it's hek massive like evrythin else in this batcrazy place. Comin over the top of it is a carvin of another lynx what looks like it's leapin across the bed but got frozen halfway. I swear Øden it musta taken a whole tree to make it. This Inglish king really likes his lynxes, that's for hek sure.

Walkin behind the bed is a lady wearin long, dark green material that doesn't look like no clothes I've ever seen before. It's gotta be the stupidest thing I ever saw someone wearin. It looks heavy and no good for runnin. The lady looks straight ahead like it's too much effort to turn her head to see who's in the room. A hek bulkin pig trots by her side with its snout snifflin up in the air. Its back is hairy with skittin black splodges on it, and its trotters clop on the stone floor, louder than what you'd expect.

Stranger than all of that is what's lyin on the bed. It's a dead body covered from head to foot in metal armour. The only parts pokin out are its hands and its face, which are withered and bone-white like the blood's been

120

drained out of them. Why they bringin a dead man in to dinner? The way evryone's bowin their heads makes me think it must be King Edmund. If it is, that means the Inglish king's dead. Well, that's a startler. But then I'm lookin closer and... Wait— The dead man's fingers... They're movin.

The eight men guards put the bed down by the door and then they pick up the movin corpse and carry it towards us. It clinks and clanks cuz of all the armour it's wearin. Right when it's close to us, its eyes spring open.

He's alive.

He stares at Konge Grímr and he stares at me. The guards put him in the chair next to me so I'm stood right in the middle of the two kings. Most of the guards step back, but two of them stay close next to their king, with one hand on each of his shoulders. The lady in green sits on the chair on the other side of him, and the big pink pig plomps down by her feet. Once the king and the lady are sittin, evryone else sits too.

"Welcome," King Edmund ses to Konge Grímr. He talks like his throat's got holes in it and all the breath's escapin. "After so many years of favourable trade with your nation, it is a pleasure to finally meet you in person."

"Likewise," says Konge Grímr in the foreign tongue, "although I'm disappointed not to witness the grandeur of your palace with my own eyes. The girl tells me it's quite something." He pulls on the chain for me to stand up again. I do an awkward sorta bow. "She is my eyes and will be with me at all times, but you can ignore her. She cannot understand us. She's nothing."

King Edmund glances at me, then straightaways looks away. His eyes are so old they've turned cloudy like curds. On the other side of King Edmund, the lady in the green leans forward to look at me too, and she gawps for much longer. She's starin at my ink. I turn my head so she can't see it no more.

"This is my wife, Lady Beatrice," ses King Edmund, pointin to the lady in the green.

His wife? She's a hek lot younger than he is. Maybe that's why she looks so sad – cuz she has to be married to that scraggin rotcorpse. Konge Grímr squeezes the top of my head.

"He's pointin to the lady sittin next to him," I say in his ear, quiet so only he can hear. "She's smilin at you in a not-real way. She's older than my mother but not by much. And she's wearin green clothes what look stupid."

"My eyes tell me you are very beautiful," ses Konge Grímr. I definitely didn't say that. If anythin, Lady Beatrice is kinda borin lookin. She's got borin colour hair what's been tied up all twirled with some bits scragglin down. Her lips are pale and her eyes haven't got no shine in them.

"That's very kind of her," Lady Beatrice ses, and she's lookin at me again when she ses it. Her right arm drifts down to the pig by her side and she scratches the harsk black hair on its snout. The pig lets out a burpin oink.

"It sounds as if our food is still alive," ses Konge Grímr.

"You mean the pig?" says King Edmund. "Oh, no, that belongs to Lady Beatrice. It has become somewhat fashionable in recent years for women to keep pigs as companions. We must allow our women their fancies, must we not?"

Konge Grímr frowns like he thinks what King Edmund said is stupid. I think it's stupid too. And I haven't heard of someone keepin a pig as a pet before neither.

The food arrives and it's the Inglish women what bring it in. They're all bowin and eyes down and careful not to make no fuss, makin me think the women in this country have got it rotten. Sept for the Lady Beatrice, of course. Why're the women doin all the servin while the men sit there gettin evrythin brought to them? If I lived here, I wouldn't stand for that, that's for hek sure. But then, I'm chained up and don't have no say about nothin, so what do I know?

I haven't never seen so much food before. There's a whole cow, a whole sheep and a whole dog for evry table. They've all of them still got their eyes but they've not got no skin. They're splayed open on big plates, all burnt red and starin. More things come like vegetables and breads and mashed things and soupy somethin else and I don't know what the half of it is.

"Let us feast!" shouts King Edmund, and he throws his hands up in the air. Even though he's nothin but

123

bones wrapped in skin, he can move hek fast. Evryone grabs at the food, pullin and tearin and chewin on. King Edmund doesn't touch nothin. He points and points and a man steps from behind him and does the pullin and the tearin and the grabbin for him. When the king's plate is overflowin, the man behind him takes a bite out of evrythin. He even drinks some of King Edmund's drink. Must be some way they have here.

I tell Konge Grímr what all the foods are and take them for him. He tells me he wants cow and sheep and dog. The meat is hot as I'm rippin it off its bones. When his plate is full, he starts eatin with both hands. I don't get to try none like King Edmund's man did, even though my stomach's crumblin. I sit back down on the floor and lick the meat grease from my fingers. It only makes me more hungry.

"I was most horrified to hear of the attack on your people," King Edmund ses in his breathwheeze voice.

"The condolences and aid you sent in its aftermath were received with gratitude," ses Konge Grímr. He picks at some food what's stuck between his nashers.

"From the last message I received, I do believe our problems are one and the same," ses King Edmund, "and that we desire the same outcome."

Konge Grímr puts down the meat bone he's been chewin and turns to King Edmund. "I seek revenge on those who have wronged me," he ses. "Namely: the servants who were meant to serve Øden but instead fled the mountain, the boy who unleashed the death shadows upon my people, and the girl who made the bats tear out my eyes."

"And these people are all Scotian, is that correct?"

"They live on the Isle of Skye, off the west Scotian coast."

"Then I too wish for them to be ... dealt with. I have heard their numbers are small, so their obliteration will be easy."

"You would be wise not to underestimate them," ses Konge Grímr. "They are more of a threat than they appear. They are in possession of an army of almost unstoppable shadows, as well as a girl who can manipulate animals to do her bidding."

"I am aware of the girl," says King Edmund.

"You know about her?" asks Konge Grímr.

"Last month, a great many wildwolves entered the north of Ingland from Scotia. Many of them were slain, but some were captured and brought to my dungeons. I wished to know why they were fleeing, so I brought a man here – one with a similar ability to this girl. He spoke to one of the wildwolves and learned about the girl's existence. Her powers sound impressive. And dangerous."

"She is both of those things, but still merely a girl. In fact, less than a girl; she was born wrong."

"What do you mean 'wrong'?" asks Lady Beatrice.

King Edmund looks hek shocked that she's spoken, as if he'd forgotten she was there.

"Her brain is wrong," ses Konge Grímr. "In Norveg

we would not have let her live."

"And yet you failed to control her, even though she was your prisoner?" ses King Edmund. He's tauntin Konge Grímr and enjoyin evry speck of it.

"As I say, she and her people should not be underestimated."

"So you do not have the strength to defeat them alone?" ses King Edmund. "That is why you came – to request my assistance?"

"Our objectives are one and the same," ses Konge Grímr, "It's true that we lost many on the Night of the Dark Mountain, but I have recruited widely from elsewhere in the country and brought one hundred warriors with me. Norvegian fighters are the best in the world, and more are on their way. When the rest of my warriors arrive, I suggest they join your army."

"And then?"

"Then we go to war."

King Edmund lifts one scraggin hand to his chin. His skeleton fingers scrape against the metal hood he's wearin.

"I like that plan," he ses. "I like that plan very much."

AGATHA

I JUMP UP QUICK. WE NEED TO GET OUT OF THE PRISON bothan. The shadow things are coming and they will get us if we don't.

"We need to get out!" I say.

"What do you think I'm trying to do?" says Aileen. She is banging on the door harder with her elbow. "Help me."

I bang it too but it is so hard it hurts me and it will not move. The noise of the shadow things is getting louder. Outside, there is shouting. The shadow things are inside the enclave and coming close and closer. I look at the window and something dark slips through between the bars. A shadow thing! Another one comes under the door. Inside the bothan it is dark, but the shadow things are even darker. I jump backwards and pull Aileen away.

"They're here! They're inside!" I say. We press with our backs against the wall. They are coming in, more of them now and coming closer to us. They slide over the walls and across the ceiling and the floor. We cannot stop them. I scream. They are going to get us. We cannot stop them.

There is a whoosh noise outside on the door and then smoke comes in. There is fire on the door. Someone made a fire on the door.

"I'm sorry," a person shouts loud. "It was the only way. I have to go. I pray you get out safe." It is Lileas's mother Edme's voice. It is her who made the fire on the door.

The shadow things inside are going around fast like they don't know where to go. The door is a big fire now. It makes the shadow things go out of the window and away. That is the good thing. The bad thing is that the fire is coming in and we are trapped and it will burn us.

"What do we— do?" I ask to Aileen. "How do we get out?"

"Through the door," she says. She steps forwards and kicks the door hard. She kicks it again and again. There is fire on it but she is still kicking it which means she is brave. Some of the wood in the middle breaks off and is cracked. It is so hot now. At first it was nice because I was cold and it made me warmer but now it is too hot. My face is all wet and I am sticky sweaty. Aileen stops kicking.

"That's as much as I can do. We're going to have to jump through," she says.

"Jump through w– where?" I say. She cannot mean the door.

"The door," she says. Oh. She does mean the door.

"But the door is fire!" I say. "It will burn me and I die."

"We'll be all right. We have to risk it now, before it spreads any more. I've broken it a little; hopefully it will be enough."

"No," I say. It is a bad plan.

"We have to be brave. Can you be brave?"

Of course I can be brave. "Yes," I say. "It is easy for me."

"Good, then hold my hand."

"Wait," I say. I take Milkwort out of my pocket and hold him close to my chest with my other hand. I tell him he has to be brave too.

"After three," she says. "One. Two. Three!"

We run forward together and jump into the fire door. It breaks when we hit it and we fall on the ground outside. Black is in my eyes and I cannot see. Milkwort nibbles on my thumb to show he is okay. Something smells of horrible burning. It is me.

"I'm on fire! I'm on fire!" Fire is on my cloak and in my hair. I hit my hair to put it out. It hurts hot on my hand. Please I do not want my hair to be fire.

"Roll on the grass," says Aileen. She pushes me down. I roll like she says with my hands over Milkwort so he is not squished.

Please stop the fire, grass. I do not want to die with the fire.

"You're all right; it's out," says Aileen.

I look all over myself to check that she is right and she is right. The fire is gone. Milkwort is not on fire too which is a big phew. He climbs onto my shoulder. My hair is a very not nice smell. I stroke it to make it pretty.

"Is my hair still— pretty?" I ask Aileen.

"Very pretty," she says, and she smiles. I like it when she says that. "Now, come on, we need to get out of here."

There are still shadow things near us. I know it because I can hear them. That is why Aileen takes some of the broken door with fire on it and gives a different piece to me. It is for the protection. I hold it in the air so there is light all around.

The Raasay people are not shouting any more. All I can hear is the shadow things. Did they get everyone and they are dead?

"Look, Aggie," says Aileen.

I look. There is a big fire on the other side of the enclave. I did not see it before. It is near the Gathering where we used to eat. Lots of people are stood next to it. I can't see their faces, only dark people shapes. Some of them are smaller ones which are children. It is all the Raasay people. They did what we said. They made the big fire and the shadow things didn't get them.

"You did it," says Aileen. "You saved them. All those people are alive because of you." She is right and I am happy, I think. It is a bit confusing in my head what I am thinking. "Let's get out of here before they find out we've escaped."

130

That is a good plan. It is our enclave so we know where the Southern Gate is. We run there quickly. There is no one at the gate and no one on the wall either. They all ran away when the shadow things came is what I think. Aileen opens the gate.

The door piece I am holding is burning more and the fire is trying to get my hand. "It's too h– hot," I say. I hold it further away from me.

"Wait here," says Aileen. She runs off. I don't know where she went. My hand is bad tingles. It's going to burn me and I don't want it. "Here, these are better." Aileen is back. She doesn't have her broken door wood any more. She has two fire torches with fire on. They are meant for holding and are better. "The Moths used to keep these in the hollow. There was a stack of them still there."

I knew that. I wish I remembered it before. Then I would have got them and Aileen would have said I was clever. I take the one Aileen gives me and throw away the broken door piece wood. It lands on the grass and the grass starts burning.

"Come on," says Aileen. She grabs my hand and we run out of the gate.

We did it! We got away and the shadow things did not get us.

I look behind me at our enclave. The fire on the grass is spreading where I threw the broken door wood. I didn't know it would make so much fire. Maybe it was a bad mistake. It is too late to stop it now.

I am so tired. We ran a long way. I'm not good at running. Also it was hard with holding the torch as well. Aileen said we had to keep running in case the Raasay people came after us. The running made me nearly be sick. After that, Aileen said we could walk as long as it was fast walking.

When the sun comes and it is day we put out the torches in a stream to make the fire go away and we drink some of the water. Aileen shows me how to do it with scooping hands. She does it good. When I try to do it, the water leaks through my fingers so I have to be so so quick before it all goes. I don't know how Aileen does it so good.

"You must have holes in your fingers," Aileen says.

I look at my fingers. They don't have holes in them so she is wrong.

We sleep by the stream for a little bit but only for a little bit. Then Aileen says we have to go. We leave the torches by the river so it will be easier to walk. I am hungry but we don't have any food. I wish I was like Milkwort and could eat the grass. I pick some good ones for him to eat and he is happy. I am not happy because grass is not people food.

Whenever I say, "I'm hungry" Aileen says, "Hello, hungry, I'm Aileen." It is a joke. I did not know it was a joke the first time and it made my face confused. Now I know it is a joke and I laugh. It does not stop me from being hungry though.

"Do you want to play a game?" says Aileen. "It might make the journey go quicker."

"Okay," I say. I like playing games.

We play a game called *raonabal* which is when you have to say a colour and the other person has to do guessing. It is a game for children but I still like it. I go first and I say green and it is grass and Aileen guesses it first time.

"Too easy!" she says. Then it is her turn and she says blue.

"The sky," I say. I think it will be sky because that is a big one.

"Nope," says Aileen.

"The sea," I say.

"Nope," says Aileen.

Hmmm. It is a hard one. "A stone," I say.

"A stone?" says Aileen, and she laughs.

"Sometimes stones can be blue," I say. I know they are not really blue but I couldn't think of another one.

"Well it's not a 'blue' stone," says Aileen. "Give up?"

"No," I say. Then I think of a really good one. "A blue flower."

"Still no..."

It is hard to think of more blue things.

"A person!" I say.

"What?" Aileen says. "You're really scraping the barrel now!"

"No, a person. There." I point to the trees where I saw the person.

Aileen stops smiling. She pulls me down and it hurts. "Quick, into the heather," she says. We crawl to where the bushes are thicker. They smell of bark and prickle my face. "Who was it? Did they see us?"

"I don't— I don't know; I didn't— see," I say. "He was m– moving."

We are both looking hard into the trees. The person moves again behind a tree. "There!" I say.

Aileen does a sound like a cough. "That's not a person, it's a stag." She stands up. "Wow, look at it. It's beautiful."

I stand up too and I brush off the heather bits from my clothes and my hair. I look for the stag. The shadow things brought us a dead stag when we were at Dunnottar Castle but I have not seen an alive one before. It is hiding a bit so I cannot see it properly.

"It's limping," says Aileen. "I think it's injured."

"Are stags dangerous ones?" I ask. They have big antlers for stabbing.

"I don't think so. He's probably more scared of us than we are of him."

Aileen walks towards it. I follow her. When I am closer I can see it is very big. Its antlers are like branches. Big tree ones. They make me remember the horrible man the king of Norveg who is called Konge Grímr. He had antlers on his crown even though he was a man and not a stag. He was a very bad man. He is dead now which is good so I will never see him again.

When we are too close the stag moves away. It is hard

for it to move because it is hurt. Aileen was right. It is its leg and also some cuts on its side.

Don't go, I say to it in my head. *We will help you.* Talking to big animals makes my head sore, but it is kind to help people and also animals when they are poorly and I am good at helping.

The stag stops and looks at me. Its eyes are big and black.

"Did you talk to it?" says Aileen in a whisper voice. "You did, didn't you?" I nod my head yes. "Incredible," she says. "What's it saying?"

It's not saying anything because she keeps talking, is what I am thinking. I do not say that, though. I talk to the stag again. I say, *Are you hurt?* and, *We can make you better.*

It is only looking at me still. It does not move one teeny bit.

Then I can hear it in my head.

We're all going to die, is what it says.

JAIME

THERE ARE SO MANY THINGS THAT COULD GO WRONG. We could get lost and never find our way back; we could be attacked by wildwolves and be eaten alive; we could find the Badhbh after days – or even weeks – of searching, only for him to refuse to help us; or he could agree to help us, but then we arrive back on Skye too late and find the *sgàilean* have already killed everyone in the enclave...

Circling through the endless negative possibilities appears to be my new greatest skill.

Everything around us – the plants, the hills, the trees – is steeped in some of my worst-ever memories. The land feels poised to unleash something terrible upon us at any moment.

Yet even my most pessimistic side has to admit that I'm a lot better prepared this time around. I have sturdy footwear and warmer clothes, we have plenty of food and material to make a shelter, and – best of all – I have people to follow. I prefer following, because it means I don't have to think.

Our plan is to go straight to the Bó Riders' camp. I explained the journey I took last time and – even though my recollection was sketchy at best – Violet thinks she'll be able to find it. I don't know how. I guess by smoke trails or hoof prints or something. Occasionally, she asks me questions about certain landscapes or whether something looks familiar, but for the majority of the time, she decides which way we should go.

I left the Badhbh's diary with Cray, which is why we decided the camp is our best starting point. Not that I can imagine finding anything useful in it; I read it from front to back several times and as far as I can remember, the Badhbh didn't leave any other clues about where he was heading. At the very least, though, the Bó Riders will help us search for him. I'm sure they will. The thought of seeing them again engulfs me in an almost giddy joy, a sensation I can't remember feeling in weeks. Cray will be there. And Mór and Finn and all the others, but it's the thought of seeing Cray that spurs me on the most. He is the friend I need right now. Everything will be better with their help.

"You doing okay?" Donal asks, coupled with the high-pitched chuckle that comes out nearly every time he speaks.

"I'm fine."

"It's tiring work this walking, isn't it? Give me a saw

and a hammer any day." He takes in a loud, drawn-out breath and then releases it. "Nice, though. It's a beautiful country. When the rain stops for long enough to let you see it, that is."

"Yes, it is."

Donal is a talker. He hasn't worked out yet that I'm really not. "Well, you let us know if you need to rest up for a bit."

"I will."

He pats my shoulder far harder than he means to. "Good lad."

He checks up on me a lot. I'd prefer it if he didn't. We're not going fast, but he's right, the walking is tough. I didn't sleep well last night – the land was alive with coos and howls and other unfamiliar sounds, and I couldn't stop thinking about the wildwolves. They fled south after their fight with the Bó Riders, but I don't know how far south, and they could easily have come back since.

Violet is walking a couple of yards ahead of us, her long legs taking big strides. She's the opposite of Donal; she only speaks when she has something meaningful to say. I couldn't tell whether I liked her or not until last night when, as we huddled together under our temporary shelter, she surprised us by telling a story. She didn't ask if we wanted to hear one, she just started talking. No one's told me a story like that for years, yet it didn't feel childish. It was the tale of a young boy who wanted to be a kingfisher. Every day the boy would scamper down to the river that ran through his enclave and watch the kingfishers as they dived into the water for fish. He tried to copy them, splashing into the river with none of their grace. The boy would not be deterred, however, and started living in the same tree as the kingfishers, eating nothing but insects and small frogs because he couldn't catch any fish. The kingfishers grew accustomed to his presence and chirruped to him in the early morning and slept close to him at night.

I was transfixed the whole time Violet was talking, but the end of the story took a dark turn: one night, a fox crept into the enclave and, mistaking the boy for a kingfisher, gobbled him up. I was left wondering what the moral of the story was, and if there was a reason Violet had decided to tell it.

Even though her back is to me now, I can picture her face almost perfectly. Her broad mouth and wide-set eyes are at odds with her long face, and she has a mole under her right eye like a permanent tear. Her hair is such a pale brown it looks like it's fading away. It streams behind her now as she walks. I don't know how old she is. Quite old, maybe about thirty.

She stops, and one of her hands drifts up, indicating that we should stop too. Her slender fingers play with the air while she peers at the horizon.

"You see something?" asks Donal.

"I don't know," she says, squinting into the distance.

"We must be getting close, I would have thought," says Donal.

"Yes," says Violet, although she doesn't sound convinced. "Let's keep going."

Midway through the afternoon we come to the bank of a river. The water speeds past us, desperate to arrive at its destination. It's flowing too fast to cross, so we follow the river upstream, hoping it will shallow. As I walk, I kick stray stones into the river with increasing force. The river gulps them down without the slightest hesitation. We've already wasted so much time today traipsing around inconvenient lochs, and now this river. I thought we'd be at their camp by now.

"It's not going to lessen anytime soon," say Violet. "I suggest we cross."

"Here?" I ask. Surely not. The gushing water mocks us with its gurgles.

"Here's just as good a place as anywhere else," says Donal. "You can swim, right, lad?"

"Well, yes, but..." I look at the river. My throat squeezes in on itself.

"It won't be as deep as it looks," says Donal. "I'll go first."

Donal takes off his boots and socks, rolls up the bottom of his trousers, and strolls into the water. His legs are like tree trunks, so of course it's easy for him. He took the end of a long rope with him, and Violet now ties the other end around a sturdy rock, pulling it hard to check that the knot will hold. Donal wiggles his end, encouraging us to join him. Violet crosses next, fast and sure-footed. She holds on to the rope, even though I'm sure she's only doing it so I won't feel bad about having to rely on it when I cross.

Copying the others, I remove my footwear and roll up my trousers. The water is so cold it feels like it's sliced off my toes. I edge out, holding my boots in one hand and keeping a tight grip on the rope with the other. The riverbed is a mix of rough rock and slippery weeds, but it's not that hard to navigate once I've got the measure of it. Donal is holding the other end of the rope, giving me encouraging looks and the occasional "That's it, lad" and "Easy does it". Halfway across, the water is up to my thighs and rages against my spindly legs. I don't know why I bothered rolling up the ends of my trousers. There's something familiar about the cold, about the way the water rushes, its power.

Sgàilean.

The memory of them swarming my body outside Dunnottar Castle comes flooding back. I picture them rampaging across Skye – the greatest threat we've ever encountered – and us with no way of controlling them. It's my fault. I should have taken the amulet from Nathara's body the moment the *sgàilean* returned to it, not left it around her neck for anyone to claim. A wave of dizziness washes over me and at the same moment, an errant torrent knocks into the back of my knees. My legs give way, I lose my grip on the rope and the water sucks me under.

I tumble downstream, surrendering to its power, with no awareness of what is up and what is down, until a mighty heave rips me from its grasp. Donal looks down at me, water dripping from his furrowed brow. He still has a hold of me even though he's dragged me several feet from the water. Violet is standing behind him, her eyes full of concern.

"You okay, lad?" Donal asks.

"Yes, I'm fine." I stand up too quickly, my legs wobbling beneath me. "Let's keep going." I hobble away from him, not wanting him to see the shame on my face. Then it dawns on me. My boots. I must have dropped them after I slipped. They'll be long gone by now.

"Are you sure you don't want to rest for a bit first?" Donal calls after me. "We can make a fire, dry your clothes?"

"I'll be fine." There's a graze on my left palm, which I hide beneath my cloak.

"I can take your packs at least." Donal catches up with me and reaches to take one of my satchels. Their straps are tangled around my neck and arms.

"I can manage them."

I increase my pace, trying to untangle the straps as I go. My wet clothes start rubbing against my shoulder blades, making me shiver.

"Wait, Jaime; you don't have any boots." Donal bounds off, further downstream, in case they've washed ashore.

"You can wear mine," says Violet, already sitting down to take hers off.

"It's fine," I say. "I'll walk barefoot."

"But you'll cut your feet. The ground's sharper than it looks," says Donal, giving up on his search.

"I'll be fine."

Donal rummages in one of his bags. "I'm sure I can find something in here to wrap around them."

"I said I'm fine," I snap, twisting around to stare at them. "How many times do I need to say it?"

They both stop what they're doing and look at me. I turn away.

"Suit yourself, lad," says Donal.

"The Bó Riders will have a pair I can borrow," I say, not loud enough for either of them to hear. We just need to reach their camp, then everything will be all right. I fix my sights on the horizon and march on, ignoring the mud that squelches between my toes. It can't be too far now.

We pass between a couple of modest hills, where the bracken looks softer than it is. Occasional stones nip the soles of my feet, and each time I swallow the pain. The sky turns darker, into a sunken grey, and the wind picks up. My whole body's shaking now. Without saying anything, Donal steps over to me and drapes a blanket across my shoulders. I pull it in tight.

Despite the cold and the wet and the throbbing in my feet, the closer we get to the Bó Riders' camp, the lighter I feel. I start to recognize certain landmarks, or at least I think I do. Maybe that's the patch of trees we passed through when Mór and Cray first brought us here, and that could have been the rock I climbed when I was being chased by wildwolves. Violet points out piles of animal excrement – which she believes came from Highland cows – as well as several hoof marks which all lead in the same direction. We walk to the top of the last gentle slope, from where we should have our first proper view of the camp.

I recognize the clearing immediately, but nothing in it is the same. There are no cows feeding on the grass, no tents, no fires, no people.

All of the Bó Riders have gone.

SIGRID

THERE'S HEK LOADS OF STAIRS IN THIS SKITTIN PALACE.
We follow this slow ploddin man up these wide ones,
then curve around, then up more stairs and along and
more stairs again. At the top of the next ones the man
opens a door to where Konge Grímr's gunna be sleepin.
Where I'm gunna be sleepin too, I guess. It's bigger than
the whole shack I lived in back in Norveg, though that
isn't sayin much. The bed is so bulkin it could sleep
six people without them even touchin. There's wooden
chests carved with patterns, a mirror taller than I am
and a bright red rug coverin half the floor, what's thick
and soft. It's not as nice as Granpa Halvor's rug, though.

The ploddin man leaves. Bolverk came up with us
and checks around the room, sniffin for I dunno what.
After I finish tellin Konge Grímr all what's in the
room, he makes me take him to the bed and he sits on
the edge of it.

"What do you make of him?" Konge Grímr asks Bolverk.

"Make of who?" Bolverk replies.

"Our esteemed host..."

"King Edmund? Well, he looks ready to drop dead at any moment, but I reckon he'll keep to his word. His desperation to kill all Scotians is apparent enough."

"Good."

"I'm not sure he trusts us, though, with all that armour he was wearing. Old fool. He'd already taken all our weapons – what was he expecting us to do? Stab him with a dog bone?" Bolverk laughs at his own joke, even though it was a measly one. "Plus, he had about thirty guards watching him while we were eating."

"Thirty-two," I say. Dunno why I said that. I'm makin a bad habit of speakin up when no one's talking to me.

"What did you say?" Bolverk turns on me.

"Thirty-two," I say again. "There were thirty-two guards watchin the Inglish king while he was eatin."

"No one asked your opinion," Bolverk snarls. "You don't speak unless you're spoken to."

"Let her talk," ses Konge Grímr.

Bolverk's head snaps up like he's been hit. Konge Grímr doesn't move none. He's waitin for me to do more talkin, but I haven't got nothin more to say. Bolverk stares at me like he wants to rip out my loller.

"There were two guards with their hands on the king's shoulders, six stood behind, two opposite him,

146

another six sat up and down our table, four by the door we went in by, four by the other door, and eight around the outside of the room."

Konge Grímr tilts his head a speck. "Well, aren't you an observant little mouse?" he ses.

"Why were you counting guards?" Bolverk asks. His face is mud and thunder.

"I wasn't countin," I say. "I just remember it."

"Exactly how good is your memory?" asks Konge Grímr.

"Good, Your Supremacy," I say.

Konge Grímr nods and grins with grottin lips. Bolverk's starin daggers at me. Don't know why he's so mad at me for answerin one question.

"Were you aware that all of the king's guards were male?" he ses to Konge Grímr. What is this – a competition who can tell him the most or somethin?

"I was not," ses Konge Grímr. "Whyever would he not have women? They are far more attentive."

"There were no Inglish women dining with us at all," Bolverk continues, "except for the king's wife, of course. I do believe they view women differently here. As inferior. My point is … perhaps you should reconsider having this *girl*" – he flings a sneer in my direction – "beside you when you are talking to him. It may be offensive in their culture."

"Don't be preposterous," Konge Grímr replies. "If he has an issue with women, that's his problem, not mine." He kicks off his boots, leavin smears of dirt over the rug. "Leave me now, Bolverk. I'm weary."

Bolverk looks like he doesn't wanna go. He's starin at me and his teeth are clamped. I smile at him as gutsick as I can, which makes his teeth clench even tighter.

"Sleep strong, Your Supremacy," he ses. He bows low then slashes me with one more look before goin.

"Take this," ses Konge Grímr after Bolverk's gone. He's taken off his antler crown and holds it out to me. He hasn't never let me touch his crown before. "Put it somewhere safe."

I take it from him. It's heavier than what it looks. Must be hek skap to lug that around on your kog all day. I lift it above my own head, thinkin maybe I'll try it on quick.

"I wouldn't do that if I were you," Konge Grímr ses. He's lookin at me with his gnarled, knotted not-eyes.

I place the crown down careful on one of the chests, pretendin I never had no intention of tryin it.

The next day I'm all aches and bones. The chain wasn't long enough to reach the rug, so I had to sleep on the hard stone floor. Not that I slept much, with it bein so cold all night. The window doesn't have no shutter, and of course Konge Grímr didn't give me no blanket.

Konge Grímr spends the day bein shown around the palace and the gardens, so I spend the day trompin around next to him, tellin him evrythin he's not seein. It was diffrunt in Norveg cuz he knew his way around for the most, and it was diffrunt on the longboat cuz

146

it wasn't so big, but here at the palace I gotta do even more for him cuz it's all so bulkin and there's so much what's new.

When he's not walkin, he's sittin and eatin and neckin with Bolverk and the other wreckers. It's a hek easy life bein a king.

I don't see King Edmund again until evenin meal. He's carried down in his gawkin lynx bed and brought to sit next to Konge Grímr, same as before. He's still clatterin with all his armour on. Lady Beatrice is there too with the fat, skittin pig trottin beside her. She's dressed in red today in clothes what are just as stupid as what she was wearin yesterday. She looks at me as she walks past but there's nothin goin on in her eyes. She hasn't got no smarts is what I'm thinkin.

Inglish women bring in all the food and top up the drinks, same as yesterday, with their bowin heads and quiet mouths. I wonder if Bolverk was right and King Edmund finds women offensive for some reason. It's not right, that's for hek sure.

I load up a plate for Konge Grímr and he starts stuffin the food in his hole. The chew smells hek scrammin. I haven't been given nothin to eat all day and my stomach's crampin like a choked squirrel. I don't wanna beg. I'm not gunna beg.

"Your Supremacy," I say in Konge Grímr's ear, "I haven't eaten nothin since before we left the boat. Could I have somethin to eat, please?" That's not beggin, it's askin.

Without stoppin his own chewin, he reaches out and grabs the first thing his skittin grubbers touch: a roll of bread the size of my fist. He chucks it on the floor, expectin me to scramble after it like some dirty rotdog. I'm not no dog and it makes me hek fiery that he's treatin me like one. I'm sure as muck not gunna leave the roll on the floor, though.

It's the most hek *rikka* bread I ever tasted. It's still warm and there's brown stew sauce on it from somethin or other. I don't care what it is, nor that there's grubmuck on it from the floor neither. I chomp on it and chomp again. I'm about to put the last piece in my mouth when I get shoved in the shoulder by a scraggin wet snout. It's the pig – Lady Beatrice's one – what must've seen the food fall on the floor and wants some for itself. I shoo it with my hands but it's not goin nowhere. It's fat enough – it doesn't need no feedin like I do. But now it's strokin me with its big pink snouter and pleadin with its beady gawpers.

I break the last of the roll into two pieces and hold one of them out for the pig. It scoffs it down, ticklin my palm with its gobbler. I scratch it under its chin, which makes its bottom wiggle. Before it gets any ideas about eatin the other piece and all, I shove the bread in my own mouth. The pig's flappy ears rise up, askin if I got more, but when it sees that I don't, it trots back to Lady Beatrice. That's when I notice she's been watchin me. Her face is so blank I don't know what she's thinkin. Maybe I wasn't sposed to feed her pig. She doesn't look angry, though. She pats the pig on its head and turns back to the table.

After evryone's finished eatin, we go through to another room. Konge Grímr leans heavy on my arm to stop himself stumbling, after all the mead he's been neckin. He squeezes my head harder than usual for me to describe the new room to him. I tell him it's much smaller than the feast hall and has soft on the floor like the palace entrance, but that this time it's blue. There's a bowl of water by the door for washin hands. I lead Konge Grímr to it. After he's washed, he shakes them dry, gettin stinkin dirt water all over me. I don't think he did it on purpose, but he might of.

We sit down at a round table and someone closes the doors. There's four people at the table: King Edmund, Konge Grímr, Bolverk and a scrawny man with skinny cheeks and chicken eyes. Two guards stand behind King Edmund, still with their hands on his shoulders, and there are six other guards in the room – three by the window and three by the door. It's a hek lot of guards for one small room.

"Well, then," says King Edmund. He clears his throat with a harsk growl what goes on for ages. "It is time for us discuss plans for the eradication of our mutual enemy."

"Of course," ses Konge Grímr, "but first, we must drink – to celebrate our union!"

Bolverk thumps his fist on the table in agreement. King Edmund keeps his lips tight and nods to one of the guards. The man goes to the flagon in the corner and pours some dark brown liquid into four metal tankards. He slops them in the middle of the table. I reach across and pick one up for Konge Grímr. It's so bulkin I gotta use both hands. I put it in front of him and place his scraggin fingers on the handle. Straightaways he lifts it to his lips and glugs down three bulk drekks.

"I trust it is to your liking?" King Edmund ses.

Bolverk's been neckin his own and lets out a grizzleburp.

"It's very fine," ses Konge Grímr, neckin one more drekk.

"On to business, then," ses King Edmund. He clicks his fingers and the scrawny chicken man next to him pulls out a long scroll. He unrolls it, and it's bigger than what the whole table is.

"This is a map of the mainland: both Ingland and Scotia, as well as all of the islands," ses the chicken man.

"Who are you?" Konge Grímr ses, cuz it's the first time the man has spoken. I bite my tongue to stop myself from sayin, *He's the scraggin man with chicken eyes, of course*.

"My name is Aldric, Your Majesty. I am an adviser to the king." He's got a high voice like a woman's. Bolverk's smirkin and I think that's why. "Perhaps you would be so kind as to point out exactly where the clan you spoke of resides?"

Evryone leans forward and is lookin at the map. Sept Konge Grímr, of course, who can't see nothin. Bolverk licks one of his fingers with his thick lollin tongue and then jabs it down on the map.

"This is the island here," he ses. "Their settlement is on this northernmost tip, but it's now occupied by people from a neighbouring isle. Unless the clan has succeeded in reclaiming it, it's likely we will find them here." He jabs his grubber down on another spot, further south. "This is the home of a different clan, who were also our prisoners; the two clans fled the mountain together, so may well be supporting each other now that they've returned."

King Edmund nods, which sets the metal chains on his hood clangin. His whole scraggin face is tight as mud cracks. "It sounds like there are more of them than I first thought," he ses. "I have dispatched spies to mainland Scotia; I shall send word for them to scout this island as well."

"As I keep saying, these people should not be underestimated," ses Konge Grímr.

"My spies are more than capable of taking care of themselves. They are, shall we say, 'special'. They're my new innovation, one I have been perfecting over the past decade. The Scotians will not see them coming ... in more ways than one." He makes a phlegmy sound in his throat what's either a laugh or a cough. "Once they return, we will have a clearer understanding of the situation."

I wanna know more about the spies, but neither Konge Grímr nor Bolverk asks, and King Edmund doesn't say nothin more about them neither. Instead, he tells them about his army, which he boasts is the most hek bulkin army the world has ever known: tens of thousands of soldiers what'll march north at the click of his fingers with nothin but killin on their minds. He talks about secret weapons and special armour and dark creatures what don't sound no good neither. What with Konge Grímr's wreckers and all, the people in Scotia don't stand a chance.

The four of them – Konge Grímr, Bolverk, King Edmund and Aldric chicken eyes – talk on forever about all the ways they're gunna wipe out the Scotian people. Although they don't use the words *wipe out*; they use more bloodsplash words like *kill*, *massacre*, and *destroy*. The more they talk, the more twistgut I feel, specially when they say about gettin rid of the kidlins and all. They speak about the girl again, the one they think can talk with animals. Sounds foolin to me, but what do I know? She's only a few years older than me, and Konge Grímr's specially keen to get his hams on her. He wants to hurt her the most. They yap on as if I wasn't there cuz they don't think I can understand, but I'm listenin tight and hearin it all.

All the whiles, Konge Grímr and Bolverk are neckin more and more. The guard keeps fillin up their tank-ards, and they're both turnin more sour with evry drekk. King Edmund hasn't supped none of his beer. Aldric takes a sip evry now and awhile, but they're so small they're not really no sips at all. I'm getting hek sapped and I wanna go to sleep, but no one cares one speck about me.

"Why do you wear all that armour?" Bolverk asks King Edmund all in a sudden. The two guards what have got their palms on the king's shoulders tighten their grip a sniff. "It's okay, it's okay," Bolverk goes on. He holds his hands up in front of him. "I'm not going to cause any trouble. I'm just wondering, that's all. We're all friends here, aren't we?"

"Yes," ses Konge Grímr, "we're all friends." Both Bolverk and Konge Grímr are smiling pigsick.

King Edmund sits up straighter in his chair, creak-clankin with evry move. "You cannot see my face, Grímr, but perhaps the girl you call 'your eyes' has informed you: I am not a young man. Quite the opposite; I am incredibly old. I plan to live forever, and so far I am succeeding rather well at it. I have defeated death." He pauses to take in three raspy breaths. "One does not escape death without extreme measures and excessive caution. I am a master of both."

"No one can live forever," ses Bolverk.

"That is where you are wrong," ses King Edmund. "I can, and I intend to. My physicians have developed elixirs to impede and reduce the effects of aging and are in the process of systematically replacing every organ in my body with a new, healthier one." No one asks what poor rotweasels he's stealin these bodyscraps from. "Besides, I already know how I will die, which gives me the ultimate advantage over death."

"And how's that?" asks Bolverk.

King Edmund smiles, makin his eyes screw into worms. "That is not for you to know."

"Oh, but we know already," ses Konge Grímr. He's the one oozin smugness now.

"Oh?" The wrinkles on King Edmund's forehead are scramblin.

Somethin's changed in the room. No one's laughin no more and the air's turned to dung.

"It's surprising what you can discover if you ask the right people and pay the right price; isn't that right, Bolverk?"

"It is, Your Supremacy."

"We discovered many things about you," ses Konge Grímr. "Including that you believe you will die at the hands of a Scotian, which is why you attempted to exterminate every last person in that country. It is also why you were so perturbed to discover there are people still alive there."

The only sound in the room is King Edmund's wheezy breathin. "Well, haven't you been busy," he ses. He pulls at the scraggin flaps under his chin while he decides what to make of Konge Grímr's snoopin. After a few strokes, he smiles a false smile and ses, "You're perfectly right, of course, and – since we are now in allegiance – I see no reason to deny it. Many years ago, I dreamt that I would be murdered by a Scotian. It was more than a dream; it was a vision, a warning, and I immediately recognized it as truth. That is why I did what I did. You know about my plague, I presume? A lethal illness that spread from person to person, leaving no one alive. It was quite ingenious. The disease was inserted into rats, which were then unleashed upon Scotia, but not before we dug the longest trench that has ever been seen. It spanned the entire breadth of the country – from the west coast of Ingland all the way to the east, right on the Scotian border. Once the rats were released, the trench was set on fire to ensure the rats could not return. It also prevented infected Scotians from crossing the border into Ingland. The trench was kept burning for over a year, during which time the plague wreaked its havoc. It was more effective than I could have ever imagined: it wiped out every man, woman and child from that dastardly place. Or so I thought. The news that there are survivors is ... unsettling – I will not deny that – and has led to certain *extra* precautions." He lifts up both his arms, indicatin the armour. "However, their numbers are small and my army is unstoppable. With the addition of yours, we will have no problem in destroying them."

This king is batcrazy. He's even more cracked than Konge Grímr, if such a thing is possible. He killed evryone in a whole country just cuz of some stupid dream. There isn't nothin right about that. I wanna scream at him. I wanna tell him he was wrong to do what he did and spit in his hek smuggin face. But I can't do none of those things, cuz I'm not even sposed to be understandin a single word he's sayin. So I just gotta stand here, pretendin like evrythin's fine while my insides swarm fire.

Finally, King Edmund announces that they've talked enough for one night and he wishes to sleep. About time too. Konge Grímr is so oafed he has to have four of King Edmund's guards drag his harsk bulk up to his room. Once we're there, the men start to take off his furs, but he pushes them away.

"Don't you touch me," he ses, his words all slurrin. "I am a king, sent from Øden. Get out, get out!"

The men look at each other unsure, then bow and leave the room. Now it's just me and him.

"Are you there, girl?" he ses in our language. Course I'm here. I'm chained to him with a mountain of thick skittin metal. Where the hell else does he think I'm gunna be?

"Yes," I say. I don't say "Your Supremacy" and he doesn't remind me to say it neither. He's not so bothered when it's just me and him.

"Take my furs," he ses. He shrugs them off and slings them in my direction. They're bulkin, but I fold them as best as I can. "And my crown." He passes that to me too, then collapses backwards on the bed. "You're a good girl," he ses. His eyes are closed and his words are slow. I don't say nothin. "I never had a daughter. Three sons ... no daughter. I don't know girls. Didn't want one. But I tell you, even you – *even you* – would've been better than the *kvillótt* sons I had. First two didn't even last a year ... sickly little weevils ... and then Knútr.

Knútr... I killed him, you know. Whiny little *bikja*. Axe in his head... Splash. Hell of a mess. Served him right..." He's really slurrin now, and smilin to himself at the memory of what he did to his son. The smile disappears. "You've got it easy. All you do is follow me around, don't have to think about anything. I'd rather be following like you." He's pointin at me, or at the ceilin, with one wild, wobblin finger. "Who'd want to be king? Everyone, that's who, because no one knows. It's not... Being a king is... And who's gunna rule after me? No one, that's who. Maybe I should live forever like that stupid... Good idea. I'll live forever too..."

His breathin gets deeper and more gravelly and, as I wait and watch, it eventually falls into snores. He's so helpless. I could probly choke him with the chain right now and he wouldn't even notice – that'd be one way for escapin.

No. I'm not killin no one. That'd make me just as bad as he is.

I'm still holdin his crown. I put it down on one of the chests and wipe my hands on my clothes. What a night. I haven't never been so sapped, but my mind's still runnin on. I lie down on the floor next to the bed. Konge Grímr's furs are in a pile nearby. I'm tempted to use them to keep warm, but I'm sure he'd find out if I did. Probly smell me on them or somethin. I wrap my arms around my knees instead. I'm about to close my gawpers when I see a small square of somethin tucked under the corner post of the bed, near where my head is.

No one else would of seen it there, it's only cuz I'm lyin so close. Could it of been left for me? No. But why else would it be there?

My fingers are unsure as they creep towards it. I slip it out from its place with a rustle. It's a piece of parchment, crisp and thick, folded over twice. I unfold it once, pause, unfold it again, then turn it into the moonlight what's drippin through the window. The message is in the foreign tongue, and straightaways I know it's meant for me.

I know you can understand us. You're being watched.

AGATHA

THE HURT STAG MOVES FORWARDS A BIT AND THEN backwards a bit. When it steps on the twigs they make snap sounds. Its eyes are moving around fast.

"It said it's afraid of the darkness," I say to Aileen. "The darkness came and it t– tried to hurt its— herd. I think it means the— shadow things. It is scared that the shadow things will come back and k– kill them all."

"Will it let us help?" Aileen asks.

"Yes," I say.

We move closer to the stag. It is very pretty. I stroke it and it likes it. Its antlers are sharp. *Don't you stab me with your head*, I say and then I say, *Please*, because of manners. It says it won't. It is happy we are helping.

It tells me its hoof is hurt. It was because it was too dark when it was running and it didn't see the sharp bushes. It lets Aileen pick up its hoof to look at it. There is a big thorn stuck in the bottom. She pulls on the thorn. It is hard to come out. Then it is out and the stag pulls its leg away. It makes a pain noise like a bark but different and stomps its bad foot on the ground one, two, three, four times. The stag is better now the thorn is out and it is happy. It rubs Aileen's arm with its head which is to say thank you and it does it to me as well.

Aileen says the cuts on its side were done by thorns as well. I was worried it was the shadow things that did the cutting. There is nothing we can do about the thorn cuts. Aileen says they are not deep cuts and it will be okay.

I'm Agatha, I say to it. *But you can call me Aggie if you like.*

It asks me, *What is an "Aggie"?*

It is a me, I say. *It is my name. What is your name?* It tells me it doesn't have a name. Everyone needs to have a name. I do a think. *I will call you Thistle-River*, I say. *Because your antlers are spiky like thistles and you are strong like a river.*

He likes his new name. He bows his head and I bow mine too.

I tell Aileen his name and she says "Hello, Thistle-River," and waves at him. She does not know that you should do bowing instead.

Thistle-River tells me that he needs to find his herd. They were split up when the darkness came. He hopes they are still alive and the darkness didn't get them. I wonder if the shadow things tried to get the deers because they couldn't get the Raasay people.

"What about tonight?" I ask Aileen.

"What about tonight?" she says back to me.

"The shadow things will come back t– tonight and try to get the deers again. They'll get Th– Thistle-River and all the other ones. We have to— help them."

"What can we do?" says Aileen. "We can't save every deer on the island."

"What if they came to Clann-na-Bruthaich's— enclave?" I say. "We can make b– big fires and they will be— safe."

"I…" Aileen says. I think she will say it is a bad plan but then she changes and says, "I don't see why not. If you can get them all there, we can at least try."

I smile a big one. I tell Thistle-River my plan. He thinks it is a good plan and he thanks me a very lot. He is going to find the rest of his deers and tell all the other ones on the island as well. I tell him he has to go to Clann-na-Bruthaich's enclave. He didn't know what is *Clann-na-Bruthaich* or what is the *enclave* so I had to do describing. Then he knows it and where it is. He calls it *Big Rock Circle*. That is a good name for it too. We will meet him there.

I say goodbye and bow my head. He thanks me again and bows his head as well. Then he says, *Goodbye, Sun-Leaf.* I ask him what is Sun-Leaf? He says I gave him a name so he will give me a name too. He will call me Sun-Leaf because suns give life and so do leaves and so do I. It is a funny name. *Okay, you can call me Sun-Leaf,* I say. He goes away through the trees. I hope he finds his herd.

We have to do walking again now and it is even worse. My head is pain and aching bad from talking with the stag. Aileen helps me by holding on to my arm. I like Aileen now. We are good friends and I hug her sometimes.

We play *raonabal* again. It makes me think less about the walking and the boring. I go first and I say white which is for goats' hair. It takes a long time for Aileen to guess that one. After she guesses it she tells me it was a good one. She is right. I was clever to think of it. Then it's her turn and she says yellow. I do lots of guesses but it is not the sun and it is not flowers and it is not a wasp and it is not teeth. It is hard for me to guess. Aileen gives me the clues and then I guess it. It is wee! That is very funny and a little bit rude. I do not want to play any more after that. My head is too hurting and it hurts more to do thinking.

We will never be there, it is so far. Sometimes I have my eyes closed and it is only because Aileen is holding me that I know which way to go. Walk walk walk walk walking.

"Would you look at that," says Aileen a long time later.

I open my eyes. All the deers are there. My head is swamp so I have to do blinking to know they are real. There are so many of them. More than a hundred even. Maybe two hundred or a thousand. They are in a group all together near to where Clann-na-Bruthaich's enclave is.

One of the stags runs all the way towards us. It looks like it is jumping when it runs.

Sun-Leaf, I hear in my head. It is Thistle-River. He found his herd and told the other deers my plan as well.

Follow me, I say. I don't say lots. My head is hurting and I don't want it to hurt more.

I walk the last bit to the enclave with Aileen and Thistle-River. There are lots of Hawks on the wall. They are looking at all the deers. One of them moves the launcher which is for firing arrows. She points it at Thistle-River.

"No!" I say. I stand in front of Thistle-River with my arms out so they won't shoot him.

"What's going on?" shouts Lenox from on the wall. On his face is big frowning eyebrows. "Where the blazes have you been?"

"We have to h– help the— deers," I say.

"What?"

"We have to let them inside. Otherwise the shadow things will— get them."

Lenox puts his hand on his head and rubs it like he is confused. I don't know why. It is easy to understand.

"I think you'd better speak to Catriona," he says.

The Upper Gate opens. The Moths stare at Thistle-River when we walk in. It is rude to stare. Don't they know that? The other deers stay outside which is being patient.

We wait for Catriona. Then she comes.

"You weren't here last night," she says. I hoped she didn't know that. "Where were you?"

"We went for firewood but got lost in the woods," says Aileen. It is a lie but I am happy she says it. Catriona will be cross if she knows where we went. She wants all the Raasay people to be dead, even the children ones. "We didn't want to risk coming back in the dark, so we made a fire and waited until morning."

"It's mid-afternoon. How lost did you get?" Catriona looks like she doesn't believe Aileen.

"We made some friends," says Aileen, and she puts her hand out towards Thistle-River. "We were helping them."

"And you've invited them to live in my enclave, I hear?" says Catriona.

"It's not— your enclave," I say.

"Excuse me?" Catriona turns her head to look at me.

"I said it's not your enclave. It is for all— all of your clan."

She does not like it when I say that. "Well, it is certainly not *your* enclave. Perhaps that's one thing we can agree upon?"

"This is Thistle-River," I say. Catriona doesn't say anything. "You're supposed to b– bow your— head when you say hello." Catriona does not bow her head and she does not say hello. "He's my friend," I say.

"I'm sure he is," says Catriona. "But why is he here?"

"Last night his herd was attacked by the *sgàilean*," says Aileen. "They need protection. We thought they'd be safer inside, where there's fire."

"Oh, is that what you thought?" says Catriona. "And since when do you get to decide what happens in our enclave?"

Aileen opens her mouth but doesn't say anything.

"They are n– nice animals, and it is what you do to be— nice," I say.

Catriona's jaw goes tight and more tight and she is thinking. She looks at me and then at Aileen and then at Thistle-River. It is a not nice way that she is looking.

"Very well," she says. "Bring them in."

JAIME

I RUN ALL THE WAY DOWN THE SLOPE UNTIL I'M STAND-
ing in the open field where the Bó Riders' tents used
to be. It's familiar, yet completely different at the same
time, as if the whole place has been sliced open and
gutted. It's so empty now, so hollow.

Donal puts his hand on my shoulder. "You did say
they were nomadic. I guess they moved on to somewhere else."

I'm nodding but it feels like there's more to it than
that. Was it the wildwolves? Did they come back for
another attack? This isn't right; this isn't what was supposed to happen.

"There's no sign of a fight," says Violet. "They had
time to pack up all their things before they left." She
crouches and examines the ground. "Although from
the marks here and over there, it looks like they left in
somewhat of a hurry."

"Can you tell which way they went?" I ask.

She doesn't have time to answer. The grass below us moves, turns into a shape, turns into a body...

It's too quick. A colourless hand flashes up and grabs hold of Donal's wrist. His body stiffens and his eyes bulge, then he collapses to the ground. The next instant, Violet is grappling with whatever it was that injured him. Its whole body looks like grass, but it's an illusion, the patterns moving in swathes beneath its skin. Contrasting colours ripple across its face.

"Jaime, run!" Violet screams.

But what about Donal? His body lies limp on the grass next to me.

I back away, shaking my head. A movement to my left and the trunk of a nearby tree comes alive in the same way the grass did. Another body, this one patterned like bark. It makes straight for me. I run, as fast as I can, without considering which direction is best. The ground booms against my naked feet, every step an agonizing slap. The satchels are weighing me down, so I remove them both and fling them from me without a second thought. My sword thuds against my legs. I try to pull it from its scabbard, but it keeps juddering back in to the rhythm of my uneven steps. I'm breathing fast, too fast, like I'm running out of air. On my fourth attempt, the sword pulls loose and I risk a glance behind me. The shape is still chasing, its bark-coloured skin fading into an almost translucent blue. What the hell is that thing? Its body is human-shaped, but that's where the similarities end. It opens its mouth to reveal colourless gums. I throw my sword at it. It swerves, dodging the blade with minimal effort. Great, now I'm weaponless. Stupid. So stupid.

I keep running; it's all I can do. Through sunken puddles and patches of wet heather, over low-rising hills and ground so brittle it decimates my feet. I ignore the pain and don't look back.

Daylight slips away and it starts to rain, the drips tantalizing my lips. I lift my head and open my mouth as I run, too distracted by the rain to notice a sudden dip in the ground. It takes me by surprise, twisting my leg at an awkward angle. I crash forwards, adding to the bruises I suffered in the river.

I flip over onto my back, lean on my elbows and try to bring my frantic breathing under control. Nothing has pounced on me. Yet. Does that mean I lost it? The soles of my feet are pulsing. They look like they've been chewed by a horde of rats. What a mess. I stand up, barely able to put any weight on them. I need shelter. The rain is coming down heavier and my teeth are chattering so hard my whole face aches. There's a rugged hillside not too far away. Maybe I can find a ledge or an alcove to take shelter in while I wait for the rain to lessen. I hobble towards it, alert to every movement around me. The dark and the rain make it almost impossible to see or hear anything.

I should go back. Violet and Donal might need me. The image of Donal lying pale on the ground hits me like a flash of harsh morning light. I have to go back; if the creatures caught Violet as well, I'm the only one who can help. Except I have no idea which direction I came from. I'm lost and I'm alone and if I don't find a way to dry out my clothes, I won't last the night. My flint lighter was in one of the satchels, along with food and everything else useful. There's no way I'd be able to find them again, not in this weather. I have nothing.

I approach the hillside, which has huge rocks clinging to its side like giant limpets. I stumble around, pressing my weight into them for strength, looking for a nook or opening I can crawl into, but there's nowhere to hide. I keep walking, keep looking. A noise draws my attention higher up the hillside. Something's there. I blink back the rain. My imagination taunts me, seeing figures in every hollow.

I turn back as a dark shape jumps off one of the rocks in front of me. My shout is cut off by the hand that clamps over my mouth. I'm spun around so my back is pressed against whatever it is that's got me. I kick backwards with my heel but don't make contact.

"Jaime?"

How does it know my name? The voice is muffled, so it takes me a few moments to realize that I recognize it. The hold on my mouth relaxes and I turn around to face her.

"Huh" is the only sound I can make.

Her gloved hand pulls down the material covering her face. Tears of relief spring into my eyes.

"Mór!" I say. I wrap my arms around her in an awkward hug, which she doesn't reciprocate. I forgot that hugging is not one of the Bó Riders' customs. The rain bounces off her hood.

"What are you doing here?" I ask, the words jolting out between cold breaths. The last time I saw her was in the harbour at Dunnottar Castle, before Agatha, Nathara and I set sail for Norveg. "We went to your camp. Where are all the other Bó Riders? Where's Cray?"

"Questions later; we need to get out of this rain."

She takes hold of my wrist and guides me further around the hill. There's a slim crack between two boulders, which we both squeeze through. It opens up into blackness. I have no idea how big the space is. I'm stooped, cramped. I raise my hand in front of my face and wave it about, but I can't see a thing.

"Stay still," says Mór after I trip over something on the ground. There's the sound of flint and a couple of blinding sparks. After the third strike, a fire begins to take hold. As it hisses into life, the hidden cave materializes around me. Its ceiling is low, but it goes back quite far.

"Where are we?" My teeth are still rattling together.

"In one of our hideouts. Come closer to the fire. You look half dead. Let me see your feet." I slump down next to the flames, greedy for their heat. "Take off your clothes and wrap yourself in this." She hands me a cloak lined with fur. "Don't worry, I won't look."

I peel off my outer layers, wring them out, and then lay them flat to dry. "Why did you leave your camp?"

I ask once I'm wrapped in the cloak's folds. "We were looking for you, but there were these ... things. One looked like grass and another one looked like tree bark. But then they changed... They attacked us. Are they the reason you left?"

She doesn't answer. She holds her hand towards one of my feet and clicks her fingers. I raise it off the ground and she inspects it by the light of the fire. From a weathered bag she takes out a wooden pot. She scoops out a generous amount of its contents and lathers it over my cuts. I scrunch up my eyes to stop myself from squealing. The balm has a pungent smell like sour spit. After the initial sting, a cooling sensation sets in that does wonders to stop the throbbing. Mór then wraps the foot in a length of tough cloth, like a second skin. It might even *be* skin; I don't ask because I don't want to know. Once she's finished my first foot, she places it on the ground and gestures towards my other one. I lift it up and she performs the same procedure again.

"Thank you," I say once she's finished. "I don't know what I would have done if I hadn't found you."

"I think it was actually *me* who found *you*." Mór smiles, but the joy doesn't reach her eyes.

"That's fair."

We sit in silence for a while. Then she says, "They're called 'imitators'. At least that's what we've taken to calling them. We don't know what they are or where they've come from. We only saw them for the first time about a week ago."

"They must have come from somewhere."

"Some people think they crawled out of the lochs, others that they've travelled from across the sea. My guess is that they're from the south, from Ingland. Maybe sent here by King Edmund, if it's true he's still alive. It seems too much of a coincidence that they should turn up so soon after we found out about him, especially when we know how intent he is on killing us all."

"You think they were sent here to kill you?"

"No. To spy on us, more likely. The first one we discovered was lurking in our meeting tent. The scuffle that followed was not pretty."

"The ones I saw looked almost human ... but also not."

"They may have been human once, but they've been altered in some way, giving them the ability to change the colour and texture of their skin."

"They reminded me of a—"

"Jellysquid? Yes. I expect that's how they were made, by extracting some element from the animal and putting it inside them."

"They attacked us, back where your camp used to be."

"Interesting. That's not their usual behaviour. They tend to just slink around, observing and absorbing information. You must have disturbed them."

"One of the people I was travelling with was hurt. The imitator grabbed him," I say. "The other one, I don't know... I have to go back to the camp, to see if I can find them. They might need my help."

"It's too dangerous. I'm sorry, but if an imitator made contact, your companion may already be dead. There's poison in their fingertips. Whatever you do, never let one touch your skin with its hands."

I let the reality of what she has said sink it. *Your companion may already be dead.* My head spins.

"I can't just leave them out there."

"Go if you like, but in this weather, without knowing the land, you'll struggle to find your way. If you can wait until morning, I'll ride you through on Duilleag."

Duilleag, I remember, is Mór's bull. "Where is he?" I ask. It's unusual to see a Bó Rider without their companion.

"Close," she says, without further explanation.

"And what about the other Riders? Where are they?"

Mór rubs her hands over her head, flinging rainwater into the fire. Her cropped hair looks dusty yellow in this light.

"In a large cavern on the west coast. Once the imitators became known to us, we had to move to somewhere less exposed."

"So everyone's all right? Is Cray there?"

"Everyone's there and everyone's fine. Like I said, the imitators appear to want to spy on us more than attack us. So far, at least."

"How many imitators are there?"

"No idea. They're hard to detect and impossible to tell apart. We've taken out a couple but, as you can imagine, they're not the easiest to track down. That's what I was doing when I found you – hunting for more of them. They're actually easier to spot in the rain because of the way it rebounds off their bodies. We're concerned about how much they've already learnt about us." Mór cracks her knuckles, one at a time. "What about you? What are you doing back here? Not that it isn't nice to see you. Did you make it to Norveg? What happened with your clan?"

I fill her in without going into much detail, telling her about the victory in the mountain and the subsequent shame of not being able to reclaim our enclave; about the *sgàilean* being released on Skye and how I was sent here to try and track down the Badhbh.

At the mention of the Badhbh, Mór's eyebrows rise. "The man who made the *sgàilean*?"

"Yes. Do you remember we found his diary at Dunnottar Castle? Does Cray still have it?"

"I'm not sure. I haven't seen it since we left there."

"I need to find it; it might be important. I don't suppose you could take me to where Cray is after we've looked for the people I was with?"

"Of course. I'm heading back there in the morning anyway, and I'm sure Cray will be pleased to see you. For now, though, you should try and get some sleep. Sorry to say it, but you look terrible."

I smile a little and rub my eyes. The smoke from the fire is making my eyelids heavy.

"Thanks, Mór," I say. "You're one of the good ones."

"I know I am," she says. "And don't you forget it."

SIGRID

"**G**ET UP."

Konge Grímr's pullin on my chain. I usually hear him wake up. I musta sunk deep. Despite bein so sapped, I was awake most of the night thinkin about them two kings sat there with their maps and their plans and their harsk ugly laughs, thinkin they're so clever and so right and can do whatever they want. I may not know much, but I know sure as the moon it's not right what they're plannin. There isn't nothin good gunna come out of all that killin. Way I see it, people should leave other people alone, free to live their lives. That's what Granpa Halvor always taught me. Not attackin people where you don't belong, not takin other people and makin them slaves, and definitely no killin cuz of some bugdumb dream.

People are gunna die. Lots of them. Even Konge Grímr's own wreckers. Don't they give no damn about that? And them people on the island what don't even know what's comin. It's not fair, none of it.

The note kept me up thinkin last night and all. *I know you can understand us. You're being watched.* It musta been too obvious that I was listenin durin the meetin. But which one of them wrote it? And is it a warnin or a threat? There was only four of them in the room. It couldn't of been Bolverk – his way is all action, not words. And it couldn't of been Konge Grímr neither, cuz I would've seen him do it. That leaves only King Edmund and his adviser Aldric chicken eyes. What game they playin? Unless it was one of the guards... Whoever it was, I gotta be more careful.

Someone enters and helps Konge Grímr into the huntin gear what they've brought for him. Once they're gone, Konge Grímr ses to me, "Are we alone, girl?"

"Yes," I say.

"Then know this: last night I was drunk. Anything I may have said to you means nothing, and if you mention one word of it to anyone else I'll skin you alive."

Charmin as always.

Someone knocks on the door. A diffrunt servant has come to show us to the stables. King Edmund's takin us on a hunt today. He suggested it late last night and Konge Grímr and Bolverk leapt on the idea. It's an Inglish thing: they let loose an animal in the woods then chase it on horses until they kill it. Sounds like a mean waste of a life to me.

When we get to the courtyard outside the stables, lots

of men are already on horses, including Bolverk and Aldric. Bolverk gives me his usual grotweasel stare. A shiny brown horse is pulled out for Konge Grímr. I show his hands the stirrup and the reins, and he swings himself up easy. It's a double saddle, what's got me thinkin I'm sposed to sit in front and do the ridin. A quick tug on the chain from Konge Grímr's got me knowin for sure. I've ridden wild horses plenty back home, but they're half the size of the beast snortin in front of me now. It takes four tries for me to get my leg up and over. Then I'm on and it's hek high. I don't usually use no reins neither, but I know how they're sposed to work. I hold them tight, hopin they've given me a horse what knows how to behave.

King Edmund is carried out of the palace by his guards and lifted onto a mustard stallion with a blond mane. His horse has got a double saddle and all, and one of his guards sits up behind him. Plenty more of his guards mount their own horses, which surround King Edmund on all sides. Lady Beatrice comes out too, dawdlin and lookin bored as usual. There isn't no sign of her pig today. She lets a horseman help her onto a black mare what's got a bright white mane and tail, and a white stripe down its nose.

A bulkin door in the side of the palace opens and four men bring out a large wooden crate. There's somethin alive in it what's bangin and howlin and tryin to get out. The men place the crate on a cart that's attached to one of the other horses. The ripshriek sound of whatever animal's inside doesn't stop, but it's soon drowned out by twenty or more hounds what come runnin into the courtyard. They're yappin and barkin all around, specially at the crate with the animal inside. They jump up, tryin to get at it, but it's too high for their scratchin paws.

"Let's go," ses King Edmund, and his guards start nudgin the horses out of the courtyard. Konge Grímr thuds our horse hard with his heels, makin it tremble beneath me. It starts movin, though, and we follow King Edmund and the others through a hek bulk gate, which is decorated with gold vines and more gawkin lynxes.

On the other side of the gate is a dirt track, which we follow for a couple of slogs. I keep holdin the reins, nudgin the horse this way or that, but I don't have to do much; it seems chirpin enough followin all the others, which is lucky, cuz Konge Grímr's still squeezin my head evry two blinks for describin what I can see. He really doesn't need to do no squeezin. I'd have to be hek foolin not to know why I'm here by now.

The track leads to a forest full of trees diffrunt from any I've seen before. Their trunks are like ogre thighs and the leaves are the size of my face. A harsk wind bickers, loosin leaves what float down to the forest floor like dyin stars.

"Bring out the prey," someone shouts, and all the horses stop. The men next to the cart pull open the crate and a grey blur shoots out. It doesn't get far, cuz the men are holdin chains what are tied around the animal's neck so it can't run off nowhere. The beast yanks

180

against the chains, wobblin the men on their toes. Its teeth are hek blades, but it can't do no gnashin cuz of the muzzle what's around its mouth.

"What is it?" Konge Grímr asks me.

"I dunno," I say. "Looks like a wolf, but it's bigger and more scraggin."

"It's a wildwolf," ses Aldric, who's next to us on his horse.

"Which is different from a regular wolf how?" asks Konge Grímr.

"They come from the north," ses Aldric. "Scotia. They are an ... after-effect of the plague. We don't usually see them in Ingland, but – as His Majesty mentioned the other night – nearly a thousand of them came running into the country about a month ago. By all accounts, it appears they were fleeing your enemies in the Highlands. Most were hunted down and killed once they crossed the border, but a hundred or so were caught alive on the king's orders and brought to the palace dungeon. They make excellent sport. Looks like it's time for the slicing."

He draws our attention back to the wildwolf in front of us. A third man approaches it from behind with a stubby blade and cuts the wildwolf across the backs of its hind legs. The howl what comes out of the wildwolf's mouth is gutsick. I explain what's happenin to Konge Grímr and don't hide that it's not nice seein it.

"You're too sensitive, girl," he ses to me. "It's a beast. Beasts are made to be hunted."

The hounds are bein held back behind us, sept with ropes, not chains. They smell the blood and start barkin hek fiery.

"Release the beast!" shouts King Edmund, excitement lightin his curdy eyes.

The men holdin the wildwolf unclip the chains and release it. At first, the wildwolf doesn't know what to do, torn between attackin the men and runnin away. It decides on runnin and disappears into the trees. The slicin on its legs can't of been deep, cuz it's off sprintin quickspit.

Soon as it's out of sight, the dogs are let go of too, and then evrythin goes batcrazy. The hounds dart after the wildwolf – barkin like hell fiends – and the horses bolt after the hounds. All in a sudden we're stormin through the trees and I'm not doing no steerin or nothin, I'm just holdin on tight as I can, thinkin I'm gunna fall off any moment and get trampled under the hooves of the horses what are behind us. That'd be a skap way to go and no mistakin.

Our horse twists and turns, weavin in and out of trees, tramplin over branches and moss. Konge Grímr's suckin in air through his skittin nashers, makin sounds like he's lovin every blink. The chase doesn't last long. Our horse comes to a halt next to the hounds, which have got the wildwolf surrounded. The wildwolf snaps at them, but it can't do no damage with the muzzle around its mouth. All the horses are stopped now, evryone watchin the poor rotten beast.

King Edmund trots his horse next to ours. "Would you like to do the honours?" he asks Konge Grímr. He means killin it. I don't know how that'd be possible, and I sure as hek hope he's not expectin me to help him.

"I can but try," ses Konge Grímr. He holds out his hand and Bolverk passes him a small throwin axe. He raises it a little, listenin for where the wildwolf is. Can he really hit it without seein? It looks like it's lined up good from where I'm sittin.

As he throws it, I tug on one of the reins with my hand. It's only a speck of a pull, cuz I don't want no one to know I did it, but it's enough to make the horse shift its weight, throwin off Konge Grímr's aim. The axe clips the hairs off the wildwolf's tail but nothin more. Lady Beatrice is starin at me from the back of her horse. I'm hopin she didn't see what I did.

"Almost, Your Supremacy," ses Bolverk. "Would you like another—?"

"Finish it off," snaps Konge Grímr.

A sniff later, Bolverk's pulled out another axe and launched it at the wildwolf. It lands in the animal's neck. The wildwolf judders once, all through its body, before fallin on its side. The hounds are still barkin, but they're less interested now the wildwolf's dead and they start to drift away. The men on the horses do the same.

"An easy victory," ses King Edmund, lookin satisfied. "The same as we will have in Scotia."

I can't take my gawpers off the wildwolf as it bleeds out into the undergrowth.

The moon's blarin tonight, splashin puddles over the stone floor in Konge Grímr's room. He's sat at a small table next to the bed, eatin again, and I'm stood watchin him eat, my stomach crampin with evry bite. He already had four meals today, but that didn't stop him wantin more. He demanded someone brought him somethin up to chomp on before he went to sleep.

The hunt this mornin left me feelin sunken. What got me most skapped was how unjust it all was. There were so many hounds, and so many horses, and the wildwolf was cut and muzzled. How was that fair? It didn't stand a chance. It was always goin to die. I hate this skittin place, and I hate King Edmund and all.

Why's the—? The door's openin, so slow it hurts. I don't know who I'm expectin to see, but it sure as muck isn't her. Lady Beatrice. When she sees Konge Grímr's still awake she looks like she might leave again straightaways, but then she looks at me and changes her mind. She steps in, creepin quiet, and puts a finger over her lips tellin me not to say nothin. The candles what are around the room flicker shadows across her face.

"Who's there?" Konge Grímr asks, turnin around so his body's facin the door. I dunno how he heard her.

Lady Beatrice shakes her head the smallest flinch.

"No one, Your Supremacy," I say, regrettin the last two words, cuz I don't usually bother sayin them when we're on our own. My heart's pumpin waterfalls; I'll be in hek trouble if he finds out I'm lyin. Konge Grímr doesn't turn back around. He stays with his face lookin straight at Lady Beatrice, tiltin his ears one way, then the other. He knows someone's here. I'm starin at him and so is Lady Beatrice. Neither of us dare movin.

"You'd better not be lying to me, girl," he ses.

"Why would I lie?" I say, keepin my voice normal. "It's late. Who'd be here now?"

Konge Grímr hawks up a phlegm glob, spits it over the table and turns back to his chew. Lady Beatrice glances behind her, then takes another silent step towards me, all the whiles keepin her gawpers on the king. She looks diffrunt. Not her clothes – they're still the stupid dangly ones she always wears. It's her face. She looks less bored, more determined, more smart. Praps there's more to her than what I thought.

There's a piece of parchment in her hands. She lifts it up so I can see it. The writin on it looks similar to what was on the folded note I found last night. It must've been her what left it for me.

Nod if you can understand, it ses on it in the foreign tongue.

I pause, not knowin what the skit's goin on. Why is she here? Can I trust her? Or is she a sneakin kerl tryin to catch me out?

Her eyes are searchin mine. There's pain in them and loss. Desperation. I read the parchment one more time, then nod.

She turns the paper around, movin slow to not make no sounds. Konge Grímr's still gobblin at the table next to me, bits of chew spittin out in all directions. On the back of the parchment there's another message.

Do you agree with the kings' plans for Scotia?

What the hell am I sposed to say to that? If I tell her the truth, I'm not only betrayin her king and country, I'm betrayin mine as well. *There are always choices. It's knowin which are the right ones that's the hard part.* Granpa Halvor's voice drifts through my kog. Somethin about Lady Beatrice makes me wanna trust her. I shake my head.

Lady Beatrice closes her eyes slow, opens them again, then reaches somewhere into her clothes. When her hand comes back out again, it's holdin somethin what catches the moonlight.

A metal file.

My gawpers go wide lookin at it. She's *handin* it to me, so I can escape. I dunno why she's helpin me, and I haven't got no time to be wonderin that now. I stretch my hand out towards it. Lady Beatrice takes another step forward. The stone floor scuffs under her foot.

"What was that?" Konge Grímr puts down the slab of meat in his hands. Dark gravy drips from the ink centipedes on his fingers.

"Nothin," I say.

He's not convinced. He stands up. "Take me to the door," he ses.

Lady Beatrice looks at me, her bottom lip twitchin. If he finds the door open, he's gunna know somebody's in here, but what choice have I got?

I take his elbow and lead him towards the door, skirtin wide, away from Lady Beatrice. She stays where she is in the middle of the room, bendin away from him as he passes. Konge Grímr's listenin hard for any sounds. We're nearly at the door. Sweat's dribblin outta my temples. Konge Grímr has his hands out, feelin the air in front of him.

Right before he touches the door, I fall to the ground, makin hek clatter with the chain to hide the sound of me closin it.

"What happened?" snaps Konge Grímr.

"I tripped," I say.

He grunts and probes at the door, then turns and stares straight at me. I know he can't stare proply, but swear Øden, right now he's lookin deep into my soul.

"I don't know what game you're playing, girl – whether you're lying to me or not," he ses, "but if I find out you're doing something you shouldn't be doing, I'll make you regret it for the rest of your life." He pauses, his mouth twisted like a dead maggot. I don't dare to swallow. "Now take me back to my food."

It takes me a few blinks to remember how my legs work. I hold his elbow again and lead him back to the table. As we pass Lady Beatrice for the second time, she holds out the file. I hesitate for the tiniest speck, then wrap my fingers around the handle and take it from her, right under Konge Grímr's nose. We both stare up at him, lookin for any sign that he knows what just happened. He's not showin nothin. He reaches his chair, sits back down and continues crammin.

I look back at Lady Beatrice. Her smile is so small it's almost not there. She nods once, then leaves the room, movin the door so slow that Konge Grímr doesn't hear her go. He's slurpin so noisy now he wouldn't hear nothin anyways.

I still got the file in my hand. I haven't got nowhere else to put it. Its handle's drippin with my sweat. I'm gunna use it tonight. As soon as Konge Grímr's buried in sleep, I'm breakin myself free.

JAIME

Once it's light outside, Mór extinguishes the fire, picks up her spear and slips back through the crack. I follow her out of the cave. It no longer hurts to put pressure on my feet; the balm and bandages Mór applied worked a miracle while I was sleeping. My clothes also dried during the night, although they're now thick with the smell of smoke.

Mór puts two fingers from each of her hands into her mouth and whistles, loud.

"Aren't you worried about imitators hearing?"

"Duilleag will get here long before they do," she says.

Sure enough, almost immediately, her mighty bull lollops around the side of the hill. Mór hops onto his back and pulls me up behind her. She gives the Highland bull an affectionate scratch, digging deep into the long, auburn hair on his head. Then she holds on to his horns and he starts to gallop, reaching a speed that dries out my eyes in a matter of moments. It doesn't take long for the familiar ache to creep into my backside... I'd forgotten how uncomfortable these creatures are to ride.

We go back to the site of the Bó Riders' former camp and circle it three times. I call out, but there's no sign of Donal or Violet. Part of me is relieved there are no bodies, although that doesn't mean much. We don't stop or even slow down, and Mór is poised with her spear, in case there are still imitators nearby.

"Where do they go at night?" I ask, the wind snatching my voice.

"We don't know. We haven't found any signs of habitation, so presume they sleep out in the open."

"Don't they get cold?"

"Apparently not. Another trait they've stolen from the jellysquid."

Once I accept that neither Donal nor Violet is here, Mór turns Duilleag away, and we start riding west. I stay alert, scanning for any signs that they may have passed through, but at the speed we're going, it's a pointless task. The further away we get, the heavier the gloom inside me grows.

Before long, the sea comes into view. At first it is just an odd glimpse behind the flowing hills, and then it spreads majestically into its full glimmering expanse. Duilleag gallops straight for it, towards a mass of hazy dots that reveal themselves to be the whole herd of Highland cows and bulls, grazing on the luscious green near the cliff edge. Once we're close, Duilleag slows a little and weaves in between the other animals. Some lift their heads and huff a greeting at us as we pass; others barely turn their sleepy eyes.

Duilleag comes to a halt at the top of the cliff and Mór and I dismount. I peer over the edge, where the land plummets into the sea. A strong smell of salt and burning wood drifts up from below. I'm guessing the Bó Riders' cavern must be beneath us somewhere, but the way the edge veers sharply inwards makes it impossible to see. The wind tugs at me in a frenzy, desperate to pull me off balance.

"I wouldn't stand that close if I were you," says Mór. "Come on, this way."

I allow the wind to pummel me for a few more moments, as if taunting it, challenging it to push me over. Eventually, I force myself to turn away from the edge and follow Mór.

We make our way down – Mór hopping from rock to rock with ease, me slipping and grazing myself at least twice – until we arrive on a sandy beach. The sea laps at it with languid strokes and the sand is soft beneath my bandaged feet.

"The best thing about sand?" says Mór, pointing at the footprints we're creating. "There's no way the imitators can cross it without us noticing."

We approach two Bó Riders standing side by side, presumably doing just that: watching for errant footprints.

"You remember Jaime?" Mór says to them as we pass.

They hold up their hands in respect and I give them a sheepish wave.

We follow the curve of the shoreline for a short while, and then the Bó Riders' new home opens up before us. The cavern is enormous, much bigger than I'd imagined it to be from above. Even though the location is completely different from their last camp, their new home feels reassuringly familiar. Their animal-skin tents have been erected in two neat semicircles, with communal fires in front of each. An ethereal light streaks in from the sea, making the tents glow with a soft golden hue.

Inside, the cavern is a hive of activity, with people cooking, cleaning, mending things, chatting. Adults laugh while children play around them. Some of the Bó Riders I recognize, others I don't. The ones who see me hold up their hands, coupled with curious smiles.

"Well, look who it is!" Finn – the young healer who helped Agatha recover after the wildwolf attack – jogs towards us. "What are you doing here?" Before I know it, he has the back of my head in his hand and pulls my forehead into his. We breathe together, in and out, and then he lets go.

I start to explain but am interrupted by Murdina and Hendry. They're the Bó Riders' leaders, I think, although they don't seem to have leaders in the same way we do.

"You're back," Murdina says to Mór. "We were worried." They touch their foreheads together in the same way Finn did to me.

"I got held up," says Mór, glancing in my direction, "but I'm fine."

"Well, this is a surprise," says Hendry.

"Nice to see you again, Jaime-Iasgair," says Murdina. "Although we didn't think it would happen so soon."

"Is Agatha not with you?" Hendry asks. "I trust she's well?"

I give them a brief account of everything that's happened and why I'm here, all the while scanning the faces around me for any sign of Cray.

"My goodness," says Hendry once I've finished speaking.

"Is Cray here?" I ask. "I need the diary I gave him in Dunnottar. The one that belonged to the Badhbh."

Murdina shakes her head. "He didn't come back last night either. Still out looking for imitators, I presume."

My heart drops. "Oh," I say.

"I can fetch you the diary, though," says Mór. "If he still has it, it'll be with his things in his tent. This way."

She leads me deeper into the cavern. Its sides have been lined with crisscrossed spears that jut out at awkward angles, preventing anyone from entering by any route other than the beach. Between what nature's offered them and what they've done to it since, the cavern is the perfect location to hide away from potential enemies.

"Are you worried about Cray?" I ask Mór, realizing as I say it that *I'm* worried about Cray. We sidestep a small group of children throwing pebbles at a piece of broken spear that's been fashioned into a target.

"He'll be fine," Mór replies.

"Is it normal for him not to come back at night?"

"No, but it's not normal for me either, and I stayed out last night as well. Sometimes unexpected things happen." She pokes me on the top of my arm. "He'll be back soon. For food, as much as anything else. That boy loves to eat."

It becomes darker and colder towards the rear of the cavern. Strange rock fingers drip down from its roof, which shine with dampness. The occasional drip echoes loudly against the hard ground.

Mór stops outside one of the tents and flips open the entrance. Inside there are six sets of blankets arranged in a neat circle, marking the individual areas of the six people who must sleep in here.

"This is Cray's," says Mór, pointing to a pile on the far side. She starts rummaging through the blankets and discovers a leather pouch buried within their folds.

"Are you sure he won't mind us touching his things?" I ask.

"Oh, he'll definitely mind, but he's not here to stop us, so..." She delves into the pouch and pulls out a handful of stuff, including – to my surprise – a candle from Dunnottar Castle, crudely cut into the shape of a heron. I carved it on our final night there but didn't realize he'd seen me do it, or that he'd decided to keep it. Seeing it now, among his other possessions, gives me a strange stab of happiness. Mór slings it onto the blankets and reaches back into the pouch for a second handful.

"Buinnig!" she says, pulling out a collection of papers bound together by a slim green cover. "I knew he would've kept it. Read it in here if you want. I'll bring some food and find you some boots; as good as my feet-wrapping skills are, you'll probably be better off with something a little more robust."

"That'd be great," I say as she slips out of the tent.

I sit on top of Cray's blankets and open the Badhbh's diary. I've already read it multiple times, but right now I'm looking for something new, some clue as to his current whereabouts.

By the time Mór returns, I've read it from cover to cover and am still no wiser as to where I might find the Badhbh. The vast majority of it is about his experimentations with King Balfour, the former Scotian king, describing all their failed attempts at creating *sgàilean*. It's only right at the end that he mentions the plague that swept across the country and killed everyone in the castle. Everyone except him and the princess, Nathara. He writes that he's going west, to the coast, as far away from the *sgàilean* as he can reach, presumably because he knew if Nathara was to die, the *sgàilean* would turn on him, just like they turned on us. None of this is helpful to me, though. It's not as if I can just scour the whole west coast looking for signs of him; the coastline of Scotia is so jagged that it'd take months to search it all.

"Anything?" asks Mór. She hands me a bowl of something warm and plonks a worn pair of boots near my feet.

"No," I say. I sling the diary to one side and start slurping down the stew. It's nutty and a little sweet, with big chunks of sinewy vegetable.

"Slow down; you'll make yourself sick. And if you're sick on Cray's blankets, he'll never forgive you."

I rest the bowl between my legs and wipe my mouth with the back of my hand.

"Also, I don't believe you've thanked me for finding the diary for you yet," Mór says.

"Thank you," I say, but my mind is elsewhere. The Badhbh's book is lying askew where I tossed it, with its final page open. There's nothing on the page itself, but across the green of the inside back cover there's a line of ink. I've seen it before and always assumed it was a spillage of some sort, but looking at it now I'm beginning to wonder if it might be something else.

"What do you see here?" I ask Mór, holding up the cover to show her.

"A line of ink…"

"But look at the shape of it – does it look like anything to you?"

"Not really. Maybe a crack or a piece of hair?"

"I was thinking more that it might be a line from a map, like part of the Scotian coast."

"I wouldn't know. We don't make maps, so I've never seen one. Hendry's good with landscapes, though, so you could ask him."

I don't waste any time. We find Hendry sitting on a flat rock near the entrance to the cavern, sewing two pieces of animal skin together into some sort of over-garment. He balances the clothing on his large belly and hums to himself as he works. When I show him the mark in the Badhbh's diary, he nods a couple of times before agreeing that it could well depict a coastline. He takes the book from me and turns it first one way and then the other.

"It's quite a distinctive shape..." he says. "My best guest would be that it's the Famhair peninsula, a little north of here. Yes, looking at it again, I'm almost certain of it."

"Good. Great. Then I have to go there. How do I get there?"

"On foot? It's a hard day's walk, possibly two. If you could convince someone to take you by bull, however..." He tilts his head to look at Mór, and I do the same.

"What, am I a free ride all of a sudden?" asks Mór.

"I don't have anything to offer you in return..." I say, my face expressing both awkwardness and remorse in what I'm sure is an unattractive combination.

"It's fine, you can entertain me with your witty company," she says, giving me a wry smile. "Once a friend of the Bó Riders, always a friend of the Bó Riders. We can leave whenever you're ready."

SIGRID

I'M STILL HOLDIN THE METAL FILE IN MY SWEATY hams. I haven't let go of it since Lady Beatrice sneaked it to me. It takes hek slogs for Konge Grímr to finish his chewin and get into bed. Even then, I gotta wait until he's sunk deep before startin.

Soon as his snores are rattlin the bed frame, I put the file to the chain and start grindin it back and forth. My workin's makin the chain rattle and its clinkin sounds awful loud all of a sudden. *Jarg!* There's no way Konge Grímr's not gunna hear that. I move the wrist what's got the chain on it between my legs, hopin my trousers will stop the sound some. It's better, but still louder than I'd want. I go slow and hard, keepin as quiet as I can. It's not easy, and before long I'm sweatin seas. It's workin, though. Little by little, it's cuttin through the chain.

I don't know how long I do it for. A hek long time. I'm

speedin up now cuz I'm nearly done. It's gettin louder but I don't care, I'm nearly through and—

"What?" ses Konge Grímr.

I stay still, not darin to breathe. My heart is speedin so fast I swear it's gunna leap straight outta my mouth. Konge Grímr doesn't say nothin else. How much did he hear? Keepin my back to him, I turn my head, slow as a sick slug. He's on his back, breathin deep. Asleep. He musta spoken in his sleep is all. A thousand horns to Øden, that was lucky. I gotta be more careful. I start my filin again, bein more careful of keepin quiet this time. Just a little more, a little more, a little more, and then—

The clank of the chain breakin is almost silent. The links slip away and I've done it; I'm not attached to him no more. There's still the part of the chain what's around my wrist, but that doesn't bother me none.

I stand up, keepin hold of the file. It's not much of a weapon, but it's better than nothin. I can't believe I'm free. On my way to the door, I pass the remains of Konge Grímr's food. It sure don't matter if he notices I ate some now. I grab a hamful of meat and shove it in my mouth. It's so rich my tastebuds are poppin. I take another fat wodge and bury it in my pocket for later. My breathin is snortin loud outta my nose cuz my mouth's so full of chewin. *Slow down,* I tell myself. *Quiet, quiet, quiet.*

I step over to the door. The bolt what keeps it locked is stiff as bones. It clunks open. I look back at the sleepin skapfiend one last time. He's gunna be hek fiery when he wakes up and finds me gone. If I get caught, it's the end of me – I'm straightaways dead and no mistakin. Well, there isn't nothin I can do about that. I made my decision the moment I started filin. I sneak out, closin the door behind me.

Now I'm outta the room, I'm thinkin breakin free was the easy part. Where the cowcrap do I go now? It's dark in the palace hallway – darker than inside the room was – and quiet. I can't hear no wind or nothin. I turn left and creep down the hall, down some steps, then down some more. If I'm gunna get out, I gotta get to the ground level first, so down is as good a way to go as any. Couple of times I hear people talkin or walkin, so not evryone's sleepin. I'm careful not to get too close to none of them. I'm sneakin around, hidin behind corners, scamperin this way and that. Lost, basically, but tryin not to think that word. Then I turn a corner and recognize where I am. I'm by the long room where we ate. Well, I didn't do no eatin – the room where evryone else stuffed their faceholes. The memory of food makes my hand reach for the pocket where I stashed the extra hamful of chew, but I stop myself. I'll need it more later.

I know where I'm goin from here, down one more hall, right and right again and then—

I stop quickspit. I'm on the edge of the first room now, the big entrance with the soft floor and the door leadin outside. Only trouble is, there's two guards standin by the door, one on each side, and another two guards on the other side of the room. There isn't no way I'm gettin past them. I need a new plan.

"Trying to escape, I presume?"

A hand on my shoulder.

I spin, holdin the file out in fronta me, my teeth gnashin.

"You won't be needing that," Lady Beatrice ses, noddin at the file. She's in the same clothes she was wearin when she came into Konge Grímr's room earlier, like she's not gone to bed yet, even though it's hek near the middle of the night. We stand there gawpin at each other. I'm breathin fast; she's breathin normal.

"Follow me," she ses. She's speakin in the foreign tongue, but I don't have no problems understandin.

I'm thinkin since she's the one what helped me break free, it can't be too foolin to follow her now. She walks, not fast, not slow. She doesn't look back to check I'm comin. We go down some narrow steps what curve as they go down. It's hek grimy here, not like the rest of the palace, and hek dark too. The air dust clings to the inside of my throat. I swallow a cough before it can come out. At the bottom of the steps there's a door. Lady Beatrice pulls out a key from inside her clothes.

"Why you help?" I ask her. It's the first time I've tried speakin the foreign tongue since arrivin in Ingland and it doesn't come out good, but Lady Beatrice gets my meanin.

"Because no one deserves to be chained to a man, nor treated the way that man treats you," she says. She fiddles with the key in her hands. "Have you noticed how few women there are in this castle? They have no place here except as the lowest servants. It makes me sick to see it, every day. And I'm the one who's supposed to inspire their obedience – 'Her Royal Modesty' they call me... Pah! You are part of my rebellion, one of the few small changes I am able to make." She puts the key in the lock but doesn't turn it. We both stand there starin at it. "What's your name?" she asks me.

"Sigrid," I say. No one's cared what my name is in a long time.

"Well, Sigrid, I have one more thing to ask you... A request. It will not be easy, so you don't have to agree, but hear me out. I'd like you to go north, to the Isle of Skye."

What's she want me to go there for? That's hek trompin; I saw how far it was on King Edmund's map.

"Why?" I ask.

"To warn the people there of the invasion the kings are planning."

But that doesn't make no sense. "You Inglish," I say. "You King Edmund wife."

"Yes, and you've spent the last few days in his company, so you know exactly what he's like. He's constantly making hate-filled choices, and I see it as my duty to amend as many of them as possible. It's the only way I can tolerate being here, in this palace, by his side. I try to make a difference. You can make a difference too."

"Why me?" I ask. She doesn't hardly know me. Hasn't she got some other person she can send, someone who knows this skittin country a hek lot better than I do?

"I've been watching you. You're strong and resourceful and you have a kind heart. If I were to send one of my own people, King Edmund would be suspicious; greater people than I have been executed for less... But you... No one would imagine it was me who set you free, nor that Skye is where you would choose to go. Please. There are children on Skye. I can't bear to think of it. If someone were to warn them – if *you* were to warn them – they would at least have a chance."

What am I sposed to say to that? What she says about the kidlins is true enough. It's one thing killin grown-up people, but killin children is stale as rot. But can I really make it all the way to Skye on my own?

Lady Beatrice is watchin my thinkin, sunken hope burstin outta her eyes. Then she ses to me, "Everyone deserves the chance to live a safe and happy life."

I'm gawpin at that, cuz it sounds a hek lot like somethin Mal-Rakki would say. It makes me think of Granpa Halvor, since he's the one always talkin on about Mal-Rakki and how great he is. My hand hovers over my pocket, the one what's still got the plum stone in it. If I go, I don't have no clue when I'll see Granpa Halvor again – if I'll ever see him again. But what else am I gunna do? I haven't got no boat, so it's not lookin like I'm goin home anytime soon. I owe Lady Beatrice and all, since she was the one what freed me from Konge Grímr. Praps if I warn the Skye people, they'll help me get back to Norveg. They know where it is, after all. Warnin them is the right thing to do; it's what Granpa Halvor would want me to do.

"Okay," I say. "I go."

Lady Beatrice kisses me hard on the top of my kog, and it's such a surprise that my arms go stiff at my side like dead sticks.

"Thank you," she ses. She lets go of me and twists the key in the lock. *Clunk*. She pushes the door open and straightaways the outside bites me like hek blades. "Directly across from here are the stables. There's a mare, ready saddled and loaded with supplies. The external gate is open and the guards distracted; if you're quick, no one will see you go. Follow the same track we rode along this morning but avoid the forest – it's dangerous at night. Turn left and cut through the city. The roads should be quiet enough."

My mouth is openin and closin like a coalfish what's been pulled out of water. This is all happenin too quick. I've got more questions to ask – there's so much I still don't know – but she's in a hurry for me to be gone.

"Whatever happens, just keep travelling north. Don't stop for anything, especially in the most northern regions of Ingland. The situation there is ... precarious. Although I have some allies in the north, there are rumours that other people there... Well, it's safer not to trust anyone. You have to reach Skye as soon as possible; the lives of everyone there depend on you. Now go, before the sentries return."

She pushes me through the door and I'm runnin across to the stables without even the time to say thank you.

AGATHA

I HEARD THE SHADOW THINGS LAST NIGHT. THEY WERE making the horrible strangle sound and it was hard for me to sleep. They were not supposed to be inside the enclave. There were fires all around the wall to keep them out, but last night there was too much rain and wind and it made all the fires not light and go out. That is why the shadow things came in. They couldn't come in the bothans though because of the inside fires. They went all around the outside. I think they were trying to find a way to put out the fires. If they do that, no one will be safe. They are angry at me for not letting them get the Raasay people or the deers. They want to get me the most.

I wished Jaime was here but he is in Scotia. Lenox told me that. I cannot even believe it. He went back to find the Badhbh man. I hope he is okay and the wild-wolves don't get him. Lenox says he will be back soon.

It is morning now and the shadow things are gone. I know that because the sound is stopped. I put on my boots and run quick out of the bothan to see the deers. They are standing in the loch so the shadow things didn't get them. That is a big phew. It was Aileen's plan that they should go in the loch and it is a clever one. The shadow things can't go in the water. I don't talk to the deers because my head is still hurting bad and I don't want it to hurt more.

I go to the cookboth. There is banging next to it. The Wasps are making something with the wood and hammers. I don't know what it is. Maybe it is a big weapon for killing the shadow things. The Stewer in the cookboth says he's not allowed to give me anything and I should know that by now. But I am so hungry so I say please and do my bestest pretty smile and he says, "Okay, but only because it's you." He gives me a bannock and a big piece of meat. I cannot even believe it! I am so lucky to get the big piece of meat. The bannock is warm and it is delicious yummy. The meat is good too and I eat it all up.

On my way walking back to the bothan I see Maistreas Eilionoir. She flaps her hand at me which means she wants to talk to me. I walk to where she is and we stand under a tree to stop some of the wind being so windy.

"Agatha," she says, "I'm glad I bumped into you. Did you warn them in time?" Her voice is a whisper one.

"W- warn— who?" I ask. I think she means the Raasay people but I have to pretend I don't know that because I was not supposed to go there and she will be cross.

"The islanders from Raasay," she says. "I know that's where you went."

Oh, she knows. That is a bad one.

"I ... I ... um..."

"It's okay; you're not in trouble. I wanted you to go there. In fact, I was relying on it. Why do you think I made you count paces outside the enclave?"

What does she mean she wanted me to go there? "You said the counting was an important job," I say. "You said we n– needed to know how many paces for the— the— to protect against the shadow things."

"I know that's what I *said*, but we didn't really need to know that. I wanted to make it easier for you to leave."

What she is saying is confusing in my head. "What—? But— What—?" I am not doing good speaking but I cannot make it come out good.

"What Catriona suggested was barbaric – allowing the *sgàilean* to kill every single person in our enclave: old people, sick people, children... The people of Raasay betrayed us, but they do not deserve that fate. However, Catriona has the authority here now, and I could not undermine her without risking severe consequences for our clan. I needed it too look like it was your idea to leave, in case anyone saw you. And it was your idea. I just planted the seed and gave you a little nudge in the right direction."

I do not know all of the words Maistreas Eilionoir said but I think I understand it.

"But how did you know I would g– go there?"

"Because it's just the kind of foolish plan only you would attempt," she says. "And it's exactly what I would have done if I were forty years younger... I recognize your stubborn determination all too well. After seeing the look on your face during the meeting, I knew if anyone would try to get there, it was you. It's partly why I mentioned your birth parents, in the hope that thinking about them would strengthen your resolve to help Lileas's parents. You must forgive me, though; I was wrong to speak of it. There are reasons such things are not spoken about in this clan, and we must not talk of it again. But enough of that. Tell me what happened while you were gone."

I want to speak about my birth parents more now because she reminded me but also she told me I'm not allowed. It is very annoying to me. I wish she never even said about them. Instead I have to say what she asked which is about how the chief of Raasay man wouldn't believe me and Aileen and he locked us up, but then Edme Lileas's mother helped us escape and we saw the big fire and the Raasay people were saved. I also tell her what Hector said about the lots of Raasay people who are sad about what the chiefs of Raasay did to us.

When I have finished saying it all Maistreas Eilionoir does something very surprising which is she hugs me. She has never hugged me like that before. I hug her back a warm one. She feels like lots of bones.

"You've done well, Agatha. Not only did your actions save lives, but you may have also paved the way for positive negotiations between us and the Raasay islanders. I knew I could rely on you."

I don't know what is *negotiations* but I know it is a good thing so I smile a big one.

"There was a– another thing the chief of Raasay man said," I say.

"Oh?"

"He said his people lived on this island first, and that our— our clan made them— leave. That's not true ... is it?"

Maistreas Eilionoir's head is a tilt on one side. "Actually," she says. "It is ... to a degree. Although it was two hundred years ago or more. Long before even I was born, and we all know how ancient I am."

"W– why did we make them leave?"

"It wasn't just us; it was all of the Skye clans. Our ancestors came here from the mainland with everyone else who now lives here on Skye, fleeing a corrupt monarchy and wanting to establish a new kind of community. When they first arrived, the people already living here didn't want to share the island with them. Our ancestors fought them for it and won, so the original inhabitants were forced to leave. It's as simple as that. And like I said, it was a very long time ago; long before Scotia was torn apart by plagues and shadows.

"Whatever the history between our people, it is the enclave that is currently in dispute, which the Raasay islanders have no right to claim. It was built by our ancestors' sweat and sheer determination, and it belongs to us."

I don't know what to think about all of that. It is true that the Raasay people were bad to take our enclave but also maybe it was wrong that our ancestor people made them leave because the island was their home.

"Can I go now?" I say. My head is filling up and I want to go back to bed. I am still tired because of all the walking and the talking to the deers and the shadow things that made me not sleep. I have to go to the wall and be a good Hawk to do my duty but first I want to sleep some more.

"Of course," says Maistreas Eilionoir. "And stay alert. The air in this enclave is heavy with uncertainty; we must all keep our wits about us."

A sound wakes me up from my sleeping. It is a horrible sound, but it is not the shadow things. It is a screech one and an animal. It is one of the deers.

My first thinking is the shadow things got them but it can't be that because it is daytime and the shadow things are not here. I go out of my bed quick to see what it is.

Outside there is a man and he is— What is he doing? He should not be doing that. There is a rope around a deer's neck and the man is pulling hard. A woman is kicking the deer from behind to make it move. The deer is the one doing the loud sounds. The pulling and the kicking is hurting it.

"Hey!" I shout. "W– what are you— doing?"

I run to them and grab the rope. I try to pull it away but the man holds it hard and he won't let go.

"What's your problem?" he says to me. He has big cheeks and nasty teeth.

"Why do you have the rope and— and— pulling on its neck?" I say.

The deer is looking at me and its eyes are scared. It doesn't have the antlers because it is a girl one.

"Well, it's not going to want to come on its own, is it?" says the man, and he laughs.

The woman laughs too. Her face is pretty but when she laughs she is ugly.

"Where are you— going?" I ask.

"To the slaughterboth," says the woman, "Now, get out of our way; we've got work to do."

The slaughterboth? Why would they—? No. They can't do that.

"You're going to k– k–" I can't even say it.

"Of course we're going to kill it," says the man. "Where'd you think your breakfast came from?"

I think about the meat the Stewer gave me. That wasn't deer meat. Please it wasn't deer meat. It was a big piece and I ate it all. I'm going to be sick. I am sick. It goes on my boots and on my chin. I wipe it on my sleeve. The taste is horrible in my mouth. I spit out three times.

"Oh, dear," says the woman. "Looks like you need a lesson in where food comes from." She laughs again and is ugly again.

The man pulls on the rope and the deer does a sad grunt sound. I try to get the rope again but the man pushes me away.

"If you've got a problem, I suggest you take it up with Catriona," says the man.

"I will," I say. "Don't you k– kill that— deer. Otherwise I'll— I'll— arghh!" I don't know what I'll do and I can't think of it.

The man shakes his head and laughs which makes me even more madder.

I won't let them hurt you, I say to the deer.

I have to find Catriona and I have to be quick. They cannot kill the deer, they cannot do it. I run to Catriona's bothan. I go in and I do not even knock. She is not inside.

'C– Catriona!' I say, even though I know she is not here. I am going to leave but I hear a noise. It is a bump from inside the bothan but there is no one there so I do not know what. The noise does a bump again.

It is coming from the chest. There is something in the chest and it is trying to get out. Is it Catriona in the chest? I step towards it. My heart is too fast. I step again. The chest bumps again and makes me jump. I am not afraid. I step two more steps. What if it is a bad thing and gets me? I have to be brave. I am brave. I put my hand on the lid. It is cold. There are two metal parts for keeping it shut. I lift them up and open it.

Nothing jumps out and gets me. I do a big breath. It is only boring things. I do rummaging through them. It is clothes and a book and a blanket. All boring. So what was it did the bumping? I close the lid and put down the metal parts. I should not be looking in the chest. I should be finding Catriona. She is not in the chest and I knew she wasn't. Also she cannot see me here or I will be in the big biggest trouble ever.

I leave the bothan. I am thinking where I can look for her when she comes from around the corner.

"Agatha," she says. "What are you doing outside my bothan?"

"I was l– looking for you," I say. I hope she does not know that I was inside. Did I close the chest properly? Yes, I think I did it.

"Why?" she says. "I'm very busy."

"The m– man and the— woman were taking the deer to the— the— to kill it," I say.

"Yes, and?" says Catriona.

"You said you wouldn't hurt them!"

"No, I didn't. I said they could come in. I said nothing about what would happen to them once they were inside."

"But it's not fair. They're not for eating."

She puts her hand on my shoulder then. I hate it and I move so it is off.

"You did everyone in this enclave – both your clan and mine – a great service when you brought those animals through our gates. Our food supplies have been dwindling fast. They were already low, but since the *sgàilean* were unleashed – since *you* unleashed them – the situation has gone from bad to worse. We now need so much firewood to defend ourselves that other duties had to be sacrificed, including scavenging and angling. And then you turn up with enough deer to keep us alive all winter. You've almost made up for your former stupidity. Almost."

"But you can't k– kill them!" I say. "We can't eat them."

"Why not?"

"I said— I said they would be safe."

"When you performed your un*dùth* trick and spoke to them in your head, you mean? Well, perhaps you should be more careful not to make promises you cannot keep. Besides, the deer are safer here than if we hadn't let them in. Had they been outside the enclave walls last night, the *sgàilean* would have killed them all. We only need one or two a day. The others will live a happy life, free from worry, allowed to graze on our grass during the day and protected from the shadows at night."

She doesn't understand. She is stupid and mean. If she will not stop the deer being killed, I have to stop it. I do not say goodbye and I leave. I need to find the slaughterboth but I do not know where it is. I run all around. I ask people and they point and I run again but my head is full of bad thoughts of the deer dying and it makes it hard to know which way to go.

Then I hear the sound again. It is the deer sad pain sound and it is near. I run to it and then I know where is the slaughterboth. I push the door open with both my hands. The man and the woman are there. The woman has a long knife. The deer is in the air. It is upside down and is hanging by one leg. Its head is turning turning and it is scared.

It's okay; I'm going to save you, I say to the deer in my head. It does not reply. It is too scared, I think. The floor is a sticky one and is red. I do not want to know it.

"Not you again," says the man.

"Catriona says you have to l– let it down," I say.

"Oh, really?" says the woman.

"Yes— really," I say.

"And why would Catriona say that?"

"Because ... because..." I cannot think of a clever why. Then I think of it. "Because she wants to give it to the shadow things. So they get the deers and not the people." That is a mean thing like what Catriona would think of.

The man and the woman look at each other. "I'll go and check," says the man.

"You don't really think—?" says the woman.

"I'll be quick," says the man. "You'd better let it down for now."

The man leaves. The woman does a huff. She moves a lever around in the circles. It is hard to do with one hand so she needs two hands. That means she has to put down the long knife, which gives me the plan.

Hello, I say to the deer. *I am Agatha but you can call me Sun-Leaf. That is my deer name.* The deer tells me she is scared of the lady with the knife. I tell her

I am going to rescue her and I say to her my plan. She is moving down cluck clunk and spinning. I don't know if she is listening. Her legs are scrambly trying to get the floor. She is nearly there. It is time to do it.

I grab the long knife and chop the rope that is on her leg. She falls the last way but it is not far.

"No, you d—" says the woman, but she doesn't finish the words because the deer does my plan. She runs at the woman and hits her in the stomach with her head. The woman coughs a yucky one and falls onto the floor. I open the door and the deer runs out. I run too and am following. I did it! I saved her so she isn't dead. We run all the way to the loch so she can be with the other deers but— What? The deer stops and so do I. We can see the loch but it is not right. There are no animals there any more.

What's happened to all the deers?

JAIME

WE DON'T WASTE ANY TIME. NOW THAT WE HAVE AN idea where the Badhbh might be, there's no point in dawdling. Mór leaves to gather a few supplies as Hendry explains to me in more detail what I should look out for and how I'll know when we're in the right area. While he's speaking, my eyes keep drifting across the beach in case Cray returns. If he doesn't come back before we leave, I won't get to see him again after all.

Mór returns and throws a pair of gloves at me.

"In case we encounter any imitators," she explains. "The less skin you have exposed, the better." She also ties strips of cloth around my ankles, at the point where my trousers meet my boots. "Best not to take any risks."

The two of us climb back up the cliff side, onto the plateau where the cows and bulls are lolling around. Going up is easier than going down, partly because of my new boots, which are a little big but much better than nothing. Duilleag trots over as soon as he sees Mór, and then we're up on his back and galloping off once again.

"Have you ridden this way before?" I ask, raising my voice so Mór can hear me over the clomp of Duilleag's hooves.

"Never," Mór replies. "So I hope you know where you're going."

If she's relying on me for directions, we're in trouble. "Hendry made it sound quite simple: around the inlet, north until we pass the ruins of an old fort and then west until we're back on the coast."

"If that's where His Majesty wishes to go, that's where His Majesty shall be taken." She's joking but – in true Mór fashion – delivers it without a hint of a smile.

Duilleag tramples the grass beneath us, filling the air with the strong scent of thyme and wild garlic, made even fresher by last night's downpour. It doesn't look like it'll rain again today; there are plenty of clouds – swarming together in fungal clumps – but they're a soft, peaceful silver, not the angry grey of an approaching storm.

As we ride, I scan the land for any signs of Donal or Violet, even though the chances of us passing them are almost non-existant. If nothing else, it helps suppress my guilt for leaving them behind.

We're riding past an area of dense forest when I hear a noise from within, like someone shouting out in confusion. The sound is cut short almost as soon as it starts.

I don't need to ask Mór if she heard it, as she immediately alters Duilleag's direction. Or maybe it was the bull himself who decided it was a sound worth investigating.

Once we're in the forest, Duilleag is forced to walk, hindered by the density of the trees.

"We should continue on foot," says Mór. She slips from Duilleag, clutching her spear tight to her waist.

"Why?" I ask. I hold on to the hair on Duilleag's back, not yet ready to give up his protection.

"Duilleag can hardly move in here. It's too risky to go that slow."

I heave myself down next to her, and Duilleag retraces his steps out of the forest.

"Don't—!" The shout comes again. Only this time I'm almost certain I recognize the voice. From the look on Mór's face, she recognizes it too.

Cray.

She starts running, deeper into the forest. I try to match her pace, but my oversize boots keep sliding on the damp soil. Mór scoots between the trees, gone one moment and then visible again the next. "Cray!" she shouts.

There's no response. I wish I had a weapon. What if there's an imitator in here, disguised as a tree or a shrub or a fallen log? It could be hiding anywhere, and I wouldn't know until it was too late.

I've been here before: running through a forest, chasing the sound of a friend's cry for help. Last time it was Lileas. Last time…

It's not going to end that way again.

I've lost sight of Mór. Which way should I go? There's a sound ahead that could have been Mór, could have been Cray, could have been nothing. I head towards it, my pace slowing with every step. Then I see him.

He is high above me, tied between two trees, at least ten feet in the air. His arms and legs are spread wide, pulled taunt with some sort of vines, forcing his body into a large cross. His whole face – including his eyes – is covered in what looks like blue-black mud, preventing him from seeing clearly. There are tears in his clothes and a cut above his ear.

"Cray!" I say. "It's me, Jaime."

As soon as he hears me, he starts shaking his head, muffled cries leaking through the gag that's been stuffed into his mouth. That's when I realize I've walked straight into a trap.

An imitator jumps down from the tree on Cray's left, a blur of leaves and air and bark. It lands with a light thud three paces in front of me. I freeze. So does the imitator. It's the same shape and size as a human but is completely naked and hairless. Colours slip across its skin like oil on water, swirling in hypnotic patterns. Its eyes are bulbous and dominated by huge black pupils – dark wells filled with a monstrous emptiness. We stare at each other for one beat, two, then it launches itself at me. I fall to the ground and we become a mess of grabbing and kicking limbs. Wet leaves fly up all around us, clogging the air with their bitter smell. I remember Mór's warning: *Don't let its fingers touch your skin.*

I grab hold of its wrists as its knee digs into my stomach. It opens and closes its mouth in a succession of silent frustrated screams. There's a fallen branch at my side. I release my grip and snatch the branch with trembling hands. The imitator's fingers hunt for my face, but I'm quicker, swinging the branch in a wild arc up into the imitator's ribs. The branch snaps on impact, causing enough of a distraction for me to scramble away. Once I'm at a safe distance, I glance back. The imitator has disappeared. Is it camouflaged in the undergrowth or did it bolt up one of the trees? It'd be too much to hope that I've scared it away. I race towards Cray. If I can free him somehow, it'll be two against one. I reach the base of tree and start to climb. The branches are smooth and cold. The higher I get, the more I worry that I'm making a huge mistake; if the imitator attacks while I'm in the tree, it'll be even harder to defend myself.

I push that thought aside and keep climbing. I reach the first of Cray's bonds – the one tied to his left ankle – and start pulling at the loops of vine that are wound around the tree. They're so tight that it's a struggle to squeeze my fingers under. The gloves I'm wearing aren't helping either, so I tear them off with my teeth and let them drop to the ground. Cray shakes his head, the gag muffling his voice. He's trying to tell me something, but I can't work out what. His shrieks become more desperate, and his eyes bulge in the direction of his waist.

A dagger. That's what he's trying to tell me. I climb a bit higher – the knots and twigs of the tree scratching me with every chance they get – and stretch my fingers towards it. It's still too far away. I'm going to have to climb up Cray's leg to reach it. I slide away from the tree and grab hold of his calf with both hands. His leg wobbles under my weight and I make the mistake of looking down. It's a dizzying drop. I focus on the dagger and inch myself upwards until I'm close enough to pull it from its sheath. Its blade is short but sharp. I clutch it in my teeth and fumble back to the tree. The vine around Cray's ankle is tough, but a few slices are enough to cut it. The first of Cray's legs falls free, but rather than look relieved, he starts shrieking through his gag again, pointing down with his foot. There's nothing there, though, only—

A hand-shaped piece of bark peels away from the tree and snatches my ankle. I slip, the branch I was standing on landing hard between my legs. A yell bursts from my mouth. I wrap my limbs around the branch except for the one leg that the imitator is still pulling down. Its fingers tug and probe at the cloth Mór tied around my ankle, hunting for the bare skin underneath. I kick with all my strength, but can't loosen its grasp. The cloth starts to unravel, the imitator pulling at it with greedy tugs.

I'm still holding Cray's dagger. It's the only way I can stop the imitator, but in the tangled position I'm in, it's going to be nearly impossible to hit it. The imitator has replicated the colours and texture of the tree bark so perfectly that it's hard to see exactly where its body is. I've only got one chance.

I throw the dagger.

It bangs into the trunk just above the imitator's head, and then plummets like a dead bird. *Tiud!* When will I learn not to throw away my only weapon?

The imitator yanks the cloth one final time and the whole strip falls away. My kicking becomes even more frantic. The imitator's fingers squirm up the side of my boot towards the newly created gap at the bottom of my trouser leg. Cray is still making distressed sounds above me. He slams the tree with his leg, attempting to shake it, but the trunk is too sturdy.

"Cray, keep still!"

Mór appears and launches her spear at the bonds holding Cray's right wrist. Her aim is good, and the spear tears through the vine. His opposing arm and leg are now free, but he's still tied diagonally between the two trees. He uses his free hand to remove the vines from his mouth.

"Imitator!" He shouts. "On Jaime's leg."

Mór doesn't hesitate. She throws herself at the tree and scrambles up towards me. The imitator sees her coming and lets go of my foot. I whip my leg up with a whimper and kneel on the branch.

"Are you okay? Where is it?" Mór asks me.

"I don't know. It was just here. It looks the same as the bark."

"Get back down. I'll get Cray."

Mór takes out her own dagger, but before she can use it, a shimmer of forest swings down from above us and shoves her out of the tree. She falls to the forest floor and hits her head with a loud crack.

"No!" I shout.

She lies there, unmoving.

The imitator has disappeared again. Cray is heaving great breaths above me, his body still pulled taught. He stretches across with his free hand and tugs at the vines around his opposite wrist. All the while, he doesn't take his eyes off Mór.

There is a sound of disturbed branches above me. The imitator is on the move again, climbing higher up the tree. As I try to focus on where it is, it leaps and lands directly on Cray's outstretched body. Cray grits his teeth and elbows the imitator in its chest, but it absorbs the blow with little sign of discomfort. It scuttles around like a spider until it is upside-down, its legs twisted around Cray's torso. Its fingers stretch toward the exposed skin at Cray's ankle. No. No way.

I hurl myself at the pair of them. For the briefest moment I'm flying and then I crash into their mess of bodies. Cray grunts at the impact. The vines holding him shudder but don't snap, meaning all three of us are now suspended above the forest floor. Flashes of red and orange ripple across the imitator's back. I slam the heel of my foot into its head once, and then again, but it refuses to release its grip. Its hand finds Cray's ankle and squeezes. Cray screams. I wrap my arms around the imitator's waist and, letting go of Cray completely, pull down on the imitator with all of my weight. My legs dangle, treading nothing. The imitator lets go of Cray's ankle and starts slapping the air behind its back, aiming for my face, as it slips a little further down Cray's body. I heave again. The imitator can no longer hold on; its legs unwind and then we're both falling. The ground comes crashing up to meet us.

The impact is softened by the imitator's body, which hits the earth first and absorbs the worst of the shock. Even so, my ears are ringing and my vision is blurred. I slide off the imitator, onto my hands and knees, and spit on the grass as I try to catch my breath. The imitator's body is a chaos of patterns. I'm wondering if the fall may have killed it, but that hope disappears the moment it pulls itself to its feet.

It opens its mouth to reveal its toothless gums, which flash purple, then red, then black. I try to crawl away, but it flips me onto my back and pins my arms to the ground with its knees. My legs flail, hitting nothing but air. A burst of yellow dashes across the imitator's huge black eyes, then it flexes its fingers and wraps them around my throat.

The effect of the poison is immediate. A long shudder ripples through my body, and tight convulsions shake my legs. The pain comes next, like a sea of scalding water flooding every part of me at once.

Someone in the sky is shouting my name.

A thud, a scuffle, more shouting ... but I'm already gone.

AGATHA

"Ah, you found another one," says Catriona.

I didn't know she was there. She is next to us. Me and the deer I saved are looking at the empty loch.

"Where are all the— deers gone?" I ask to Catriona.

"They're safer where they are now," Catriona says. "Thank you for bringing this one back to us." She is looking at the deer next to me. Something is bad.

Run! I say to the deer in my head.

The deer does what I say and runs but people are there. They are holding Reaper sticks. The deer goes a different way but a man with a net is that way and he throws it. It goes over her and she falls and is tangled. I don't know how to help. The net man and another man try to get her but she kicks one of them and gets out of the net. She runs away and they can't stop her this time.

"Find it," says Catriona to the net man. "And then put it with the others."

"W– w– w– where—?" I say. It is hard to get the words. "W– where are all the other ones? Why are they not by the— loch?"

"I'm doing as you asked, Agatha. I'm keeping them safe," says Catriona. I do not understand. She is smiling that is not a nice one. "If they are free to roam the whole enclave, we have no way of knowing where they are. They could get lost or injured and we wouldn't know. If that happened, they would be at the mercy of the *sgàilean*. We can't have that. So we've extended the old goat enclosure. Tonight, we'll light fires all around it so they'll be safe. Isn't that what you wanted?"

"No," I say. "That is not— not what I— wanted. You can't keep them there."

"Why not?"

"They're not the same as g– goats."

"What's the difference? They're both animals, Agatha. And we're humans. If they're stupid enough to wander into our enclave, then we're going to be smart enough to keep them here. It's as simple as that."

It's not as simple as that. I said for them to come here. I made the promise.

"Where is the goat en– en-? Where are they?" I say. I have to see them.

Catriona looks at me and her mouth is chewing slow but I don't think there is food in it. "Next to the cookboth," she says.

I turn to go there but Catriona holds on to my arm hard.

"Let— go," I say. She does not let go. I try to pull my arm away but she holds it too tight. "Let go!" I say again.

She slaps me. It is hard and it stings and I am shock. Her face is too close to my face. "This is the way it is, Agatha, and that's not going to change," she says. Her eyes are big. There are red lines in the white parts. "I'm doing what is necessary for the survival of my clan – and for the survival of yours, even if you're too stupid to realize it. Don't go causing trouble or you'll regret it; I can assure you of that."

I pull away again and she lets go. I am hot and angry all the way through. I want to hit her or kick her. My teeth are crunching. She is just looking. She wants me to hit her. Then she will hit me again and harder. I do a breath and then another breath, like how Maistreas Eilionoir taught me. I am better than Catriona. I do not hit her. I run away.

I cannot run for far or very fast so I stop after a bit and I walk. I am shaking and my face is stinging. I hate her. I hate her so much. She should not have hit me and she should not have taken the deers away. She is bad bad and mean.

It is easy to see the deers next to the cookboth because there are so many of them altogether. Most of them are already behind the long fence. It is what I saw the Wasps making this morning. There are people with Reaper tools and sharp sticks and they are making the other deers go in. They hit the deers who try to go not the right way. It is like when the deamhain made all my clan go on their boats to be slaves and hit them if they didn't do it. The last deer goes in and the people shut the gate. It is small inside and not enough room.

I go to the side of the fence away from the people. I have to talk to Thistle-River. I cannot see him and it is all a big jumble of deers and antlers and heads and bottoms. *Thistle-River?* I say in my head. There are too many voices and it is all the deers and they are scared and angry and frightened. I call for *Thistle-River* lots of times.

I am here, says Thistle-River. He puts his head higher and I see him. His eyes are sad. All the other voices go away. *You have betrayed us, Sun-Leaf.*

No, I say. *It wasn't me.* I tell him it was Catriona and that I didn't know it. He shakes his head. *I will get you out,* I say. *I promise it.*

He turns his head away. He does not believe me.

I will show him. I will do it. But how can I do it? The fence is too strong to break and the people are guarding the gate so I cannot open it.

"Agatha," says someone behind me. It is Aileen. She is running towards me. "I just heard. This is terrible."

"We need to f– free them," I say.

"Yes," says Aileen, "but we have to go about it the right way. Let's find Maistreas Eilionoir."

We go to the Lower Gate which is where Maistreas Eilionoir is. She is telling the people with the chopped trees where to put them.

"Excuse me, Maistreas Eilionoir," says Aileen. "We need to speak to you."

"I'm busy," says Maistreas Eilionoir. "Find me later."

"But it's— it's— important," I say. "The deers— the deers…"

"Catriona has locked up all of the deer," says Aileen.

"And she's going to— kill them," I say. "For everyone to eat!"

"Well, we do need food," says Maistreas Eilionoir. "Our supplies are worryingly low, as you know. Maybe it was the right choice."

"It wasn't!" I say. Why is everyone wrong? "They are not— food! It was me who said them to come here. It is my fault. Please. Please, you have to tell C– Catriona not to— do it."

"Hmmm," says Maistreas Eilionoir. Her nose sniffs. "The problem is, we are guests here, Agatha, and I have very little sway over Catriona." She holds one of her hands in her other hand. They are old wrinkle hands.

"Please talk to her," I say. "Please, you have to try it." Maistreas Eilionoir does not look like she is going to say yes so I say it again. "Please. I promised they would be— safe."

"Okay, I'll talk to her," says Maistreas Eilionoir, "but I doubt she'll change her mind. She's as stubborn as an old boot. Much like myself, I suppose, although I like to think my judgement is a little better than hers. Our only real hope for change is to make her people see her for the brute she is."

"How do we do that?" asks Aileen.

"I have no idea, but she's hiding something, I'm sure of it. No one that young commands the respect she does without a few monsters in her chest... Anyway, if I'm to talk to her, I need the two of you to stay here. Tell anyone who returns from the forest to leave their wood in a pile and I'll distribute it when I get back."

Maistreas Eilionoir walks away. After she is gone, I go too.

"Hey, where are you going?" Aileen asks me.

"I have to g– go," I say.

"Maistreas Eilionoir literally just told us to wait here." Aileen shakes her head and does a little laugh. "Is it impossible for you to stay still?"

"No," I say. It is not impossible for me but I cannot be still right now. I had a thought. I had it when Maistreas Eilionoir said about the monsters in Catriona's chest. I do not know if it is a clever thought but I have to find out.

I have to go back to Catriona's bothan.

JAIME

I CAN'T SEE ANYTHING. ALL I CAN FEEL ARE THE hands. They're still on my neck, pumping their poison into my veins. I tear at them, digging in my nails. My scream is wild, but it's trapped in my throat.

"Hey, take it easy; it's me. It's me."

I'm so hot. It's too hot. I can't feel my toes.

"Can you open your eyes?"

Someone sealed my eyelids with tree sap. I'm still in the forest. Who's talking to me? I know him. I do. The ground's shaking, or is that me?

"Stay with me, Jaime, okay? You're going to be all right. I promise."

The world spins. Am I flying? It's cold, so cold. I don't think I'll ever be warm again.

There's fire in my throat and my head is pounding. My memories are slippery, flitting away like river sprats. Time has passed, but I don't know how much. I was being carried, the sky was burning, someone was talking... It's all a series of blurs.

I'm lying down. The ground is hard, but there's something soft beneath my head and someone is holding my hand. I grip the hand with the little strength I have and the hand squeezes back; a strong squeeze, full of concern. The kindness makes me want to cry. I peel apart my eyelids. It feels like my face is cracking in two.

"Welcome back," says Cray, giving my hand another squeeze.

I smile at him, then glance at our hands. I peel mine out of his grip.

He helps me sit up and I try to speak, but nothing comes out. Why can't I speak? My heart starts pounding against my rib cage. It's as if my whole throat has been torn out, taking my ability to speak with it. I raise my hands to my neck and probe at the tender skin. It's all rumpled and clammy. What did that thing do to me? My breath is coming out faster and faster, even though breathing at that speed makes everything hurt more.

"Whoa, Jaime, slow down, slow down." Cray places one of his hands behind my neck and leans in until our foreheads are touching. I try to pull away, but I don't have the strength. "Breathe with me. Just breathe," he says. "It's okay. You're going to be okay."

His breath mixes with mine. Slow. Slow. Slow.

* * *

The next time I wake up, my head is clearer. Everything still hurts, but the pain has lessened. Cray is leaning over me, his face pasted with apprehension. I start to cough, which makes my throat a hundred times worse. Cray turns me onto my side and rubs my back until the coughing stops.

"Thanks," I say. It comes out sounding like a drowning frog.

Cray tries to repress a smile. "Sorry, I shouldn't laugh," he says.

"No, you shouldn't," I say, hiding my own smile. I'm just glad I can speak again.

"How are you feeling?"

"Honestly? Like sheep crap."

Cray places a hand on my forehead. A rush of heat floods my cheeks. From the fever.

"You're still hot," says Cray, "but not as hot as you were." He takes his hand away. "I have to admit, I hoped I might see you again one day, but this isn't quite how I imagined it."

"Where are we?" I ask. The words are like wasps, stinging the inside of my throat. From where I'm lying, all I can see is the sky above me and grass sloping up on either side. Morning light leaks through the tangle of clouds; I must have been unconscious all night. There's a sound I wasn't aware of until now – a slow, repeated rustle and crunch.

"You're in a small ditch outside the forest you found me in. I thought we'd be safer away from the trees but couldn't move you too far, not with Mór injured as well."

Mór. How could I have forgotten about her? "Is she all right?"

"She's fine. She has a headache from hell, but other than that she's all good. She'll be back soon. Here, drink this."

He helps me sit up and hands me a leather flask. The liquid inside is sticky and hard to swallow, but as soon as I've taken a few swigs my throat feels a little better. The ditch we're in is roughly the size of a small bothan, with tall spear thistles growing up its steep sides. Their fluffy purple flowers sway in the breeze. The big hairy faces of Bileach and Bras look down at us from the top of the ditch. Duilleag wraps his tongue around a thistle and rips it from its base. The long spiny plant soon disappears into his mouth.

"What happened? The imitator—?"

"It got away. I managed to land a few blows before it could finish you off, but then it bolted into the trees. I don't know where and I haven't seen it since. It was injured, but it's still out there somewhere, and they seem to be able to heal remarkably quickly." The veins in my neck start pulsing. "Thanks for pulling it off me when you did," says Cray. "If you hadn't done that…"

"Hang on; are you saying I saved your life?"

Cray brushes a few stray hairs away from his face. "Well, I'm sure I would have found a way to deal with the situation had you not dropped by."

"Stop it. I saved your life and you know it!"

"All right, let's not get carried away." He smiles at me. "Besides, I saved yours almost immediately afterwards."

"I wouldn't have needed saving if you hadn't got yourself tied up in the first place," I say.

"Let's not dwell on the specifics."

"Okay, fine, so I saved yours and you saved mine. We're even."

"You say that, but I happen to remember a time not so long ago when you were stranded on a rock surrounded by wildwolves, about to face certain death, until this strapping hero turned up." He points to himself and puffs his chest. "Which I think you'll find makes it two-one to me."

A short laugh huffs out of me, which makes the coughing start again. Once it's died down, I ask, "How *did* you end up tied between two trees?"

"Funny story, actually..."

Before he has the chance to explain, Mór appears at the top of the ditch, holding a fistful of green leaves. She picks her way down to us. Her head is wrapped in a bandage of ferns and her skin is pale, but she smiles her modest smile when she sees I'm awake. "Welcome back," she says.

"How are you feeling?" I ask.

"Like I was pushed out of a tree and hit my head really hard," she says. "But I'll live. It's a shame I was knocked out when I was. Sounds like I missed all the fun."

"If you call being strangled and poisoned at the same

time fun, then yes, you missed out on that," I say.

She crouches beside me and gives the top of my arm a gentle squeeze. "You're looking much better than you were, that's for sure. You were lucky; if that thing had held on to you for much longer, I doubt you would've woken up again. You're going to be left with some impressive scars, though."

"Really?" My hands rise towards my neck but stop before they reach it.

"Afraid so. Cray's been applying a poultice, which has drawn out the poison and should prevent infection, but even once it's fully healed, there's likely to be some scarring."

"Oh." I don't know why that bothers me so much.

"Don't worry, I've got one too," says Cray. He lifts the bottom of his trousers to show me the ankle the imitator touched. The skin is creased and raw in fingerprint-sized ovals.

"I found some more knitbone," Mór says, waving the leaves in her hand at Cray, "so we can make more poultice. Although now you're awake, Jaime, I suggest we all head back to the cavern. Finn will be able to heal you much better than we can. He probably even knows a few tricks to lessen the scarring."

I'm tempted – I don't want to be scarred for the rest of my life – but it'll take us half a day to retrace our steps and come all the way back again, and that's half a day I can't afford to lose.

"I have to keep going," I say. I turn to Cray. "Did

Mór tell you where we were headed? That I need to find the Badhbh?"

"Yes, she told me," he says. "But she can't take you any further; it's not safe for her to ride at speed after a head injury like that."

"Sorry," says Mór. She taps her head. "Got to protect my pretty little brain."

"Of course," I say.

"But I'm happy to take you the rest of the way if you want me to," says Cray.

"Really?"

"Think of it as returning the favour for that *one time* you *may* have saved my life."

"Thank you," I say, and I really mean it. I struggle to my feet. "Can we leave now? I'm feeling much better." My words are undermined by another bout of harsh coughs.

Cray raises his eyebrows. "If you're sure?"

"I'm sure."

The three of us stagger out of the ditch, avoiding scratches from the hostile thistles. Mór gives the fresh knitbone to Cray, and the two of them touch foreheads.

"Come home soon," she says to him. "And stay out of trouble."

"Always," he replies.

They hold each other for a moment, and I find myself longing to be included in their closeness.

"Goodbye, Mór," I say once they've separated. I give her a small wave.

"That's not good enough for me, I'm afraid," she says. She places her hand on the base of my skull and brings our foreheads together. "Don't let this one push you around, okay?" She indicates Cray with her head, our noses still touching.

"I won't."

"And good luck." She lets go, and our heads drift apart. "Take this with you." She reaches into a pocket and hands me a small pot carved from the trunk of a thin tree. Inside is a gloopy paste with a pale green shimmer. "For your neck. Put it on whenever you're in pain."

"Thanks."

"Here, you can keep it in this." Cray slings a flimsy satchel at me. I stumble as it hits, still a little unsteady on my feet. "Oops."

Mór slaps his arm. "You're supposed to be taking care of him."

"Don't you worry about us," says Cray.

Mór mounts Duilleag, gives us one final nod, and then plods off in the direction of the cavern.

Bras steps forward and pushes his big wet nose into my face.

"Sorry, Bras, was I ignoring you?" I say. "It's good to see you again." I delve my fingers into his long hair and scratch him behind his ears, where I know he likes it. Cray leaps onto his back and then pulls me up behind him. I wrap my arms around his waist, my heart beating a little faster as I feel the warmth of his body through his clothes.

"Just like old times," he says, looking back at me.

"I can hardly wait."

Cray holds on to Bras's enormous horns, and the bull responds by trampling the ground, finding his footing before he breaks into an unrestrained gallop.

It's hard to talk properly on the bull, so we mainly travel in silence. A fine drizzle sets in and before long my hair is clinging to the sides of my face. I lift my head and let the droplets trickle past my chin. The coolness of the water soothes my neck.

The old fort Hendry told us to look out for is easy to spot: a ramshackle cluster of crumbling stones speckling the top of an ochre hill. We turn west as instructed and, when the coast comes back into view, take a break to have some food under the skant shelter of some measly trees. I dismount Bras – something I'm still unable to do without looking like a drunken crow – and stretch my back.

Cray swings down and offers me a strip of dried meat. It's hard to swallow and irritates my throat, so I don't eat much. I take out the poultice Mór gave me and smooth some over my neck.

"So tell me: what have you been up to since I last saw you?" Cray asks. "Mór said you managed to rescue your clan."

"Yes, I suppose I did." I tell him what happened in Norveg, although I'm scant on the details. It's still strange remembering it all, like it didn't actually happen or that it wasn't really me.

"Wow," says Cray once I've finished. "Sounds like you were a real hero. Spending time with me must have rubbed off on you."

Now that I'm with him, I don't know why I was so keen to see him again; I'd forgotten how arrogant he can be.

"What about you?" I ask. "You still haven't told me how you ended up captured and totally helpless." I can't resist the opportunity to batter his ego a little.

"It wasn't really my fault... I presume Mór told you that a group of us went out searching for imitators the other night? We were supposed to stay together but thought we'd be able to cover more ground if we split up. We're faster than the imitators when we're riding bulls, and they'd seemed much more intent on spying than attacking, so we thought we'd be safe. We were wrong. I was further east, on my own, when one of them ambushed me. It jumped out of a tree and landed on top of me. There was a scuffle, and it fled soon after, but it had made a fatal mistake: the tree it'd been hiding in was a bleeding birch, which stains anyone who touches its bark. The imitator was covered in blood-red smears, making it impossible to fully camouflage. I couldn't waste the opportunity, so I left in pursuit of it. I tracked it for the rest of the day before finally defeating it."

"And the part where you ended up in desperate need of rescuing?"

"I'm getting to that... I didn't realize it at the time, but the whole while I was pursuing the imitator, it was leading me straight into the hands of another of its kind – the one you encountered in the forest. I was hit over the head with what felt like a tree branch and the next thing I know, I'm stretched out like an animal hide, way up in the air. I don't know what it was planning to do to me. They don't have teeth, so I don't think it was going to eat me."

"Maybe it was going to suck out your blood," I suggest.

"Nice image, thanks. I think it was more likely to torture me, or maybe it was always its plan to use me as bait and lure in other people. Which is exactly what happened, of course, when you and Mór showed up. They're unpredictable creatures; I can't work them out. Lucky for me, it underestimated my rescuers." He turns and grins at me. "That was a compliment, by the way."

"I know," I say. I look down and pick a handful of grass so he can't see me blush.

"That's half the reason I agreed to come north with you; my mother is going to be furious when she finds out I got caught. She didn't want me heading out in the first place."

"Who's your mother? Have I met her?" I forgot that the Bó Riders are told who their birth parents are.

"Murdina. You remember her, don't you?"

"Wait. Murdina is your mother?" How did I not know that? I suppose I didn't ask many personal questions last time we were travelling together. There must be lots of things I don't know about him.

"Yes, and Mór's my sister. Did you know that one?"

"What?" That's a lot of information to take in at once.

Cray laughs at my astonished face. "I thought you knew that too."

"I didn't, I..." The subject of birth parents and siblings is *toirmisgte* in my clan – no one's allowed to speak about it. All of the grown-ups are my parents and the other children are my siblings. Maybe that's why I never thought to ask. "Do you know your father as well?"

"He died when Mór and I were young."

"Oh. Sorry."

"It's fine, I didn't know him well." Cray picks a leaf out of Bras's hair and rubs the bull on his nose. "Shall we keep going?"

The western coastline is rugged and beautiful despite the rain's attempts to taint it. We pass great sloping mountains of luscious green and serene bays tinged with mist. Dramatic rock formations burst out of the sea, repeatedly assaulted by explosions of water. I scour the view for any signs of habitation, but the burning in my neck makes it hard to concentrate. I close my eyes to shut out the pain and am struck by a surge of tiredness. I rest my head against Cray's back. It's warm in contrast to the cold of the rain, and I feel safer than I can remember feeling in a long time.

I jerk awake as Bras comes to a sudden halt. I don't know how long I was asleep. We're on the edge of a gritty beach, which has been ambushed by long streaks of black seaweed.

"Look over there," says Cray, pointing to a tiny islet a short distance out into the sea. At first I don't know what he's talking about, but then I notice the hut. It's been built on the islet in between two boulders, making it well hidden and hard to spot.

"A hut," I say.

"Think it's him?"

"It could be."

"How do you want to do this?"

I hadn't planned that far ahead. "I suppose we just go in and ask for his help. If it is him ... and he still lives there."

"As you wish," says Cray. He whistles, and Bras trots towards the water. As he crosses the seaweed, it squelches and pops, filling my nose with its briny stench.

"Maybe I should go in by myself?" I say as we draw nearer. "We don't want to startle whoever's in there."

Bras stops as if he's heard me.

"Okay," says Cray. "I'll wait here." He slides his spear out of its loop beneath our legs. What does he need that for? I'm suddenly regretting my suggestion to go alone. Well, I've said it now. I jump down from the bull into a receding wave and start to wade towards the islet. The frigid water rises almost to my waist before I'm close enough to clamber up the islet's steep sides.

The hut doesn't look at all sturdy; whoever made it was no expert. Boulders on either side make up its walls, so it's really just a front, a back and a roof, made of driftwood and withered leaves. There are no visible windows, just a door, which is open a crack. I creep over to it and knock three times. The dull clunks are answered by nothing but the soft lapping of the waves. The only other sound is my blood pulsing in my ears. I creak the door open.

"What do we have here?" says a voice from within the darkness.

There's a man sitting on the floor in front of me. It's him, it has to be.

The Badhbh.

SIGRID

Swear to the high sky, the further north I go, the colder it gets. I'm freezin my kog off here, despite the extra clothes Lady Beatrice put in the saddlebags for me. She was right that leavin the palace grounds would be easy. Well, the leavin part was. The gettin up on the horse and makin it move part was trickier. I recognized the mare Lady Beatrice'd got ready for me; it's her one, the one she rode on the hunt. It's a beauty of a horse – all shiny black, with white hair bright as a mountaintop and a white stripe gushin down from its forehead to its nose. It was patient with me and didn't move none while I heaved myself up, which took me six tries cuz it's hek bulkin. Once I was on, I couldn't make it move for war nor peace, and in the end I had to kick it on its sides. I didn't like doin it, but it seemed to know that meant time for movin, and out we went.

I did what Lady Beatrice told me and left through

the same gate we used for the hunt. There weren't no guards, just like she said, and before I could sniff twice, I was away from the palace and stompin hooves. The stars winked above me and the wind whipped at my hair and I knew that I'd done it: I'd escaped; I was free.

When we got to the edge of the forest, I turned the horse towards the buildins where all the people live. Rows and rows of tall shacks, all squished next to each other, lookin ready to slip over. The knock knockin of the horse's hooves was hek loud as we clopped through the streets. I couldn't go fast cuz the ways were all scraggin and uneven. All I knew was I had to go north, and the Bright Star was peepin through the clouds just enough to show me the way. As we got further from the palace, the streets got more skittin. I swear I nearly gagged on the reek of them. Then there were less buildins and less still until it wasn't nothin but fields and we could go proper fast after that.

We've passed a hek lot of settlements, big ones and small ones, but I don't slow down for nothin, like what the Lady Beatrice told me. We go tramplin right past them all, past what I reckon musta been Oxenford and then Waringham. I only saw the map of Ingland and Scotia once, when King Edmund put it out on the table, but it's in my head clear as chickenspit. Lucky it is and all, cuz Lady Beatrice didn't give me no maps in the saddlebags. Maybe she couldn't find one, or maybe she knew I wouldn't need it.

I've called the horse Eydis. I didn't like her not havin

no name. Not when I'm bein so mean to her, really, makin her go so fast the whole time. I rode her hard all through the night and the whole of yesterday, with only short stops for eatin and drinkin. When dark dropped, I stopped for us to have a few blinks nappin, but I didn't dare sleep for long cuz I think we're bein followed. I can't be certain, but I got this twistgut feelin. Two times yesterday I thought I spotted someone a long ways behind me. Someone ridin a big white animal, and ridin it fast. A dip in the hills and then it'd be gone.

I've been tryin my best to lose them: changin direction all in a sudden, goin through rivers to cover my tracks, pushin Eydis to go faster and faster. I haven't seen no sign of them today so I'm hopin they finally lost my trail.

It makes sense that Konge Grímr would've sent someone to hunt me down. He woulda woke up and found me gone, and – from the file marks on the chain – realized it was me what'd done it. He would've got hek fiery at that and demanded I be found. He won't want me makin him look no fool. Also, I know too much. Even though I pretended I couldn't understood his meetins with King Edmund, he had plenty of conversations with Bolverk and the other wreckers what he knows I overheard. And then there's the confessions he made when he was turned sour with slosh. As long as I'm alive, there's a thousand reasons he'd want me not to be. If I ever get caught, he'll punish me rotten in fronta evryone and no mistakin – make an example of me; that's how he works.

"Sorry, girl," I keep sayin to Eydis, strokin her hair and pattin her neck. "I'm sorry, but we gotta keep goin."

As we tromp norther, I watch the land get more and more harsk. The fields were bright greens and deep yellows in the south, but up here they're moth brown and decayin. The settlements are more harsk too, and the few people we pass ogle at us in a way I don't like one speck. There's somethin not right about them, somethin about how they look: pale faces, hollow eyes, sunken cheeks.

"This sure is a wreckmess of a place," I say to Eydis. Talkin to her helps keep me awake and focused and makes me feel less alone. "Reckon we need to start avoidin anywhere we might find people, like what Lady Beatrice told us, don't you think? We'll rest again soon. You must be tired. So am I, and my backside's killin. Sorry to be the one to tell you, but you're not as comfy as what you look. Anyways, just a little bit longer and we'll find somewhere safe for stoppin."

It's gettin dark. I've been findin my way by what I saw on the map, and by readin the sun like what Granpa Halvor taught me, but what little sun there was has gone now. The sky's hek cloudy, so it doesn't look like I'm gunna be able to read the stars neither. It starts to rain. Time to find somewhere to rest. We could do with some food and all; the handgrab I stole from Konge Grímr's table didn't last long, and neither did the bits what Lady Beatrice put in the saddlebags, even though I was hek stingy with the eatin of them.

Fwihsss!

What in hell thunder was that? Somethin just shot past my face, fast as lightning.

Fwihsss!

And another. Someone's shootin skittin darts at me!

"Faster, Eydis, faster." I kick her flanks, hatin myself for doin it, but if we don't get away soon, both of us are gunna be dead. She strides forward a little, but I've been pushin her hard for the past two days and she hasn't got much left in her. I can feel her body weakenin beneath me. Another dart flies past us, so close it nips the top of one of Eydis's ears. She whinnies and shakes her head. Her eyes are wild, rovin round and round all over. I kick her again. We gotta go faster.

The next dart falls short. We're gettin away. I kick again. Faster. Gotta be sure. I don't hear no more darts, but whoever was firin them could still be followin. Kick again, just a little bit further. *Come on, Eydis, just a little bit further, gotta get away, gotta be sure—*

Her front leg goes first, then her whole body follows as she trips. She twists her head up to the sky, brayin with throatsick fear. For a moment I'm weightless, then I'm fallin too. The ground, my face, the two collidin.

A crash shriek sigh.

Blackness.

"Where is horse?" I ask.

"I keep telling yer, there wunt no horse."

I don't know if I believe her. I don't know if I believe a single word she's said. She told me she found me

250

unconscious on the ground, but that she didn't see my horse. She brought me back here, to her shack, which is fallin down and skittin as hell. I woke up on the floor with a thin blanket round me. The woman gave me water and bandaged my head, so I spose she can't be that bad. But I gotta find Eydis – all my supplies were in the saddlebags, and I'm hek hopeless without her.

There's a small fire in the corner, with a person huddled next to it, arms wrapped around his twigbone legs. He looks too old to be the woman's kidlin but too young to be her husband. I'm cold and I wanna go join him, but somethin stops me. He's starin at me with deep, sunken eyes. He looks kinda wild.

"My brother," ses the woman when she sees me lookin.

"Person shoot me," I say in my cowcrap foreign tongue. "Dart."

"I dunt know anything about that," ses the woman. She speaks soft, like her words are wrapped in leaves. "But yer safe here. Trust me. Try and get some rest." The way she talks the foreign tongue is diffrunt to King Edmund and evryone else in the palace, but I can just about understand her.

Truth bein told, I wanna do exactly what she ses. Sleep. But it don't feel right doin it in this strange, harsk shack with that weird brother of hers watchin and this woman who I don't know nothin about. And course there's Lady Beatrice's warnin goin round my head that I shouldn't trust no one I meet up here.

The woman puts a cold hand on my forehead. There's no tellin how old she is. She's so scrawny it's like all the flesh has been sucked out of her and all that's left is bones wrapped up tight.

"Where'd yer come from?" She looks at my ink – at the neck-snapped raven – then down at the chain what's still clingin to my wrist. "How'd yer end up in these parts?" I don't know if I should tell her or not. My gut ses I shouldn't tell her nothin. I shake my head and keep my tongue still. "Fair enoughs if yer dunt wanna say, but wherever yer came from, I suggest yer turn right around and go straight back there. Int nothing good round here."

I'd worked that much out for myself.

"Water?" I ask. It sounds like beggin, which I hate, but my throat is dry as sand.

"Of course," ses the woman. She picks up a bowl what's by her side and tilts it against my lips. Whatever the liquid is, it sure as the moon isn't no water. It's got a bitter edge what lingers at the back of my mouth. "Drink up, petal," ses the woman, tippin the rest of the liquid down my throat. "I'd offer yer something to eat, but I've got nowt to give yer. I wish I did, but times are harder than hard." A single tear dribbles outta the corner of her eye. She wipes it away before it reaches her cheek.

"I go," I say, startin to get up.

"No," she ses, puttin a hand on my shoulder. "Yer tired, and it's dark out. Int no point leaving now. Rest some. I'll get yer on yer way tomorrow."

I let her push me back down. I really am tired. I haven't

napped proper for days, and even before then I was sleepin on a cold floor, so not no proper buried sleep at all. My eyes are shuttin before I even know what's happenin. What if the person what was followin me...? Gotta keep goin... Warn the Skye people... She's strokin my hair now. So tired. Just a quick sleep. Only a quick one.

I wake up and straightaways I know somethin's not right. It's still dark out, but I know I slept too long. That's not the worst of it, though; it was a noise what woke me – one that's got me panicked – but I can't hear it no more, nor remember what it was neither. Maybe a scream or a shout or people arguin. I'm still in the shack, still on the floor, but the woman and her brother are gone. The fire in the corner is burnin bigger, and there's a pot over it now with somethin bubblin. My arm's gone dead from sleepin on it funny. I try to move it, but— Why can't I—? My hands won't move. They're tied behind my back, hek tight. I try to stand up, but my legs are tied and all. What the skit? That lyin sneaksnake has gone and tied me up. But why? What's she done that for?

I flip myself over onto my stomach, which bangs my chin, and then up onto my knees. I need somethin to cut through the ropes but there isn't hardly nothin in this whole skittin place.

The door creaks and she's there, stood in the doorway. Pale face, thin hair, hollow eyes. The same woman from before. And in her hand, a knife.

"Ye're not supposed to be awake yet," she ses. What

in Øden's name is that sposed to mean? "I'm sorry... We haven't got a choice."

It's not a very long knife, nor a very sharp one by the lookin of it, but I'm sure she can still do some hurtin with it if she tries hard enough. She's walkin towards me now, the knife held out in front of her.

"No!" I say. "Stop! Why?" I'm throwin words at her, but they land soft as snowflicks and melt into nothin.

"I weren't going to, I swear. But I have to." She's closer now, and I'm surprised to see she's cryin. Proper harsk streamin-down-her-face cryin.

"No," I say. "Please."

"My brother... I have to for my brother." What's she wailin on? I never did nothin to her scraggin brother. The hand with the knife in is shakin. "I've tried. I've tried so hard. But there's nothing. That bastard King Edmund. He's to blame, for all of this. The dead land, the no food. The whole north has fallen, but he dunt care one bit for us, sitting down there in his fancy palace with his fancy foods and fancy ways." There's black anger in her now, talkin about the king is gettin her teeth grindin. "The things people've started doing... I made a promise to myself that I never would, even when others did, but there's nothing left. There hasn't been anything for weeks."

Then it all comes clear in my head. The words she's sayin, the pot on the fire, the way her brother was lookin on at me earlier... It's the same look what this kerl's givin me now.

Hungry.

JAIME

THE BADHBH AND I STARE AT EACH OTHER FOR A LONG time – if that's who the person in front of me is. He's sitting cross-legged on the floor with his palms resting on his knees. There are no windows in the hut, but the crude manner in which it's been constructed has left large gaps, through which stark sea light streams in. Slices of daylight slash across his face.

"You're the Badhbh?" It comes out as a hoarse question, not nearly as assertive as I was aiming for.

"I was once known by that name." He has the richest voice I have ever heard, a voice that demands instant respect. He speaks slowly, giving reverence to each individual word. I knew he'd be old, since he was middle-aged at the time of the plague, and that was over forty years ago, but I'm still taken aback by how aged he looks. His jowls hang limp from his cheekbones as if they've melted in the sun, and a peppery white beard clings to his jawline. The hair on his head is long and grey and twisted into thick, greasy locks. Yellow toenails curl out from beneath his weathered feet.

"And now? What name do you go by now?" I ask.

"Now I have no name."

"Then what should I call you?"

"Why call me anything at all?" He raises two over-grown eyebrows, which burst from his forehead like the wings of a bird.

Is he expecting me to answer that question? He hasn't moved once since I entered the hut.

"We need your help," I say.

"No, you don't."

His reply knocks me off guard. "We do – my clan – we need—"

"Need does not exist," he interrupts me. There's a piercing intelligence in his eyes.

"What?" I say, my forehead creasing.

"There is nothing we truly need."

What game is he playing? "Of course we need things," I say. "What about food? Or water? Air?"

He shakes his head as if pitying a dying animal. "You require these things to live, true, but what need does the world have for your survival?"

Now I'm really confused.

"You may *seek* my help," he continues. "Or *want* my help. Or *request* my help, even. But you do not *need* my help."

"Okay..." I start again. "Then I'm here to request your help."

"Better. I refuse. You may now leave."

"But ... I haven't..." This isn't going well at all. "It's the *sgàilean*," I try. His face gives away nothing upon hearing the word. He doesn't move or respond, but he doesn't throw me out either, so I carry on talking. "They were contained in the onyx amulet, but they broke free. Now they're all over the Isle of Skye, where my clan live, and they're trying to kill us. We need you to make them go back inside the amulet. I mean, we want you to. We hope that you will."

The Badhbh does not reply for a long time. Then he opens his mouth and utters a single, resonant word.

"No."

"What do you mean 'no'?" I don't care that he's old, or that this is his home, or that he's some sort of powerful mage; right now, he's really starting to boil my blood. "You created them. It's because of you that they exist. And now they're killing people. Innocent people. Not the Inglish, not your enemy, but innocent Scotian people. Doesn't that mean anything to you?"

"It does not."

I'm about to speak again, but he silences me with the most minimal of hand gestures.

"I prefer my home silent," he says. "It is time for you to leave." An edge of hostility has sharpened his voice, warning me that I should obey him, but I can't leave now, not when I've come all this way. I have one more idea.

"Nathara is dead," I say.

The Badhbh's perfectly composed body betrays him with a flicker of a reaction; his shoulders slump a fraction and a glimpse of emotion wanders across his eyes. Surprise? Sadness? Regret? A beat later, whatever it was disappears and he is impassive once again.

He doesn't speak, as if waiting for me to say more.

"Nathara, the princess, the little girl you left in the tower. Don't pretend you don't remember her."

It was all in his diary: how the plague killed everybody in Dunnottar Castle except for him and Nathara and how – even though she was only a child at the time – he left her behind, locked in the highest tower, all on her own.

His lips are pursed. He swallows.

"What happened to her?" he asks.

"Does it matter? The truth is you abandoned her. How could you do such a thing?"

"I…" He struggles to find the words for his excuse. "You have no idea. Everyone was dead. *Everyone*. I had to start again. I knew if I took her with me…" His whole face stiffens. "I don't have to explain myself to you."

"Well, you should know that she survived. She broke out of her room and spent her whole life in that castle, fending for herself, with only the *sgàilean* for company. I'm sure you can imagine the effect that would have on a child. Growing up without love, without family or friends."

He breaks eye contact and stares past me, at nothing.

"I've thought about her every single day. Not one day has passed where I've not regretted my decision to leave her there."

"So why didn't you go back? You could have rescued her at any time!" The thought makes me rage – that Nathara could have been saved from her tragic existence if only this man had had a little empathy.

"You know nothing about me, about the life I've led, the choices I've had to make." Flecks of dust float through the streaks of light. "How did she die?"

"I only met her about six weeks ago. My clan was taken prisoner by deamhain, and she wanted to help rescue them. She thought we were going to rescue her family, and I couldn't convince her otherwise. We sailed to Norveg and defeated the deamhain, but she died in the fight. She was very brave."

The Badhbh nods, a slow, repeated bob of his head. I don't know what he's agreeing to.

"Her death means there's no one left to control the *sgàilean*," I say. "No one except you. So will you help us?"

He's still nodding, which is a good sign. Then he stops and says, "No."

One word, one decision that will affect the lives of thousands.

I open my mouth to say something more, to convince him to change his mind somehow, but he cuts me off before I can speak.

"Get out," he says with pounding authority. "Leave this place and never come back."

"But—"

He raises his hand with terrifying force, as if he's about to strike me or throw something at me, even though his hand is empty. I stumble backwards, compelled by a sudden need to leave the hut.

Once outside, I slam the crooked door and kick it as hard as I can, letting out a guttural cry of frustration as I do so. I turn away and the brightness of the daylight smacks me in the face. Cray and Bras are where I left them, a short distance from the islet. Cray jumps off the bull's back and comes towards me, dragging his spear as he walks. It leaves a dark snake in the wet sand.

"Well?" he asks as I tumble down from islet and slosh through the water towards him.

"He said no," I reply. "He's not coming. He won't help." This whole trip has been a complete waste of time.

"Need me to try a more assertive approach?" He raises his spear and flicks it in an elegant circle.

"I don't think that's a good idea; I get the impression he's still quite powerful."

"Pah! I can handle one old man."

"No, I just ... I need to think."

I trudge away from the islet, following the line of the shore. My trousers are sodden and my legs are freezing. All I want is to go home. My neck is starting to throb again as well. Without slowing my pace, I take out Mór's poultice and smear it on. It cools the pain a little. Bras trots along beside me.

"Jaime," Cray calls from behind me. I don't answer. Right now, all I want is to get as far away from the Badhbh as possible. He's not going to help us. I tried, and I failed, just like I always do. How can one man be so insensitive, so heartless?

"Uh, Jaime..." Cray's voice is a little louder now. "I think you'll want to see this..."

I turn around. At first I don't know what he's talking about. Then I see the Badhbh. He's left his hut and is wading through the water towards us. A weathered bag hangs limp at his side. I retrace a few of my steps, still wary. The Badhbh reaches Cray first but doesn't acknowledge him. When there are only a few strides between us, he stops.

"Take me to where they are," he says.

The Badhbh has agreed to come with us on three conditions: number one, that I ask him nothing about himself; number two, that I mention nothing about the past; and number three, that I have no expectations about what he may or may not be able to do for us. I'm fine with all of those. More than fine. I don't know what made him change his mind, but I'm elated. He's coming with us! I was sent to find him and convince him to help us, and against all odds, I've succeeded in doing just that. Now we need to return to Skye as quickly as possible; it's been three days since I left – who knows what could have happened since then?

My only other worry is that I won't remember where

we left the boat, as I wasn't paying that much attention at the time. I presumed Donal and Violet would be with me to lead the way. I'm struck by yet another pang of guilt at the thought of leaving them here.

A strong gust of wind nearly blows me off my feet. It's been really windy all afternoon. We walked a little inland to escape the worst of the sea breeze, but it's still cold enough to make my ears sting. Ahead, two crows bicker over a morsel of food. The wind flings their bodies this way and that as they squabble mid-air.

Cray and Bras are still with us. I didn't ask Cray to come, or expect him to, but I'm grateful that he has. For some reason it's easier to breathe when he's around. I thought he'd want to head straight back to his tribe's cavern, but he volunteered to take us as far as the boat. It's a good job really, since despite being fit for his age, I'm sure the Badhbh would have struggled to walk the whole way. He's sitting on Bras, and Cray and I walk on either side of him. Occasionally we jog for a short stretch to keep our pace up. Even so, we won't make it to the boat before nightfall, which means another night my clan will have to spend fending off the *sgàilean* on their own. As long as they keep the fires burning, they shouldn't be in too much danger.

Bras stops and so does Cray. "What is it, friend?" Cray asks the bull.

Bras puffs air through his nose and turns his head first one way and then the other. Cray's knuckles tense as he tightens his grip on his spear.

The Badhbh dismounts from Bras with more grace than I've ever managed. "Something's near," he says.

I don't know how he knows it, how they all seem to know; I can't see or hear anything.

"An imitator," says Cray.

"A what?" asks the Badhbh.

"An imitator. They're—"

Before he can explain, the imitator strikes. It does something to Bras that spooks him into a gallop. Cray runs after him, leaving me alone with the Badhbh. The imitator's disappeared. The Badhbh looks intrigued and not the slightest bit afraid. He doesn't know what they're capable of.

"Look out!" I yell as the grass-and-sky-coloured imitator grabs the Badhbh from behind. One of its hands is around the Badhbh's waist and the other is reaching for the exposed skin of his face. Still, there is nothing but fascination in the Badhbh's eyes. Then a bright spark emanates from the Badhbh's body, and the imitator is flung several yards away from him. What the hell?

I keep my focus on the imitator as its skin spasms green and brown, replicating both the colour and the texture of the bracken on which it landed. As long as I don't blink, I'll know where it is. It jumps up and runs at me. *Ò daingead!* My neck burns. I grit my teeth and raise my skinny arms in front of me, willing them to be stronger than they are.

Just before the imitator reaches me, there is a rush to my left as Bras comes charging with Cray on his back. Bras lowers his head and smashes into the imitator's chest. At the moment of impact, an orange-brown burst – the same colour as the bull's hair – spreads all over the imitator's skin. Soon after, the imitator is prostrate on the grass, violent flashes of purple and red streaking its body from head to toe. Cray jumps down and stalks towards it. He raises his spear and throws it at the imitator's neck. The imitator's reflexes are lightning-fast. It catches the spear inches from its face and leaps back onto its feet without using its hands. They stare at each other, the imitator holding the spear, Cray now weaponless. The imitator lunges.

Cray bats away the spear as the imitator thrusts it again and again. He's defending himself well, given the disadvantage he's at. He even manages to land a few punches, although the imitator makes no sign of being hurt. Bras hovers nearby, inching forwards a little, horns lowered, before backing away again. I know how he feels; I'm also looking for an opportunity to help, but the spear is swinging so wildly I can't get close.

Cray is tiring. He misjudges a feint, and the imitator lands a kick to his ribs. As he stumbles, the imitator jabs with the spear once again. This time it makes contact, its sharp point slicing through Cray's upper arm. Cray cries out and falls backwards onto the ground. The imitator's going to kill him. I look around for a weapon, a rock, anything I can use to stop it, which is when I see the Badhbh. I'd forgotten he was there. He's standing watching the fight with no emotion on his face whatsoever.

"Help him!" I yell. "It's going to kill him."

The Badhbh looks at me as if he hasn't even considered that as an option. The imitator raises the spear above its head, preparing for a final strike. I'm about to throw myself at the imitator when the Badhbh thusts his hand in its direction. His fingers twitch as if pressing holes on an invisible set of pipes, then he twists his hand to the left in one sudden jerk. The instant he does it, the imitator's neck makes the exact same motion. There is a sickening crack, and the imitator collapses to the ground.

I'm so shocked it takes a couple of moments to process what just happened. I approach the imitator and flip it over with my foot. Swirls of colour drift away from its skin like clouds swallowing a sunset, and then all that's left is a body. Without the patterns camouflaging its skin it looks more human than ever. Did it ask to be made this way or was it forced into it, the result of some sick experimentation? It looks so cold and exposed, its lips already tinged blue. Part of me wishes we could stay and bury it, but we don't have time for that.

"It's the same one that attacked us in the forest," says Cray, nudging its body with the toe of his boot. "There's the knife wound I gave it before. You okay?" I nod. I should be the one asking him; it didn't even touch me. He prods at the spear wound on his arm and then dismisses it as unworthy of his attention. "Thank you," he says to the Badhbh, "for ... whatever it was you did."

The Badhbh doesn't acknowledge him. "Let's keep going, shall we?" he says.

Without further discussion – and with no one mentioning the fact that we all just watched the Badhbh snap someone's neck without even touching it – we carry on walking, leaving the imitator's cold body behind us.

SIGRID

No way. That's the first thing I think. No way in high hell am I endin up in some scraghag's dinner pot. I'm gettin out of here. This is not the way I die.

The woman who's got me tied up sees my resolve, cuz all in a sudden she gets serious. She stops cryin and her harsk gaunt face grows mean. "Yer can't escape," she ses, "so don't even try."

"Watch me, you skittin grotweasel," I say in my own language, cuz I don't know how to say words like that in the foreign tongue, and hek sure this is a situation what needs swearin.

The woman's surprised hearin me speak foreign words. Don't know why; she knows I'm not from round here.

"Don't make this harder than it already is," she ses, almost like she's beggin me now. Tight, hard-faced beggin. "I should've killed yer sooner – I could've done, you know." Too right she shoulda, cuz I'm a whole lot more skapped now than I woulda been if I'd of been nappin.

She comes at me then, swingin the knife wild. I duck it once, then lean back, missin her second strike. She's not trained for fightin, that's for hek sure. Her stance is off, her slashin's erratic, her left side's wide open. Doesn't mean it's gunna be easy, though, what with me bein tied up and all. After her third swing, I make my move, launchin from my knees, batterin my head straight into her legs. I slam her left kneecap and somethin cracks. She falls to the floor in an ugly twist, lettin go of the knife, which goes off spinnin. She's screamin and wailin and holdin her busted knee. I crawl on my side towards the knife like some drunken caterpilly. She sees me doin it and starts crawlin too, like we're in some mad drunken-caterpilly race. It's easier for her cuz she's got her arms, so she reaches the knife first. She grabs it and starts lumberin up on one leg. I turn so I'm lyin on my back, then kick my tied-together feet smack into her ankles. She doesn't scream nothin at first, she's too shocked by what she didn't see comin. She stumbles away from me some, her knee gives way again, and she falls backwards straight into the pot on the fire. The pot tips, splashin water all over her, and I know from her screamin that it's hot as hellfire. I scoot back, away from where it's spillin. The fire's spreadin now too, twistin out of its place and jumpin up the walls. The woman tries to get up, slips on the water, tries again.

She's in a bad way, manic, hek crazy. She knows the fire's comin for her. She struggles up once more, headin for the open door, but she's so batcrazed she misses it and runs straight into the wall. *Bam!* and she's on the floor again, not movin.

I dunno what I'm waitin for. The whole shack's on fire now. I gotta get out of here. I push myself up onto to my feet, then jump outta there with plenty of stumblin.

I'm outside and the air is fresh and I'm gulpin it in, but it's not over yet. I'm still tied up and she could wake at any moment. I gotta get free. There's a nail stickin out of one corner of the shack. I drop to it. The walls are turnin black from the fire inside. It's hek scorchin and I'm sweatin seas just by bein near. I find the nail with my hands behind my back, and use it to scratch away the rope. The fire is burnin my wrists through the wall, but I'm nearly there, nearly there.

The rope splits and my hands come free. I crawl forward, away from the burnin shack, and rip at the ropes on my ankles. Soon they're off too and I get up, ready to run, only somethin stops me. The woman. She's gunna burn to death if I leave her in there. Even though she tried to kill me, I can't let her go that way. It's not her fault she's been thrown a rotten's life after all.

I go back into the shack. There's so much smoke I can't hardly see nothin but black. My breathin turns to chalk and my eyes are streamin. I get down on my knees and feel around. She was near the door some-where; that's where she fell. Unless she woke up and moved. There's a tearin ripcreak and part of the roof falls down, far too close to my head for likin. Sparks fly up like lightnin dust, then disappear into nothin. I feel around some more, quicker now. I'll be hek skapped if I die tryin to save this skittin kerl. I grab somethin. An ankle. It's her. *Jarg*, she's heavy. I pull and pull with all I've got until we're outside and I keep pullin, away from the shack, away from the fire, just in time, as the whole place collapses in on itself, dead. The fire looks mighty pleased with its doin.

I wipe at my eyes and my hand comes away black. I'm black all over. A cough rolls out of me, and once I start I can't stop. I'm coughin so hard it feels like my insides are gunna come right outta my yapper. I spit black and spit some more. Then I lean down and feel for the woman's heart. She's alive. Whatever nearly happened, I'm pleased about that. Now I gotta get outta here quickspit.

I stand up, ready to run, but am stilled to stone when I see the boy – the woman's brother – standing at the edge of the trees. He looks at the burnin shack, then at his wreckmess of a sister lyin on the ground, then at me. His eyes turn hek fiery and he starts comin towards me.

"Stop," I say. Somethin about the way I say it makes him obey.

"You killed my sister," he ses, showin me all of his teeth.

"No. Alive." I give her leg a small kick with my foot, but she doesn't move, which doesn't help prove my point none. I'm weighin up my chances of bein able to outrun him. He's a lot older than me and his legs are long. Also, he knows the land here a hek lot better than I do. He pulls out some sorta stick from his belt and puts it to his mouth. A blowpipe. It musta been him what was firin at me before.

I hear the *fwihsss* of a dart and dive outta its path in a sideways roll that gets me straight back on my feet again. Then I'm runnin and I'm not lookin back, followed by the sound of him chasin, close behind.

Up ahead is a hump in the ground which I run towards as fast as my flamin lungs will let me. The slope beyond it is steeper than what I'd hoped, but I haven't got no choice but to go down it. I'm half runnin, half slippin-slidin. I can hardly hear nothin over the scrunchin of the branches beneath me and the pantin of my breath and the thunderboomin of my heart. I can hear enough to know he's still followin, though. I slip on wet mud and land bamsmack on my backside, sharp stones grazin my hands. *Jarg!* I haven't got time for bleedin. I get back up and carry on stumblin.

I reach the bottom of the slope and don't stop for one blink, even though my throat is burnin and my legs are sapped. The ground is flat again. I risk a look back and there he is, comin down the last part of the slope, lookin even more skapped. Only good thing is he can't run and use the blowpipe at the same time, and for now he's focusin on runnin. The grass starts sloshin beneath me and then drizzles away, replaced by thick mud what sucks at my feet, makin it hard to lift them. If I don't get outta here soon, I'm gunna get stuck, makin me easy pickins for that rotweed what's chasin me. The mud's gettin deeper the further I go, but I can't turn back nor reach the side neither. I've slowed down so much, it's given him a chance to get closer. He stops and lifts the blowpipe to his mouth, gettin ready to fire another dart.

A whinny to my left. I'm foolin myself that I recognize it, but swear Øden I do. Then I see her. Eydis, my hek brimmin horse, runnin straight for me. I can't think where she's been or what she's been doin or why she's comin to rescue me now, but holy godsmite am I glad to see her. Only problem is, how in a hundred winters am I sposed to get on her back while we're both runnin? It's hard enough when she's stood still, and I never had no madfire boy tryin to get me at the same time before neither.

A dart flies past my head, makin me flinch some. I can do this. I *have* to do this. I'm still sloshin along, and Eydis is runnin beside me, mud flyin out in all directions. All I gotta do is jump at the right moment, grab the reins, jam my foot in the stirrup and swing myself over. Easy. Easy. She's close. Okay, okay. I jump.

My left foot finds the stirrup, but I miss the reins and am grabbin at her hair. She doesn't seem to mind none. I'm danglin, my right foot draggin through the mud as she keeps runnin. I gotta get up quick, before my foot catches on somethin sharp what'll snap my ankle bones apart. I try to pull myself up, but the speed we're goin, with the bumps and all, it's too hard. Mud is flyin in my face, in my mouth. It tastes of salt and bitterbread. I try to swing myself up again, and this time Eydis lowers her head some, makin it easier for me. I reach for the saddle and heave my right leg over. I'm up! Only skap thing is I'm facin backwards, but I'm not bothered about that none. I trust Eydis to keep goin. I don't care where, as long as it's forward. She doesn't seem troubled by the mud. The woman's brother is gettin further and further away from us. He fires one more dart, but it doesn't even come close.

"You're a good girl, Eydis," I say to her, huggin her rear end. "A hek *ríkka* good girl."

She snorts outta her nose and carries on runnin.

AGATHA

I HAVE TO FIND CATRIONA'S BAD SECRET. THAT IS what Maistreas Eilionoir said and what made me have the thought. That is why I am going back to Catriona's bothan. Maistreas Eilionoir said there are monsters in Catriona's chest but she is wrong. I looked in the chest and it is clothes and a book and a blanket. The only thing is the bump noise though. I don't know what it was but maybe it is Catriona's bad secret and I am going to find it.

I put my hood on my head and pull it all the way down which is disguise. It is not a very good disguise but it is a bit of one. I do not want anyone to see me go into Catriona's bothan because it is naughty to do it. This is my one, two, third time going into Catriona's bothan when I wasn't supposed to. That is my bad secret. It is important so I have to do it.

When I am at her bothan I look around and no one

is seeing me so I go in. It is the same as when I was here before except the only thing is it is more brighter. I look at the bed and the chair and the chest and am thinking where the bad secret can be. I open the chest again and look again. Maybe I didn't look properly enough. No, it is still clothes and a book and a blanket.

'No bad secrets in there,' I say, which is talking to myself.

I stand up and am thinking where to look next when the bump noise comes again. It is the same one from before. It is quiet bumps from far away. I do not know where it is the bumps.

I take Milkwort out. He has good ears for hearing. I ask him if he can help me find where the bump noise is and he says yes. I put him on the floor and he runs first one way but then the bump noise comes and he turns quick around the other way. He stops next to the chest. It is not in the chest because I looked. Doesn't he know that? Then Milkwort says to me the bumps is under the chest. How can it be under the chest? Under the chest is the floor. Milkwort says again that is where it is. I say okay I will look.

The chest is heavy so it is hard for me to pull it. When it is away from the corner I go to the other side and push it which makes it a little bit easier but still hard. Underneath is just the floor like I knew it would be. But, oh – there is a hole. I go on my knees to see closer and it is a hole for a key I think. Why is there a key lock hole in the floor?

The bump noise does again and it is a surprise and I do a yelp. I put my hand over my mouth. I shouldn't do that yelp sound. It came out of me because of the surprise. Something is bumping from inside the floor. What if it is a monster or a wildwolf and it gets me? I have to be brave. I put my eye next to the hole lock to see inside but it is only dark and I cannot see. The bump comes again and again and is harder and loud. I move away from the hole. Maybe Milkwort can see. He has good eyes in the dark and little ones that can see in small holes. I ask him if please he can look in and see it but be careful in case there is a monster or a wildwolf inside.

He runs to the hole and puts his nose close. He says he can see something. He says it is a person. There is a person in the ground!

Is the person alive? I ask Milkwort. *Are they moving?* He tells me yes and yes. I say to him thank you for being the best most brilliant vole and he is happy. He comes back into my pocket. I bend down on my knees and hands on the floor.

"Hello?" I say into the hole with my mouth close. "Can you hear me?"

Then I put my ear next to it for listening but there is no speaking back only faster bump bump bumps. This is the most strange ever. I put my finger in the lock hole and wiggle the floor but it won't come. It is locked. I have to find the key. Then I will open the floor and the person will be free. That is the clever plan. But where is the key? It is not in the chest because I looked in it twice and I know. I look under the bed and it is not there. I look under the chair and it is not there as well. There isn't any other places in the bothan to hide it. Maybe Catriona took it with her when she went. I look around again. There's nothing except the chest and the chair and the bed and the pillow. Oh, the pillow! I haven't looked in the pillow.

I pick it up and pull out the straw. It is yellow and hard spiky on my hands. It goes all on the bed. I am making the mess. The door does a creak and opens.

I stop pulling out the straw and look at the door. It is wide open. My heart is bumping like the person in the floor but only harder. No one comes. It was the wind I think. I close the door tighter and look out of the window. Still no one is there. I am not found.

I go back to the bed and hold the pillow at the end and shake it so all the straw is out. There is no key. That is sad. I did not find it. The bumping is still louder and faster but I have to go now before someone comes. I think someone will come soon. Before I go I have to make the room right again so Catriona does not know I was here. I pick up a grab of straw in my hand and put it back in the pillow sack. Then – what is that shiny? It is a key! It was in the pillow. I didn't see it when it came out but I see it now. It is a clever place to hide it in the pillow and I am more clever because I thought to look in the pillow and found it.

I pick it up. It is cold like puddles. I go to the key lock

hole and put it in. It goes in. It is hard to turn it but then it does. There is a loud sound that is clunk. The bump noise stops. I try to pull up but it won't open. It is too too heavy. Or maybe the key is wrong. Then the ground moves below me. I am lifted in the air a small bit. The floor hole is opening but it is not me doing it. The person from inside the ground is pushing up. I am on top so they cannot do it high. I move away to next to the bed. The person is going to come up. *Please be a nice person* is what I am thinking. The floor moves again and now I am not on the top it can open all the way. A head comes up. It is a man. His face is all dirty and his eyes are scrunched. In his mouth is a rope which is tied. I think I do not know him but then I look more and I do know him.

It is Kenrick. His eyes are squinty ones and blinking a very lot. I am in big surprise.

"K– Kenrick?" I say. "W– why were you in the h– hole in the— ground?" There is a very bad smell that is nasty like poo. I go to him and take out the rope in his mouth. He tries to speak but he cannot do it and he coughs.

"W-water," he says. His voice is different. It is croaks like dry. Behind me there is a jug next to Catriona's bed. I pour some water into a bowl and tip it by Kenrick's mouth so he can drink. "Thank you," he says. "Could you help me out of here?"

"Yes, I will h– help you, Kenrick," I say.

I hold him under his arm and help him to come out

which is kind. His hands are tied behind his back. They are dirty and so is all his clothes. I do not mind dirty. I try to undo the knot but it is too hard for my fingers.

"Don't worry about that for now," he says. He moves his body one way and then the other to do the stretching.

"Catriona said the— shadow things t– took you away," I say.

"Catriona lied."

"W– why?" I ask.

Kenrick shakes his head to get some of the dirty off but it is still dirty. The shaking makes him woozy-wobbles. "She did not agree with how I was leading this clan, with the hospitality I was showing your people. But even I did not think she would stoop this low."

"It was Catriona who locked you in the— floor?" I say.

"Yes." He swallows the gristly in his throat. "She took advantage of the *sgàilean* attack and struck me over the head when no one was looking. Next thing I know, I woke up in that hole, scarcely able to breathe. The choke-hole's an old punishment: leaving your enemies to rot in the very ground beneath where you sleep. I believe it was her plan to let me die in there."

Kenrick is Catriona's bad secret! I knew it and I found him.

"Do you know where Catriona is now?" Kenrick asks me. "We have to get out of here."

"She locked up all the deers," I say, "and she is going to— kill them." I tell him about Thistle-River and the other deers and how Catriona is mean and the other people hit them with the sticks.

Kenrick is looking out of the window. "I think it's time my people knew the truth," he says. "Catriona has a lot to answer for."

We walk outside the bothan and through the enclave. It is hard for Kenrick to go fast and he stumbles a lot of times. People from Clann-na-Bruthaich are surprised to see him and they run to us. One person undoes the tight knot so his hands are free and other ones put his arms around their necks to help him do walking. They want to know how he is alive and if he is okay and where he has been.

"Gather the clan and bring Catriona" is all he says, and some people go.

We stop by the loch. It is raining now and cold. The wind is blowing on the loch and makes the water tremble. Lots of people come. Maistreas Eilionoir is there and she looks at me like she wants to say why am I standing next to Kenrick and what happened.

"Get your hands off me" is a shout and it is Catriona. Two people are holding her arms but she doesn't let them and she pushes them off. "What's this all about—?" She stops when she sees Kenrick. Her mouth goes open. "Kenrick," she says. "We thought you were dead."

"Did you, now?" says Kenrick.

"Thank goodness you're alive. We thought the sgàilean took you." She is lying. She knows the shadow things did not take him because she is the one who locked him in the ground. She is the worst bad liar.

"You knew full well that the *sgàilean* did not take me," says Kenrick, "but I don't doubt that you thought I was dead. After all, how many days has it been now since you locked me in the choke-hole?"

There is gasps and people are speaking shocked.

Catriona looks at them. "I have no idea what you're talking about. I would never—"

"Catriona-na-Bruthaich." Kenrick stands up very straight. Everyone is quiet. "You stand accused of treason and conspiracy to kill your fellow clansman. How do you plead?"

"This is ridiculous," she says. "How dare you accuse me of such things?"

"So you deny it?" Kenrick asks her.

"Of course I deny it," Catriona says to everyone around. "Look at the man. He's clearly deluded. He must have hit his head when the *sgàilean* dragged him away."

"It's not true," I say. "She's lying. Kenrick was i– in the— ground in Catriona's— bothan. She locked him in. I know it because I— I f– found him."

Everyone is talking again.

"Lock her away," says Kenrick. "She will stand trial for her crimes once the current crisis has been averted."

The two people grab Catriona's arms again and pull them hard behind her back. One of them has a sword.

"Wait! You can't—!" says Catriona. The people start taking her away. She looks at her clan around her. "Fine,

I admit it," she says. The people stop dragging her. "But I did it for you. For us. For Clann-na-Bruthaich. Look at yourselves. What's happened to us? We used to be the greatest clan on all the islands. Now look at what we have been reduced to: ordered around by outsiders and *retarchs*." That is a very rude word. She looks at me when she says it. She should not say that word to me. "We cannot survive here, all of us together. Nor should we want to. This is *our* enclave, and it's time for us to reclaim it; it is time to send Clann-a-Tuath home. This man," she points her finger at Kenrick, "is weak, and refused to make the hard choices necessary to secure the future of our people. You need a strong leader, and that leader is me. Together we can be strong. Together we *are* strong! Who is with me?"

Nobody speaks. Only the rain is the sound.

"No one? Not one person?" says Catriona. Her hands are tight in fists. She spits on the ground. "Then you deserve every misery that's coming your way."

"It looks like you are on your own," says Kenrick. "So that is what you shall be. You are hereby banished from this enclave. You are no longer a member of Clann-na-Bruthaich. You are to leave at once and never return."

"But... No. You can't," says Catriona. "The *sgàile-an*." She looks scared and it is the first time I have seen it. "I'll have no way of protecting myself. If you banish me, you're sentencing me to death."

"It is no more than you bestowed upon me," says Kenrick. He steps forwards and his legs do wobbles again. People move to help him but he says he doesn't need help. He stands up tall and stares at Catriona. His eyes are hard ones. "You wanted strong leadership, and now I am showing it. If you are ever seen near this enclave again, you will be shown no mercy. Am I making myself clear? Now take her out of my sight."

Some Moths go to move her but she shakes so they are off. "I can take myself," she says.

She walks away from everyone and we follow. When we are near the Lower Gate, the Moths open it. The rain is harder now and makes outside look dark. Catriona does not slow down. She goes straight out of the enclave. When she is lots of steps away she turns back to look at us.

"One day, I'm going to make you regret this," she says.

I think she was talking to me.

JAIME

WE MAKE CAMP AT THE BASE OF A HILL, WHICH CRAY says will help protect us from the wind, as well as being safer should another imitator turn up. It feels like we're exposed out in the open like this – especially with the fire we made, lighting up our location – but Cray pointed out that we'd be much more at risk if we camped beneath trees, given the imitators' affinity for climbing them. There's also some solace in having the Badhbh nearby, after his display of power against the imitator earlier, even if his allegiance to us is still somewhat questionable.

"How's your throat?" Cray asks.

"A little better, thanks. And your ankle?"

"Barely even tickles."

A small pot of watery soup rests on the grass between us. We've been taking turns to drink from it. We offered some to the Badhbh, but he wasn't interested. He's sitting on the opposite side of the fire with his back to us, staring at the stars. His hands are resting on his knees, palms facing up, in the same way they were when I walked into his hut.

Cray picks up the soup pot and looks inside.

"You finish it," he says. "There's only one slurp left."

"I've had enough."

"Come on, you need it more than I do."

I take the pot from him and glug down the remainder of its contents. There's not much sustenance in the soup, but it's warm and slips down easier than the meat I tried to eat earlier.

"Do you want first watch or second?" Cray asks as I wipe my mouth with the back of my hand.

"Um ... first?" I reply.

"In that case, I'm going to snatch myself some sleep. Here, take this." He unsheathes his dagger and hands it to me, handle first. "Just in case." It's the same dagger I took from his waist belt yesterday. He must have picked it up after I threw it at the imitator. I take it from him, then he crosses over to Bras and lies by his side, in between the bull and the fire. "Wake me up when you're ready to swap over or if you hear anything suspicious."

I don't want him to go to sleep. I'd prefer it if both of us stayed awake all night, but of course that's not possible. Cray closes his eyes, and within moments his breathing relaxes into a soothing faraway rhythm. What I wouldn't give to be able to fall asleep that quickly, to not be constantly haunted by the spectres of the past few months. Even now, without Cray's conversation as a distraction, my mind starts wandering into dark places filled with *sgàilean* and wildwolves and Lileas and death... I scrunch my eyes closed and shake my head. If only ridding myself of my thoughts could be that simple.

"I'm taking first watch if you want to get some sleep," I call to the Badhbh.

He doesn't move or acknowledge that I've spoken. Perhaps he's already asleep, or maybe he doesn't sleep at all. Who knows with that man?

The wind batters the fire, bending its glow in eerie directions. Cray positioned Bras to block the worst of the gusts, but there's only so much one bull can do. Outside the small ring of light created by the fire, the night is oppressively dark. Staring out into it makes my eyes weary. I should be afraid; we're out in the open, and we know there are more imitators around somewhere, yet all I really feel is indifference – full of sickness from the past and numb to the future.

A long while later, the Badhbh stands up, his body unfolding like a blossoming plant. He turns around and then sits back down, so that he's facing me from the other side of the fire. He looks at me, the flames fidgeting across his taut face.

"Hello," I say, to break the weird silence between us. He doesn't reply. "Were you asleep before?"

He takes his time before replying. "No."

"You can sleep now if you like? I'm keeping a lookout."

No reply. He's really not one for chatting.

He sits watching me for so long that I wonder if I should get up and move or turn around, but something makes me hold his gaze. He's older than me – a *lot* older than me – so I really shouldn't be staring back at him the way I am, but I don't care. It feels like he's looking deep inside me, and right now, I want to let him.

"Do you know where the imitators came from?" I ask after a long silence.

"What's an imitator?"

"That person-creature-thing that attacked us earlier. The one you—" I hold up my hand and twist it to one side while clicking my tongue.

The Badhbh does not react.

"Have you ever seen one before?" I ask him.

"No."

"Weren't you interested in what it was?"

"No."

"But it could have been created by magic. Isn't that what you used to—?" I stop myself, remembering the promise I made not to mention his past. "I read your diary," I say.

"I am aware of that."

A giant moth circles the fire in two irregular loops and then disappears into its smoke.

"It used to be human, but it wasn't made through blood magic," he says. "I sensed that when I—" He twists his hand and clicks his tongue, copying the same actions I made.

"How did you do it?" I ask. His eyebrows rise a fraction. "Am I allowed to ask?"

"You want to know about blood magic?"

I don't know. Do I? Magic is not *dùth*, no matter what sort it is, so even showing curiosity is a violation of our clan rules. Yet something inside me is eager to know more.

He continues before I can answer. "Blood magic is fed by blood. The more blood you feed it, the more powerful it becomes. That is why it is the darkest of all magics, and the most likely to corrupt."

"Did it corrupt you?"

"Not the magic, no."

He stares at me even more intently than before, as if daring me to probe further. I don't know what game he's playing. He's goading me into asking questions about his past, even though he's forbidden me from mentioning it. Of course I want to know more –about his life, about blood magic, about how he survived the plague – but his whole demeanour is so intimidating.

"The darkness inside you is of your own creating," he says to me then, knocking me off guard.

"What?" I reply.

"I can see your darkness, but it is not necessarily a bad thing."

"What are you talking about? I don't have 'darkness' inside me." My fingernails are sharp against the palms of my hands.

"Have you ever considered taking up magery? Inner

darkness is a strong foundation for a powerful mage. Blood magic in particular is strongest when it comes from a place of darkness."

"No, of course I don't want to... You're wrong." My voice is loud over the silence of the night. I lower it so as not to wake Cray. "You know nothing about me. And stop staring at me like that." I shift my body until I'm side-on to him. The next time I glance in his direction, he's turned back around to look at the stars.

The Badhbh doesn't say a word to either of us the whole of the next morning. He rides Bras in silence as Cray and I walk along beside him. Neither of us has seen him sleep or eat since he started travelling with us yesterday.

While we walk, Cray jabbers away about anything and everything – imitators, King Edmund, his tribe, my clan... It's nice, just listening to him talk. A couple of times, he even makes me laugh with some stupid joke or another. It's been so long since I properly laughed, I've forgotten what it feels like. It reminds me of a version of myself I wasn't sure existed any more. I know I have to go home, and of course I want to – my clan is relying on me after all – but part of me wishes I could stay here longer.

The weather's been kinder today: not exactly sunny, but certainly less windy. The harder ground that we were walking through most of yesterday has succumbed to dense grassland filled with red clover and yellow rockroses. It's unusual to see so many flowers this late in the year. A dark orange butterfly flits from blossom to blossom.

"I'm going to run up that hill and check we're still on track," Cray says. "Keep walking. I'll catch up with you."

I don't want to be left alone with the Badhbh – not after the strange things he said to me last night – but I mutter a weak, "Okay," and Cray jogs away. I watch as his body shrinks up the hillside. Even when he hits the steep incline, his pace doesn't falter. I sometimes forget that Cray is only a year or so older than me. He's so strong, so self-assured. I can't imagine ever being like that.

"Be careful how close you get to that one," says the Badhbh.

"What do you mean?" I ask, immediately defensive.

"It will never end well."

"I don't know what you're talking about," I say. "We're friends. What's wrong with that?"

The Badhbh gives me a condescending look but doesn't comment further. The longer I spend in the Badhbh's company, the less I like him. I swipe at the midges that hover around my head. I've already been bitten a couple of times, which I know is going to infuriate me later. There aren't any around the Badhbh, as if they know to avoid him.

"I'm not a bad person," he says out of nowhere. "You think I am, but I'm not."

"I never said you were a bad person," I reply.

"Correct. But it is your thoughts I am accusing, not your words."

One of the midges bites the top of my ear – or at least I imagine it does – and I slap it away, which probably hurts me more than it hurts it.

"I don't understand some of the choices you've made," I say, "but then I don't really know you."

"That's right; you don't. Yet you think that you do. From one book. A book that I wrote – true – but you are unaware of the circumstances in which I wrote it. That diary is not the whole truth. It certainly isn't *my* truth."

I don't know what he wants from me. Once again, he seems unexpectedly keen to discuss the forbidden topic of his past.

"So what is your truth?" I ask.

The Badhbh continues looking straight ahead. "What is my truth...?" he mutters. For a long time he says nothing, making me wonder if he's changed his mind about talking to me. Then his lips drift apart and he says, "I had a daughter."

I don't know why I'm so surprised by his revelation, but I am. I can't imagine him with a daughter, having someone he cared about. He never once mentioned her in his diary.

"What was her name?" I ask.

The Badhbh ignores my question. "She was a similar age to King Balfour's daughter, to the princess, Nathara. In fact, the two of them were friends at one stage, until Balfour took my daughter away."

A blast of wind pummels the long grass around us, making it quiver and shriek. I already know this story isn't going to end well. There is a long silence, which I feel compelled to fill with another question. "Why did he do that?"

"It was right at the start of his obsession with creating the first *sgàil*. He wanted me to help. He *forced* me to help. I was merely a court physician at that time, although I read extensively on many topics and knew a little about the theory of magics. Balfour's need to eradicate his enemy, King Edmund, consumed him. He was convinced that creating a *sgàil* was the only solution."

Bras plods on, disinterested in whatever the Badhbh has to say.

"At first, I was complicit," the Badhbh continues. "I'm not ashamed to admit that. I'd long been fascinated with blood magic and was eager to learn more about it. But then the people we were experimenting on started to die. True, they were mainly thieves and war criminals, but it still made me uncomfortable. I approached Balfour one night and informed him that I no longer wished to assist him. He replied that it was not a matter in which I had a choice. I still refused, so he had my daughter and my wife imprisoned, with the threat that they would only be released after I'd succeeded in my task.

"Of course, once I'd created the first *sgàil*, the conditions of our arrangement changed: he wanted a whole army of them. And by the time we'd completed that, it was already too late. The plague killed my daughter and it killed my wife, just like it killed everyone else. If I was with them, I could have used my abilities to save them, the same way I saved myself, but I never saw them again – from the moment he took them away to the day they died. The last years I could have spent with my family, and he stole them from me." He swallows, followed by a single laboured blink. "That is my truth."

The sun sneaks out from behind a cloud, then changes its mind and slips away again. I don't know what to think any more. If what he's saying is true, it's atrocious how he was used – but it doesn't justify all the wrong he's done since.

"Is that why you left Nathara in the tower?" I ask him. "To punish King Balfour for what he did to you, even though he was already dead?"

"It is not a decision I am proud of, but it is the one I made."

I want to ask him if that's why he changed his mind and agreed to come with us – to seek redemption for the wrongs of his life – but something tells me our conversation is over. Whatever his reasons for helping us, I'm not sure anything can make up for abandoning a small child in the way that he did.

Cray bounces back down the hill and catches up to us. He notices none of the heaviness that the Badhbh's revelation has created.

"We're nearly there," he says. "Well, I could see an island from the top and it was huge, so I presume it's Skye."

I look past him at the sweeping vastness of the Scotian landscape. Donal and Violet are still out there somewhere. The whole time we've been travelling, I've been secretly hoping they'd come running out from wherever it is they've been hiding and then laugh as we exchange stories of our different adventures. But no, I really am leaving them behind. My only solace is that as soon as I get back, I can alert the clans that they're missing, and they'll send a team of Scavengers to find them. If they're still alive.

My first sighting of Skye brings me none of the joy I was hoping it might. I don't know why. Maybe because it's not our true home I'm returning to, maybe because I'm not quite ready to say goodbye to Cray again just yet. I keep thinking about the Bó Riders' cavern. They haven't lived there for long, and yet in the short space of time I was there, I felt such an overwhelming sense of belonging. I haven't felt like that since we lived in our own enclave, since before the deamhain, before any of this happened. It's not the same staying with Clann-na-Bruthaich. I want to go home, to our real home.

"Anything look familiar yet?" Cray asks.

"Yes, we definitely came up this way. At least I think we did... If I'm right, we left the boat in the copse at the bottom of that ridge."

We wander further down towards the shore. A strong smell of gannet droppings hangs in the wind. We reach the copse, but the boat is nowhere in sight. At first

I think we must be in the wrong place, but then I recognize the rock that looks like a goat's head, which Donal pointed out when we first arrived.

"What's this?" asks Cray, holding up the end of a torn piece of rope. The other end is still wrapped around a tree. It's the rope Donal used to tether the boat, but the boat is no longer there.

SIGRID

Me and Eydis watch the sunrise together, and it's hek beautiful. We're up the top of a hill, so we've got a clear view of the ripped-up clouds what are soaked with orange as dark as egg yolk. I feed Eydis another apple and she thanks me by leavin a thick trail of slobber on my palm. I wipe it off on her neck. "You dirty slobberin beast," I say.

There are apples aplenty up here. Couldn't believe my luck. Eydis has already gobbled close to twelve of them. Truth bein told, they taste like sourpickle, but they're better than nothin.

Eydis nuzzles me, wantin another. "You're gunna be squittin apples all afternoon," I say, but I grab another and rub between her ears as she eats it. I'm beginnin to think she isn't no ordinary horse. She's bulkin for one, and can run for a hek long time for two. And then there's how she found me and saved me from that crazy skittin dart boy. I owe her my life and I'm never gunna forget it.

As the sun gets brighter, I can make out somethin else and all. A dark strip what runs through the ground as far as I can see in both directions. It's the Scotian border, the hek bulkin trench what King Edmund was talkin about. Lookin across into Scotia, it's a bit disappointin. Dunno why I thought it would look diffrunt to Ingland, but the land on the other side of the trench is the same as it is on this side. The same dull, sunken brown.

"Come on then, greedy face," I say to Eydis. "Time we got movin."

Before we go, I load up one of the saddlebags with apples to feed her later, then we're off and trottin.

It doesn't take us long to get to the border trench, which is hek wide, with steep, crumblin sides. In my head I imagined it'd still be burnt and black from the fire, but course not; that was decades ago. The grass has grown back, but it's sad, beige grass what doesn't look like it can grow proply, same as the land on either side of it.

It's hard for Eydis to get down into the trench, and even harder for her to get up again, but with a bit of pushin and shovin, some whisperin and some encouragin, she manages.

We're here. Scotia. We made it. I sure am chirpin to be leavin Ingland behind. It's a scraggin wreckmess of a place. I don't never wanna go back there again.

We don't see no people the whole rest of the day, but

that's not surprisin. King Edmund said evryone here was dead. It's nice bein just me and Eydis. Peaceful. We still ride hard – Lady Beatrice's voice, tellin me I gotta get to Skye quick, never leaves my head – but there's calm in the air.

Once we get a little ways away from the border, the land starts comin back to life. Greener trees, fuller fields, even patches of flowers and gorse bush. It's nice and not what I was expectin. It's cold, though, and there's a harsk wind bitin. Not as cold as Norveg, praps, but colder than Ingland for sure.

I talk to Eydis the whole time. She's the best listener. I tell her about Norveg, with its long, bright summers and the winters where the sun doesn't hardly bother risin; I tell her about Granpa Halvor and how pleased he'd be to know I'm helpin people what need it; and I tell her about my mother and what she used to be like before she started neckin. There was a time when my mamma was a diffrunt person: she'd make up stories for me evry night before I went to sleep, she could make the most hek *rikka* chew outta nothin at all, and she always used to mess up my hair cuz I pretended I hated it. I explain to Eydis how evrythin changed after my pa was sent off to fight in some stupid bloodsplash for Konge Grímr and never came back. My mother wasn't never the same after that.

I lean forward and hug Eydis's neck. It's warm and smells of rich dirt and sweat. "Thanks for listenin," I say. She whimmies loud and keeps on gallopin.

By mid-afternoon she knows hek near evrythin about me, so I start tellin her about Øden and how he grew the world out of a tree, and about the High Halls of Heaven, where we'll go to when we die, providin we done good in this life. Then I say all about Konge Grímr and what a skittin grotweasel he is, and about his brother, Mal-Rakki, who's hidin out in the ice caves in the north of Norveg.

I pretend I'm Mal-Rakki now, ridin on my own, out in the wilds. We do have things in common, after all: we both fled north to escape Konge Grímr, we both wanna help people what've been done wrong, and the king is hek keen for both of us to be dead...

"*Mal-Rakki* means White Fox," I explain to Eydis. "He wasn't always called that, but that's what evryone calls him now."

He's still alive; I'm back to bein sure of it. He must've known Konge Grímr didn't die durin the battle in the mountain, so he's still bidin his time and preparin his army. He'll only get one chance and he knows it. When he does come back, he'll lead our people to a new kind of livin, just like Granpa Halvor always says.

We stop before the last of the light goes so I've got time to gather some wood for a fire. We're gunna need a big one tonight, cuz the tips of my fingers are already frostin. I found a bridge for us to sleep under. It's tumblin in places, but it'll keep out the worst of the wind, as well as the rain if the sky starts spewin. It's only just tall enough for Eydis to fit under, but she doesn't seem to mind none. I get the fire goin and she stands near it, not scared one speck.

My nappin is deep but brief. Soon as I wake up, I know I'm not gunna be buried under sleep anytime soon. It's spewin heavy and the drips are findin their way through the skittin bridge. I was wrong about it keepin us dry. The fire is hissin, reduced to almost nothin. Eydis is awake too. I expect it was the drips what woke her.

"Can't sleep neither?" I ask. She moves her head from side to side, shakin out a sad sigh. "Spose we might as well keep goin, then."

I don't mind the rain. In fact I kinda like it now we're out and ridin in it. I think Eydis likes it too. We ride so fast that it doesn't feel cold. The wind yesterday was hek skap, but the rain is refreshin.

Now that I'm in Scotia – now that I'm gettin closer to Skye – I've started thinkin about what I'm gunna do afterwards, after I tell the Skye people what I gotta tell them. I was thinkin before that I'd try to get back home somehow, but it might not be that simple. I haven't got no way of gettin there for starters, and – even if the Skye people did have some way of helpin me – once Konge Grímr gets back, nowhere'd be safe for me. Øden knows my lyin, drunken kerl of a mother won't miss me, although she'll struggle gettin by on her own. Too bad. She chose her fate when she swapped me for neckin pennies. What about Granpa Halvor, though? I miss him so much. But his shack'd be one of the first places the king'd look, and if he found me there, he'd punish

Granpa Halvor and all. I can't do that to him; I can't risk Granpa gettin hurt.

So that's it, then. I can't never go back home. The realization hits me like a thunderpunch in my stogg. I'm never goin back.

My face is drenched but none of it's tears. I wish there was a way I could let Granpa Halvor know I'm all right, that I'm doin somethin important, somethin I believe in. I miss him so much. The thought of never seein him again makes me... All I want is one hug from him. One hug. And for him to tell me I'm doin the right thing.

I'm not cryin. It's rain, I swear it.

I prefer this to my old life any day: on my own, not relyin on no one but myself, no one pullin me this ways and that, tellin me what I gotta do for all the days long.

Here, I'm free.

I wipe the rain from my face.

Here, I'm free.

JAIME

THE BOAT'S GONE. I SLUMP AGAINST THE TREE IT WAS tied to, staring down at the limp rope. Who could have taken it? An imitator? The only people who knew its location were Donal and Violet, and it can't have been them – they wouldn't have left me stranded here. If they had taken it for themselves, they would've sent someone back with it, surely? With no boat, we don't have any way of crossing the channel. We're stuck here.

"What are we going to do?" I say, hating the desperation that has slunk into my voice. I turn to the Badhbh. "Is there anything you can do?"

He cocks his head. "You overestimate me if you think I can walk on water," he replies.

"You'll have to swim," says Cray.

I almost laugh, until I realize he's not joking.

"I can't, it's too far. The water's too deep."

"I'm not sure you have any other choice," says Cray.

302

"Unless you want to spend the next couple of days making a raft."

I haven't got two days to waste. My clan need me to return with the Badhbh today. Now.

"How deep do you think it is?" I ask.

The Badhbh clears his throat. "I'm afraid you're still overestimating me if you think I can swim."

He can't even swim? What sort of person can sever shadows from people's bodies and snap people's necks without touching them but never learned to swim?

"What if I came with you?" asks Cray.

My heart leaps. "Would you do that?"

He shrugs. "Sure. That way you can stay on Bras," he says to the Badhbh.

"Bras can swim?" I ask.

Bras huffs at me as if to say, *Obviously.*

"All Highland cows can," says Cray. "Better than you'd imagine."

I'm even more surprised that Bras can swim than that the Badhbh can't. Okay, so it looks like I'm swimming, then. Great. Maybe it won't be so bad if Cray and Bras are beside me...

We wander down to the shore. The water stretches out in front of us like a field of dead grass. Crossing the sea in a boat is one thing; swimming in it is a whole new world of terror. Cray must notice the intensity of my breathing, because he puts a hand on my shoulder and says, "It's not as far as it looks. We'll be fine."

That's easy for him to say – he's never encountered a

rush of deathfins. What's to say there isn't a whole load of them waiting for us out there? All water is connected, so there's no reason they couldn't have swum into this channel. We're entering their world now.

"The only danger is the cold," says Cray. "So whatever you do, don't stop swimming." When a deathfin attacks, I might not have much choice. "We're going to be fine," he says again. His reassurance does nothing to ease the cramping in my stomach.

We reach the water's edge. It's painfully cold, even through my boots. Bras lumbers in ahead, the Badhbh wobbling on his back. The bull seems strangely at home in the water and swims with unexpected elegance. His head lolls on the surface, lifting every now and then to stretch over the larger waves. Cray is standing in the water beside me.

"Why are you helping me?" I ask him.

"What do you mean?"

"You've done so much already – for both me and my clan – but you don't owe us anything. So why are you doing it?"

He looks at me like the answer is obvious. "Because I like you, of course."

My whole body feels hot despite the icy water licking at my feet, and sweat prickles my armpits. I don't know what he means by that, so I choose to ignore it, sloshing into the water to end the conversation.

I shudder all over as my body submerges. The first few strokes are the hardest. My lungs feel like they've frozen and my eyes ache at the thought of what's hiding in the water below me. It doesn't take long for Cray to overtake, but he keeps glancing back to check that I'm okay.

Once I hit my stride, it becomes a little easier, and I soon get used to the cold. In fact, the salty water helps soothe the sores on my neck. If it wasn't for my overactive imagination, this could actually be enjoyable. Then I make the mistake of looking behind me. We've come further than I realized. Scotia is now far away, but so is Skye, leaving us stranded between the two, at the mercy of the sea. If something were to attack now, I wouldn't be able to reach either shore in time.

Don't stop swimming.

Bras and the Badhbh are way ahead, and the distance between me and Cray is increasing. I'm falling behind.

What was that? Something on my leg, I'm sure of it. I lash out, kicking with the heel of the opposite foot. Nothing there. But there was. I carry on swimming, faster than before. My arms are tiring. A side wave takes me by surprise and salt water rushes into my open mouth. I have to stop to spit it out. It leaves a stinging sensation in my nose. I'm treading water, my legs dangling beneath me. I shouldn't have stopped.

A jolt on my leg, one I definitely didn't imagine. Something curls itself around my ankle and starts tugging me down. I cry out, kicking at it again and again.

"What's wrong?" Cray is next to me in an instant.

305

"Something's on my ankle," I say. "I can't get it off."

I'm gasping desperate breaths, my neck straining to keep my mouth above water. There isn't enough air.

"Keep breathing," says Cray, then he dives under the water. He tugs at whatever is on my leg, but he can't dislodge it. When he next breaks the surface, there's concern on his face, which he tries, but fails, to hide.

"You have to keep swimming," he says.

"But what is it? I can't."

"You have to. It's... I think it's a sucker eel."

Then I understand. I launch myself forward. I need to get to land. Now.

Cray's suspicions are confirmed when a second one wraps itself around my other leg. A scream finds its way through my clenched teeth.

"Another one?" asks Cray. He's swimming backwards so he can watch me at the same time. I nod, spitting out more water. He turns his head and whistles for Bras, but the wind steals the sound; the bull is too far away, oblivious to the danger I'm in. As I'm staring at Cray, the left side of his body dips and he stifles a yelp. He's got one on him too. "They're not poisonous," he says. "If there's only a couple of them, they can't hurt us."

But there are more than a couple of them. Another one twists around my right knee, and a fourth is circling my stomach. It's how sucker eels hunt: they work together to drag their prey under water until it drowns, then feast on its remains. That's what's going to happen to us.

My arms thrash at the water, creating great splashes all around me. I know it's not helping the situation, but I'm losing focus.

"Jaime," says Cray. "We have to stay calm. The only way we can get them off is to reach the shore, and we'll only make it there if we keep swimming."

Another tug on my right leg, stronger this time, more insistent. How much easier it would be to give in, to let them drag me under and not to have to worry any more. About anything.

I'm only vaguely aware that Cray is still talking to me. "We can do this. Jaime, look at me. Look at me!"

I steady my arms long enough to concentrate on his face, at the worry lines that are spread across his forehead. He's right: we can survive this. And, more important, I *want* to survive this. I give a quick nod, and the two of us swim side by side with renewed energy. There are so many sucker eels on me now that I've lost track of the number. My whole torso is a mass of writhing bodies. They snake up and down my legs and under my clothes. Every now and then a new one attaches itself, the tug of their combined efforts pulling my head a little further beneath the water. Each time, Cray reaches down and heaves me back up again. I do the same for him. He's better at disguising it than I am, but he's struggling too.

At some point he takes my hand and I let him. It's harder to swim while holding hands, but it also makes me more determined to keep going. We coordinate our arm movements and look at nothing but the land as it inches slowly, slowly towards us.

By the time we reach the shore I've swallowed so much seawater my guts feel like they've been turned inside out. I let go of Cray's hand. There's no beach here, just stony ground with the odd tuft of coarse grass poking through. My head throbs and my arms pound, but I have to keep moving; the eels will only release their grip once they sense they're too far from water. They redouble their efforts, squeezing and squirming in protest at being removed from the sea. The skin on my legs feels tight enough to burst. I drag myself across the hard earth on my hands and knees without once looking down. The sound of the eels' squelching is sickening. Ahead of me, the Badhbh stands next to Bras, watching. He makes no attempt to help.

Once I've crawled a little further, the eels start to leave. It's only a couple to begin with, but the others soon follow. There are dozens of them, all over my body. I turn and shake my legs, pelting the eels with the backs of my hands, desperate for them to be off me. One by one, they slither along the stones, their grumpy bodies lurching back to the surf. I pat myself down to make sure they're all gone, then lean on my elbow and throw up in a shallow rock pool. What comes out is mainly seawater with the smell of putrid fish.

As I sit up, an eel appears in front of my face. I shout and slap it aside, but it swings back at me, almost hitting my nose. I jerk my head away.

"Careful!" says Cray. He's holding the creature by its tail. Its body is a thick strip of brown, flecked with mud-yellow spots. It fixes one of its eyes on me: a small black dot in a pool of white, as if it's been taken by surprise.

"That's not funny," I say to Cray, shuffling back another few inches. "Get it away from me."

"Thought you might like to see one close-up." He smirks. "Pretty creatures, aren't they?"

"Stunning, yes, thanks so much for sharing," I say.

The eel opens its mouth, revealing two neat rows of tiny teeth – teeth that would have ripped us apart had its ambush been successful. I resist the urge to throw up again.

Cray places the eel on the ground with great tenderness, and it slides away.

"Well, we made it," he says. "Just like I said we would."

I'm cold and I'm wet and I stink of vomit. "Hooray for you always being right," I say as I drag myself to my feet.

"You said it's only a short walk to the enclave you're staying in, right?" says Cray. "I could do with drying my clothes and maybe getting something hot to eat before Bras and I head back."

I have a sudden image of Cray in Clann-na-Bruthaich's enclave, talking to people from my clan.

"Um…" I don't know how to say this. "That'll be fine, but… When we arrive at the enclave, maybe…

Well, you know my clan thinks differently about some things to yours, so maybe don't mention the fact that you ... you know...?"

"Don't mention what?" he asks. He knows exactly what I'm talking about. He wants to make me say it, but I don't want to. Not here. Not in front of the Badhbh.

"You know, about ... you..."

"What about me?" His brow is well and truly furrowed now. Why is he making this so difficult? "Are you ashamed of me, Jaime?" he asks. "Ashamed to be seen with me?"

"No! Of course not. I just... It doesn't matter."

Does it matter? I don't even know any more. We walk the rest of the way to the enclave without talking to each other.

Clann-na-Bruthaich's enclave is easy to spot; even though it's only mid-afternoon, fires are burning all around the outer wall. The wind whips the flames up into a frenzy. At times, they look like they're in danger of going out. As we draw nearer to the Lower Gate, chimes sound to announce our approach and the Hawks and the Moths eye us with suspicion. They probably don't recognize me, and they won't have seen a Highland bull before. With the addition of Cray and the Badhbh, they're right to be cautious.

I'm about to speak when someone calls, "Crayton! It's C– Crayton. He's my favourite one!" Agatha beams down at us from the top of the wall.

Cray waves at her, making her smile grow even wider.

The gates open and we walk inside. We're only a couple of paces in when Agatha comes running down from the wall and throws her arms around Cray. He hugs her back.

"I'm very— very h– happy to see you, Crayton," she says.

"It's nice to see you too, Agatha," he replies. "Jaime tells me you helped save your clan?"

Agatha does several overemphasized nods. "I did the very clever plan. Do you want to touch our heads together?"

"Sure." He places his forehead against hers and they breathe in three slow breaths.

"Jaime says you like to kiss boys and not— girls," Agatha says.

Cray flashes me a bemused look as I glance around to make sure no one overheard.

"Well, yes, that's true," says Cray.

"It's not *dùth* to do that," says Agatha, "but I don't mind." She gives him a big smile.

"I'm very pleased to hear it," he says.

"Um ... hello! I'm here too," I say to Agatha.

"Yes, Jaime, I saw you," Agatha says. She breaks away from Cray and wraps her arms around me.

"What happened to your n– neck," she asks mid-hug.

"Long story," I say. "But you should see the other guy." Agatha laughs, way harder than I expected her to. "Do you know where Aileen is?"

"She's in the enclave somewhere," Agatha replies,

"but I don't know w– where." There's something strange about the way she says it, as if there's more that she's not telling me. She turns her attention to Bras and scratches him between his horns.

"Who are you?" she asks the Badhbh.

"He's come to help us," I say, once it's clear the Badhbh has no intention of replying. "Where's Catriona?"

A small crowd has gathered around us while we've been talking. At the mention of Catriona, there's an uncomfortable silence.

"Welcome back." A deep voice breaks the quiet. The crowd parts and Kenrick steps forward. I'm sure my face doesn't hide my surprise. "A lot has happened since you left," he tells me. "We have much to discuss. But first I suggest we find you some dry clothes."

"I had to leave Donal and Violet in Scotia," I say. "We were attacked. You need to send someone to help them."

"Calm yourself, Jaime," says Kenrick, holding his palms up towards me. "They have already returned, and both of them are fine."

"Really?" Relief floods through me. "When? That's… That's great news!"

Kenrick gives me a sympathetic nod. "Go and get yourselves warm, and then we'll talk. I'll be waiting for you in the meeting bothan once you're ready."

The many questions I have remain unasked as we're led across the enclave. We pass the loch and at first I think my eyes are playing tricks on me, but no: there are hundreds of deer all around it. The only stag I've seen before was the one the *sgàilean* dragged into the courtyard at Dunnottar Castle, which I was forced to mercy-kill. Watching them grazing on the grass now, I'm taken aback by how incredible they are. I had no idea they were so graceful. Bras ambles over to join them.

"Nice place you have here," Cray says to me.

"Like I said, it's not our enclave," I reply. "Ours is better."

"Maybe you can show me that one day too?"

I give him a weak smile and catch up with the others. Something doesn't feel right about Cray being here, but I know he'd hate me if I admitted that.

We're shown into a small bothan with a large fire burning in its centre. I peel off my sopping outer layers and let the warmth seep into to my bones. I've never appreciated heat so much in my life. Someone brings us clean clothes, and I slip into an adjoining room to get changed. Once I'm done, I return to find that Cray has also changed. He looks completely different in the woven garb of our clan as opposed to the crude animal-skin attire I'm used to seeing him in – so much so, I let out a hearty laugh.

"What?" says Cray, posing first one way and then another. "Don't you think it suits me?"

"I'm saying nothing," I reply.

The Badhbh stands by the fire, watching us. He refused the clothing that was brought for him, preferring to stay in his own tatty robe and cloak.

We step outside and are led to the same meeting bothan that Catriona took me to the morning after the *sgàilean* broke free. Kenrick is there, and so are Lenox and Maistreas Eilionoir, who greet me with open arms and proud smiles. My palms start sweating when I introduce them to Cray, but they seem nothing but pleased to meet him and grateful for his help. Kenrick grasps Cray's fists for a long time to show the extent of his gratitude. He then turns to do the same to the Badhbh, but something in the Badhbh's gaze stops him from making contact.

"I'm guessing you're the one they call the Badhbh?" Kenrick asks. The old man lifts his shoulders and tilts his head in a half-nod, half-shrug. "And it was you who helped create these shadows?" The Badhbh gives another non-committal gesture. "Well, we know they'll return at nightfall," says Kenrick. "How do you plan on returning them to the necklace?"

The Badhbh runs a finger down the length of his nose. "If that is what you are expecting from me, I'm afraid you have been misinformed," he says. It's the first time he's spoken since we arrived on Skye.

"What do you mean?" asks Maistreas Eilionoir.

"Exactly what I said. The *sgàilean* were made to serve the royal family, to obey only them. If Nathara is dead, there is no one left alive who can control them. Including me."

What? "So why are you here?" I say, my voice rising. "Why didn't you tell me that before now? Why did we

go all the way to bloody Scotia and risk our lives bringing you back if you can't even help us?"

Everyone stares at me while I catch my breath. It felt
liberating to shout, like something inside of me was released, if only a little.

"I said I'm unable to control them. I didn't say
I couldn't help you." The Badhbh's lips relax into a hu-
mourless smile. "I see my previous lesson on semantics
was lost on you."

Maistreas Eilionoir raises her hand and takes a
step forward. One look from her is enough to know
I shouldn't say anything more. "Perhaps you would be
kind enough to explain how you can help us," she says
to the Badhbh. "How do we get rid of the *sgàilean*?"

"There is only one way," says the Badhbh. He looks
at each of us in turn as if measuring our worth. "You
must fight them."

SIGRID

THERE ARE HEK LOADS OF LAKES IN THIS PART OF Scotia. I knew there would be cuz I saw them on King Edmund's map, but there are even more what weren't on his map, which is hek skap, cuz I hadn't planned for those ones. We have to keep windin round them, which makes the journey even longer. No one can say they're not wondrous lookin, though. When the sun shines through, they ripple with star sparks, and when the skies are dark, they look like they wanna suck you in and drown you in blackness.

Today, while we've been trottin, I've been imaginin I'm the last person left in the whole world. It's easy to imagine that here. Me and Eydis, with nothin but the whole world to explore. I think about the places we'd go and the things we'd discover. Just the two of us, trottin on forever.

My imaginin comes crashin down the moment

I see him. He's sat atop a white elk on a ridge not two hundred yards away. The elk's antlers stretch up into the air like lightnin claps. It must be the same animal I saw followin me the day after I left. Even from this far, I know exactly who's ridin it.

Bolverk.

I shoulda known it'd be him who came after me. I bet he volunteered straightaways. He's been wantin to get his grubby hams round my throat since the first day I met him. The elk tosses its head from side to side. Bolverk knows I've seen him. He *wanted* me to see him. That's why he put himself up high on the ridge: he wants the chase. He's too far away for me to see his face proper, but I know he's smilin wicked.

Holy skap, what am I sposed to do now? I click my tongue and jiggle Eydis's reins. She sets off at a gallop. She don't need tellin that we gotta go fast. From up on the ridge, Bolverk spurs the elk too, only he does it with a kick hard enough to crack its ribs. The elk's screech echoes through the rain towards me.

There's a forest to my left where I can maybe lose him. As soon as we enter, I wonder if I've been bugdumb goin in. The trees are rammed so dense it's hard for Eydis to go fast. They're like spruces, only spinier and more hateful. Eydis is weavin in and out, but one wrong step and we'll both come crashin. The needles claw at my hair, tryin to rip me down. The whole forest hums with their sticky sweet smell.

"You can't run forever, little raven," I hear from

317

somewhere. In front? Behind? Beside? I can't tell. It's gettin lighter ahead: the end of the forest. *Keep goin, Eydis. You can do it, you can do it.*

We burst out of the trees at a speed what makes my stomach gulp. I don't know where Bolverk is. I'm hopin his elk isn't nimble like Eydis, with its hek bulkin antlers and all. Maybe it tossed him head first into a tree. I can only pray.

No such luck. He's out of the forest a little ways east of us. He turns in my direction. There's a lake in front of me, blockin off the way, so I head up the hill on my left. Eydis is faster than the elk, I'm sure of it. It's really spewin down now; evrythin's smeared through the blur of rain. The hill turns steeper, the ground beneath us rockier. Eydis's hoof-clops change from sloppin to crackin. We're nearly at the top, and from there I can decide what's the best way to go.

The hill is higher than what it looked from below. There's a thin ridge that runs for as far as I can see, although the rain is still obscurin my view. We're goin so fast and the rain is so hard that I don't see the drop until we're right on top of it. Eydis rears up, nearly throwin me from the saddle. She shuffles backwards, her front hooves loosenin stones, which fall over the precipice. It's like someone's cut the hill in two and taken a thick slice outta its middle, creatin a hek bulk gap. It's too wide to get across; we'll have to go back the way we came. I turn Eydis around, but while we've been stopped, Bolverk's had a chance to catch up. He's on the hill, waitin to see which way we turn so he can cut us off. We're trapped. Unless... I look over my shoulder, tryin to judge how big the gap is. It's too wide for a horse to jump. But then, Eydis isn't no ordinary horse. I jostle her forward, towards Bolverk. He doesn't move none. He just watches me come towards him, smug as a goosefart. When I'm halfway between him and the hill edge, I turn Eydis back around. Bolverk realizes what we're gunna try to do.

"Don't even think about it," he ses. "It's suicide."

He must've been given orders to take me back alive, cuz I know sure as muck he doesn't give two hells about whether I live or die.

"We gunna do this, Eydis?" I say into her ears. She snorts, tellin me she's ready, then starts gallopin towards the drop without me needin to encourage her. She knows what we gotta do.

From what I saw of the drop, it's at least a hundred yards down. If we don't make it, we'll both die quickspit and no mistakin. We're drawin closer, Eydis's hooves thunderin, the rain thunderin, the blood thunderin in my head. We reach the edge and Eydis launches herself over the gap. We're in the air and time disappears. There isn't nothin in my ears but silence. I don't look down, I can't look down. Eydis stretches her legs forward, reachin, reachin for the other side. We're gunna make it, we're gunna make it, we're gunna—

Her front hooves hit the other side, but the edge is loose and crumbles away beneath us. By the time Eydis's back hooves make contact, there isn't nothin there for them to stand on. She's scramblin, her legs fightin for purchase. All the muscles in her neck tense with the strainin. I lean forward as far as I can, tryin to help tip the balance with my weight. One last, desperate push and then she finds firmer footin and stumbles us onto solid ground.

"We made it!" I'm rubbin her white hair and huggin her neck. "You did it, Eydis. You're the most *ríkka* horse in the world!"

There's no way Bolverk's elk'll be able to make the jump. Now's our chance to get away.

I glance behind me just in time to see Bolverk pull out a *bjark* – a studded stone what's attached to a short length of rope. He spins it above his head then hurtles it across the gap, too quick to avoid. The stone slams into my chest and I fall from Eydis's back, landin on the ground with a shudderin headsmack. Eydis whimpers and turns in a frantic circle.

There's a thud beside us. I was wrong about the elk not bein able to make the jump. Bolverk slides off the animal and takes two mighty strides until he's towerin above me. His smile is pigsick.

"Hello, little raven."

JAIME

"WHAT DO YOU MEAN 'FIGHT THEM'?" KENRICK ASKS the Badhbh.

"Exactly what you think I mean," the Badhbh replies. "You must draw the *sgàilean* into the enclave and destroy them, one at a time. That is the only way you can be rid of them for good."

"And how are we supposed to do that?" Lenox asks.

"With one of these." The Badhbh reaches into his cloak and draws out a concealed sword. I don't know why it surprises me that he's carrying a weapon, but it does. Maybe because he hasn't taken it out before now, not even when the imitator attacked. The hilt is worn, with dusty gaps where gemstones used to be. In contrast, the blade looks clean and new. Where it catches the light, it glows a dark berry red. "King Balfour was insistent that only the royal family have control over the *sgàilean*. I argued against him, but he would not heed my warnings." A deep frown crumples the Badhbh's forehead as he talks about the old Scotian king. "I enchanted this blade in secret, to protect myself and those I loved."

"You're saying that blade can destroy *sgàilean*?" asks Kenrick.

"I believe so, although the opportunity has never arisen to test it."

"One blade is not going to be much use against a thousand *sgàilean*," says Lenox.

"Correct," says the Badhbh, "but I can make more."

"No," says Maistreas Eilionoir. "Permitting you to practise your unlawful art is one thing, but placing corrupt weapons in the hands of my clan is quite another. Magic has no place on this island. If that is the only option you have for us, we will find our own solution."

The Badhbh's eyelids close and then float open again. "The *sgàilean* were created with ancient blood magic," he says. "Whether you like it or not, magic is already here, and my solution is the only way for you to be rid of it."

The room is cocooned in silence. Maistreas Eilionoir's tiny nose flares and twitches. Kenrick looks at her and then back at the Badhbh.

"Tell us what we must do," he says.

"Bring me all of your weapons and the largest cooking pot you have. If you want them ready before nightfall, I will have to start straightaway. I will also need a sacrifice. Blood magic cannot occur without blood."

* * *

The enclave is a hive of activity. Word has got out that we are fighting the *sgàilean* tonight. People are busying themselves by carting great armfuls of weapons to the Badhbh, reinforcing the defences, cleaning their armour. The apprehension in the air is so heavy it makes my skin prickle. Everyone knows what a great risk we're taking by goading the *sgàilean* into a fight.

In front of us, a goat is dragged by its legs towards the meeting bothan. It shrieks as its head knocks against errant stones. I wish they'd lead it to its death with a bit more dignity. It has a lot more suffering to come.

Cray and I are on our way to see Aileen, who I've been told is helping out in the sickboth. Apparently all duties have been suspended while the threat of the *sgàilean* remains, so everyone's assisting wherever they're needed. I know Aileen will be mad at me if I don't introduce her to Cray before he leaves, plus I still haven't had the chance to apologize for the way I've been treating her recently.

The moment I step inside the sickboth, a voice calls out, "Hey, good to see you, laddy!"

"Donal!" I run straight to his bed. "I'm so glad you made it back!"

"Likewise," he says with a chuckle. "You found the boat, I presume?"

"No, it wasn't there. You took it?"

"We did, but it was brought back for you. Did you not see it? It might not have been in exactly the same spot, but I told them the general area."

Great, so I swam the whole way and was nearly devoured by sucker eels just because I didn't look properly. I swallow my frustration. "Where's Violet? Did you come back together?" I ask.

"We did indeed – who do you think did the rowing? I was in no fit state. That thing – whatever it was – got me bad. I was delusional, slipping in and out of consciousness. If it wasn't for Violet, there's no way I would have made it back. She was a little unsteady herself – poisoned by the one that grabbed her wrist." His eyes flick up to the sores on my neck. "I'm guessing you may know a thing or two about what that feels like. Anyway, they left us in pursuit of you – presumably thinking we were too injured to recover. We tried looking for you, but the state we were in, we weren't much help to anyone. Sorry we had to leave you there."

"Don't apologize – I'm just glad you're both alive."

"What about your mage? Did you find him? I'm guessing it's not that handsome lad behind you, unless he's *really* good at hiding his age."

"I'm afraid I'm just your average strapping hero," says Cray, standing up to his full height.

Before I can introduce them properly, there's a thump on my arm. "Have I got to beat you up to get some attention?"

"Aileen!" I offer her a timid smile, and she wraps me in a tight hug.

"I'm so glad you're back," she says. "When Donal and Violet turned up without you..." She breaks away and tucks her hair behind her ears. "Wait – what happened to your neck?"

I tell her about the imitator and how it tried to strangle me. She bounds off, only to return a moment later with a small bowl filled with balm. It smells of dead grass and goat hair.

"This worked well on Donal and Violet," she says. Her eyes keep flicking to Cray when she thinks he's not looking. "Their scars have already started to die down a bit."

"I can vouch for that," says Donal.

"Thanks," I say.

While she's lathering it on, Cray looms over my shoulder. "Hi," he says. "I'm Cray. You're bracelet girl, right?"

"Oh, you've heard about me?" Aileen gives me a pointed side-look.

"Of course," says Cray. "The first time we met he wouldn't shut up about you. It was actually quite annoying."

A blast of heat flares in my cheeks.

"He's told me about you too," says Aileen, wiping her hands on her trousers.

"About how great I am, I hope," says Cray.

"Mainly that, yes."

My face is getting even hotter. Why did I think the two of them meeting would be a good idea?

"Anyway, Cray needs to be getting back to the mainland," I say.

"Actually," he says, "I think I'm going to stay for a while."

"Are you?" I ask.

"Are you?" echoes Aileen.

"Why?"

"To help you fight the *sgàilean*, of course. I've seen you swing a sword, Jaime... I need to make sure you don't accidentally stab someone. Or yourself." Aileen laughs, which grates on me more than it should. "Besides, at this very moment, the Badhbh is in a room somewhere enchanting weapons. He's making me a *magic* spear. Capable of destroying killer shadows. That's not an opportunity I'm going to pass up in a hurry."

"Oh," I say. "Okay..."

"Wait, the Badhbh's here? You found him?" Aileen asks, grabbing me by my wrists. "I can't believe that wasn't the first question I asked."

"You three are making far too much noise," says one of the Herbists, coming over to hustle us out. "This is a place of rest. All of you, out. You too, Aileen. You need to prepare for tonight."

"What's happening tonight?" Aileen asks.

"Only the most terrifying fight imaginable..." I say, surprising myself with my ability to make light of the situation. "Come with us; I'll explain everything."

I say goodbye to Donal, and then Cray, Aileen, and I walk towards the loch. I tell Aileen about the battle that's planned for tonight, and her face tightens with unease. She goes on to tell me about her journey north with Agatha, about their encounters with *sgàilean* and the deer and how, when they got back, Agatha discovered Catriona was keeping Kenrick captive. It sounds like the two of them have been even busier than me.

We stop and watch the deer for a bit.

"So they stay in the water all night and it prevents the *sgàilean* from getting them?" asks Cray.

"That's right," says Aileen.

"Clever. Hey, let me introduce you to Bras." He whistles, and Bras slips away from his new friends and trots over to us.

"Wow," says Aileen, stroking his flank. "He's incredible."

"Want a ride?" Cray asks her.

"Absolutely!"

Cray jumps on and then pulls Aileen up behind him. She holds on around his waist and then the two of them speed off in a large loop around the loch. I smile as I watch them, but my cheeks are tight. I don't mind them riding together. Of course I don't; I'm glad they're getting on. It's just strange. It's like two worlds colliding, and I can't work out how I feel about it.

As they're returning, the Fifth chimes out from around the wall. Bras comes skidding to a halt.

"What does that mean?" asks Cray.

"We're being called to a meeting," I reply. "This way."

Cray and I stroll to the meeting tree, while Aileen rides next to us with a big smile on her face. I've always hated bull-riding, but for some reason, right now, all

I want is for Aileen to get off so I can ride Bras instead.

A large group has already started to gather around the meeting tree, or what's left of it. It used to be so majestic, a symbol of all that was great about this clan. Now it's just a burnt-out husk, a giant claw grasping at nothing. We wait at the back as the last few people drift over. Agatha joins us and, to my surprise, so does Donal.

"If I'm well enough to stand, I'm well enough to fight," Donal says.

Kenrick climbs up onto one of the tree's blackened branches.

"*Fàilte,*" he calls out to welcome everyone. The crowd falls silent. "I'm sure most of you have already heard, but for those who have not, here is the truth: we are fighting the *sgàilean*. Tonight. This man on my left is known as the Badhbh, and he has travelled here from Scotia to assist us. We are indebted not just to him, but also to three other people who risked their lives to bring him here: Donal, Violet and Jaime. *An gaisge is urramach.*"

A few people turn their heads in my direction. I stare at the ground, hoping it might crack apart and swallow me whole.

"No mention of me," Cray whispers in my ear. "Always the unsung hero…"

I nudge him with my elbow.

"The Badhbh has … past experience with the *sgàilean*. He has forged weapons for us capable of destroying them. These are no ordinary weapons, and the decision to create them was not made lightly. The destruction which the *sgàilean* have already wrought on this island is all the confirmation we need that our ancestors were right in declaring magery un*dùth*. However, if we are to defeat them, we have no option but to combat their dark magic with our own. It may not feel right, but it is a necessary evil. So, take up arms and we will use them to strike the shadows down."

"How do we know the weapons will work?" someone calls out.

"We don't," replies Kenrick. "But there is no way to test them without the *sgàilean* discovering what we are doing. They are intelligent entities, and we must utilize the element of surprise. We will fight from the edge of the loch, keeping our feet submerged in the water's protection. That way we can always retreat further into its depths if necessary."

"What about the children?" shouts somebody else.

"As soon as the sun sets, all fires will be extinguished with the exception of those in the sickboth and in the nursery, where all the children will be. The magic within the weapons will attract the *sgàilean* to us like moths to a flame – the Badhbh assures me that once the first few come, the rest will follow. Then we fight. Clann-na-Bruthaich and Clann-a-Tuath side by side. Together we will overcome this darkest of foes. Tonight we rid ourselves of the shadows' curse!"

On his last word, he pulls a sword from the huge feast pot in front of him and raises it into the air. It glows the same red as the Badhbh's sword. Everyone in the crowd raises a fist and shouts out in support of his words. Then those closest to the pot reach in and start passing back the many weapons that are inside. Swords, knives, bows and arrows, all manner of weapons pass from hand to hand, each one emanating the same soft, ethereal light. Cray pushes his way forward to ensure that no one else takes his spear. Once he has it, he spins it in the air, the red glow of its tip making impossible circles above his head.

The woman in front of me offers me the choice of two swords – one long and sharp, and the other a short, metal practice sword. I choose the practice sword; it'll be easier to wield, and its bluntness shouldn't make too much difference against the *sgàilean*. Aileen dismounts from Bras and accepts a large meat hook from someone else.

"What w– weapon can I have?" Agatha asks anyone who will listen.

"Ah, Agatha, I'm glad I found you," says Lenox, stepping through the crowd. "I have an important job for you."

"I know what is an important job," says Agatha, "and it is— fighting. I have to do the f– fighting. It is the most important one."

"Actually, Agatha, we think you'd be most useful staying with the children."

"No!" she shouts. "I am not a— child."

"I know, we know, but we need your help to look

after them. You're good at helping people, aren't you?"

Agatha nods, but she's still frowning. "But I am the hero," she says. "I want to be the h– hero."

"Being a hero doesn't necessarily mean swinging a sword," says Lenox. "Helping people is being a hero too. You've never been trained to use close-combat weapons, so I'm reluctant to place one in your hands now. Besides, there aren't enough for everyone. So make your way over to the nursery – they're expecting you there."

Agatha spins on her heel with a growl and storms off. I'm glad she won't be fighting. Part of me wishes I'd been given that option too. It's all happening so quickly. I've scarcely had time to catch my breath since arriving back on Skye. Exhaustion from the past few days weighs heavy on my shoulders. I suppose I can rest when I'm dead...

"To the loch!" someone shouts, and I'm swept along with everyone else. Once we're there, we spread around its edge, facing outwards. There's a nervous excitement in the air, which hangs over us like a swarm of hungry bees. Cray stands on one side of me and Aileen is on the other. Maistreas Eilionoir is nearby, swinging her sword in a double loop. I've never seen her use a sword before, but it looks comfortable in her hands.

All of the deer have moved into the safety of the water behind us. They know what's coming. Bras is there too – this is one fight Cray does not want him involved in. One of the Hawks rings a chime: the signal for all of the external fires to be extinguished. Water is poured over them, and they fizzle out with sad sighs.

The sun starts to set, hidden behind a mess of lumpy clouds. We all look in its direction and watch as the sky slowly dims through shades of grey.

"Are you ready?" Aileen whispers.

"Definitely not," I reply.

Maistreas Eilionoir is the first to raise her sword, then everyone else follows her lead, creating a ring of magical light to attract the *sgàilean*. The only sounds are the distant shrieks of crickets and the occasional splash as one of the deer slides through the water. Everything else is still.

Now we wait.

SIGRID

Rᴀɪɴ ɪs sᴘᴇᴡɪɴ ᴅᴏᴡɴ ᴀʀᴏᴜɴᴅ ᴜs ɪɴ sɪᴄᴋsQᴜɪᴛ lashes. My ribs are sore from the *bjark* and my head's throbbin from fallin off of Eydis, but I haven't got no time to be worryin about none of that right now.

From where he's standin next to his bulk elk, Bolverk pulls out a length of rope – I'm guessin for tyin me up. There isn't no way I'm lettin him do that.

"You've been a very naughty little raven," he ses. "The king is not happy with you one bit."

"I don't give two hells about the king," I say.

Bolverk whistles. "I'd advise against saying anything like that in front of His Supremacy." I can't stop starin at his scar, at the way it slices through the ink goat's neck. I have a twistgut feelin that I'm about to share its fate. "Not that it'll make much difference. The way he was talking when I left, he's going to skin you alive. In fact, I might ask if I can have the pleasure of doing it

333

myself. A reward for tracking you so successfully – do you think that sounds fair?"

I'm not really listenin. All I'm thinkin is I need to get away. But how?

He sees my eyes flickin for an escape route. "There's no way for you to escape, so let's do this the easy way, shall we, and save ourselves a whole lot of pain?"

He doesn't know me at all if he thinks I'm just gunna let him take me easy. But I sure can pretend that's what I'm gunna do.

"Fine," I say, standin up.

"Show me your hands," he ses. I put one of my hands above my head. "And the other one," he ses. But the other one's busy pullin out the file Lady Beatrice gave me from the back of my waistband. I sneak it out slow, then, soon as it's free, I launch it at him. Before I see if it hits, I'm turnin and jumpin and stretchin for the lowest branch of the nearest tree. The first time, I miss. There's growlin behind me. I've only got one more chance. I jump again, and this time I grab it. I heave myself up and scurry higher, out of reach.

Bolverk is directly below, blood tricklin from a small slash on his arm where the file hit. He's too heavy to follow me up the flimsy branches and he knows it. It's makin him hek fiery.

"You can't stay up there forever." He bellows loud and smashes his fist into the tree trunk, sendin it wobblin and cuttin his hand and all.

Eydis whinnies and rises up on her back legs.

"It's okay, Eydis," I call down to her.

That was a mistake. Bolverk looks at me, and he looks at Eydis. Then he bends down slow and picks up the file I threw. He takes a step towards Eydis, then another one.

"You leave her alone," I say. "She didn't do nothin to no one."

"Shhh. Me and your horse are just making friends." He strokes the back of his hand down her neck. "Aren't we, pretty horse?"

"Don't you touch her."

"*Such* a pretty horse." He raises the file level with her eye. "It'd be a shame if something were to happen to her."

"Stop it. Stop it!"

"You've got until the count of three, little raven, until I have an accident with your horse here. One. Two." He's countin too fast. "Th—"

"Okay. I'm comin down."

I crawl back down the tree and drop onto the wet ground.

Bolverk barks a single laugh. "I've got to be honest, I'm a little disappointed. It's a horse. You know that, right? A horse that you've known, what? Less than a week. You're giving yourself up for a skittin horse? I thought you'd be stronger than that."

I don't say nothin. I don't care what he ses.

He walks towards me, loomin over me like the hek massive oafogre he is. "It's over, little raven; there's nowhere left to run."

I don't wanna run. All I wanna do now is hurt him – for

tormentin me, for threatenin Eydis, for the way he thinks he's so much better than me and can do whatever the hell he wants. I lunge towards him, but he bats me aside with his thick skittin paw as easy as if I was trampwheat. I'm on the ground. My lip is cut. He grabs a fistful of my tunic and drags me to the drop like he's gunna toss me over, but I know he won't; Konge Grímr will want me alive.

"You probably think I won't throw you over, that the king wants you alive" – rot him to hell for bein right – "but I don't trust you, little raven. I don't trust you to behave yourself on the journey back. You're a slippery little wench, and I sure as hellfire don't want any more trouble out of you. Much easier to say you fell, and return with your broken body." He means it, I can tell; he's gunna throw me over. He laughs then, and a thin line of dribble lands on my face. He's got my arms tight so I can't wipe it away. "I've always enjoyed the irony of your ink," he ses. "You know the meaning of the raven, I presume?" Course I know – all kidlins are taught the meanins of the diffrunt inks. "What could be funnier," he ses, "than a tattoo that's supposed to represent hope, looking like it's already dead?" His scar is even more gawkin ugly when he smiles.

I grit my teeth. "Wreck you to hell!" I shout. I grab and pinch and scratch at his harsk scraggin arm, but it's like tryin to hurt a growler bear.

"Enough talking. It's time to see if the little raven has learnt how to fly." He grins at his own joke and lifts me off the ground.

336

Somethin charges at him, a black blur that crashes into his side. Eydis! She hits him bamsmack on his arm with her head. He's so surprised he drops me and trips over my legs, stumblin forwards, only there isn't nowhere forwards for him to go. Only the edge, the drop to nothin below. I haven't never seen someone look so angry as what Bolverk looks in that moment. And then he's gone, his shouts fadin fast. I scramble to the edge to watch him fall, but I can't see nothin: he's already been swallowed by the rain.

I wrap my arms around Eydis's neck. "You really are the most hek *ríkka* horse there ever was!" I'm shakin all over, from the cold or the wet or the shock or somethin. Eydis nuzzles into me, and I rub the white stripe down her nose just how she likes it. Bolverk's giant elk stands a few yards away, watchin over us with indifference. The rain splashes off its bulkin antlers.

"Come on, Eydis," I say, turning my back to the elk. "We gotta find us some shelter outta this spew." My voice is tremblin and my legs are hek wobblin, but I lean on Eydis and she supports me.

One last push and we'll reach the channel what separates the island from the mainland. It didn't look wide on King Edmund's map, and I'm pretty sure horses can swim. I hope they can cuz I'm not leavin Eydis behind, that's for hek sure.

Then we'll be on Skye. We're so close now. We're gunna make it, I know we are. Isn't nothin gunna stand in our way.

JAIME

THE WAIT IS AGONIZING AS WE STAND IN SILENCE around the edge of the loch. The wind has picked up and careens around us with reckless abandon. I clench my teeth together to stop them from chattering.

After what feels like forever, the final shreds of daylight disappear and the whispering begins. At first, it's not easy to hear it over the wind, but it soon grows louder – that foul, aggressive sound I've heard so many times before: the *sgàilean* are coming. Lots of them. We all take a collective step backwards until our feet and ankles are submerged. *Sgàilean* can't move through water, so as long as we stay in the shallows, it should prevent them from grabbing us.

My heart gallops in my throat. What if the weapons don't work? Or the *sgàilean* find a way to force us out of the water? I've seen what they're capable of: ripping, tearing, snatching, slashing. It's all they know how to do.

"*Hè!* Where are you going?" Kenrick calls from further around the loch. A man has broken out of his position and is hobbling away from the line. "Come back. Everyone else, hold your ground!"

It takes me a few moments to realize the fleeing man is the Badhbh. I sprint after him.

"Jaime!" shouts Aileen, but I don't stop.

I grab the Badhbh's elbow and spin him around. "Where are you going?"

He shakes me off. "This is not my battle."

"Yes, it is. The *sgàilean* exist because of you. You made them; you need to take responsibility for them." I can't let him abandon us. If he doesn't have faith that we can beat them, what hope do the rest of us have?

"I did what you asked: I helped your people; I made your weapons. Now, leave me alone."

He sets off again, in the direction of the nursery. So he's planning on hiding with the children. And I thought *I* was a coward.

I let him go. I need to get back to the loch before the *sgàilean* reach it. Suddenly, everything around me grows darker and the whispering drowns out all other sounds. The *sgàilean* are inside the enclave. They drift as one, like the shadow of a storm cloud. They hit the loch's northern rim first, the area furthest from me. There is shouting and confusion, then an earth-shattering scream pierces all other noise. I've never heard anything like it. There's no way that it was human. Another scream rings out, even higher in pitch, containing even more

337

agony. Is that the sound of a *sgàil* dying? The fighting ripples down both sides of the loch. The screams continue, becoming more and more frequent.

People are running towards me: Cray, Aileen and Donal. Their weapons sway in their hands as they run.

"Come on," says Donal when they're near, "we need to get you back to the loch."

"Not your smartest move, running off like that," says Aileen as we race back.

"I thought I might be able to change his mind," I say.

"We thought you were bailing on us as well for a moment," says Cray.

He means it as a joke, but it stings, especially because it's not true. I can fight and I intend to. No one saw what I did in Norveg, but I'll show them now.

We arrive back at the southern shore and step into the water moments before the *sgàilean* sweep in on us. Cray strikes first, stabbing his spear into a shifting darkness on the ground. As it hits, the end of the spear glows ember orange. The shriek is so loud it batters the insides of my ears. The *sgàil* explodes in a swirl of black and then it's gone, leaving nothing but the thick smell of burnt meat. Cray is in his element. It's mesmerizing to watch. It's as if his spear is an extension of his body; it spins and turns and strikes with lethal precision.

"I'm enjoying this," he says. He edges out of the water, seeking more targets.

Just because the weapons work doesn't mean we can't get hurt. As if to prove my point, I see a man dragged away by his ankle, his sword arm flailing as he tries to stop the heinous entity that has a hold on him. He must have stepped out of the loch as well. No one tries to rescue him; he's gone before they can.

Aileen slashes a *sgàil* with her hook, then another. They both disappear with monstrous screams. I try to hit one as well, but they're moving too fast and they're not coming close enough. I risk half a step out of the water and something digs into my toes with razor claws. My eyes widen and I stab the ground in front of me. The pressure on my foot vanishes and so does the *sgàil*. I got one! I look up to see if anyone saw, but they're all too busy fighting their own battles. I should be doing the same. A *sgàil* takes advantage of my lapse in concentration and nearly pulls me to the ground. Its grip on my leg is like a rush of icy wind. Aileen reaches out and digs her hook into the *sgàil*, turning it into wisps of dust.

"Don't say I never do anything for you." She winks at me, then turns away to attack another shadow on her left.

I retreat back into the loch and continue trying to hit the *sgàilean* from the safety of the water.

"I'm sorry," I say to Aileen, raising my voice over the *sgàilean*'s screams.

"Sorry for what?" she asks with her back to me.

"For the way I spoke to you the other day, when we were in the meeting tree. And for how I've been since we came back from Norveg. For everything. I know I've not been a very good friend."

She glances at me over her shoulder. "Seriously? You're choosing now as the time to have this conversation?"

"What if this is the only chance we get?"

"Oh, very optimistic!" She strikes another *sgàil*. The burning smell makes my eyes water. "Look, you can tell me how sorry you are – and how great you think I am – once we've defeated these damn things. Deal?"

Fine, but I'm not doing much to help while cowering in the loch. Nearly everyone else is fighting outside the water, since it's the only way to get close enough to the shadows. I take a deep breath and step forwards, my sword poised. A *sgàil* darts straight for me. I drive in my sword and it explodes with a burning scream. I get another one soon after. The sword feels lighter in my hands now, more responsive to the strokes I've been practising. And the Badhbh was right: the *sgàilean* are attracted to the magic within the weapons' dark red glow, making them easier to destroy. They're vanishing all around us. The black smoke of their dissipating bodies curls across my vision, and their death howls rattle the air.

I lunge towards one right in front of me, but it pulls back at the last moment. The next one I try to strike does the same thing.

"They're retreating!" someone shouts. It's true: they're pulling away from us all around the loch.

"Hold your ground!" shouts Kenrick.

The *sgàilean* have stopped about ten paces away from us. Their whispering grows more intense, as if they're communicating with one another, plotting something.

"On my command, we charge at them," says Kenrick, and the order is echoed along the line. "They are no match for our weapons," he continues, "and they're close enough that we can still return to the loch if necessary. Three, two, one, charge!"

Everyone runs forward, weapons raised. At the same time the *sgàilean* rush at us at an impossible speed. It happens so quickly. A few are taken out, but the majority slip past. By the time we turn around, they've formed a black barrier between us and the loch, cutting off our safety net.

"What do we do?" someone shouts.

"We need fire!" shouts somebody else.

"No, we have to stay together," says a third voice.

Panic forces people in different directions, and within moments, everyone has dispersed. Individual *sgàilean* break away from the group and hunt down those that are fleeing. The screams of the fallen are even worse than those of the *sgàilean*. Without saying anything, Cray, Aileen, and I huddle together, our eyes alert. Not far from where we're standing, two *sgàilean* sneak up on a woman from Clann-na-Bruthaich.

"Look out!" I shout, but she doesn't hear me.

While one of the *sgàilean* distracts her, the other slips up her body, then down her arm and tears at her wrist. She drops her sword. Cray takes a few paces towards her, but the moment she is weaponless, more *sgàilean* descend on her, and there's nothing we can do.

The discarded sword sways into the air; one of the *sgàilean* has picked it up. Something within the sword allows the *sgàil* to rise up off the ground until it is upright in front of us: a faceless mass of pulsing darkness. It's getting a feel for the sword's weight. It doesn't take it long to figure out how to wield it. Cray takes half a step backwards, raising his non-spear hand in the air as if trying to calm a wild animal. The *sgàil* swings the sword in a swift figure of eight and then launches itself at us.

AGATHA

I DON'T WANT TO BE WITH THE CHILDREN. I AM NOT A child. Lenox says it is an important job to do helping the children but I want to do the more important job which is fighting the shadow things.

All of the children are here in the nursery. It is a long room and a big one. Some children are asleep and one of them is crying which is more annoying. He is from Clann-na-Bruthaich. If he was our clan he would know not to be scared. I am not scared. There is no point to be scared. A woman is trying to make the boy stop crying by stroking his hair. She is one of the people here to look after the children with me and her name is Una. She has a sword which glows because the Badhbh man made it magic. It is for killing the shadow things. It is covered up by her side so the shadow things don't see it. She is the only one with a magic sword in here. Lenox says we don't need magic swords. He says the shadow things won't come in here and he is right. Una's one is only for the emergencies.

I listen for the shadow things but I cannot hear them. All I can hear is the fires and some wind outside. There are four fires in the nursery. They will stop the shadow things from coming in no problems. The wind outside is very loud. We closed all the windows so it didn't blow in. Now it is hot because of the fires and there is smoke which makes me cough.

It is dark outside. I know it because Una said it to another man and I heard. It means the shadow things will come soon.

There is a sound. Was it a shout? I think it was, yes. It was from outside. Everyone is quiet. The boy who was crying is not crying any more. One girl says, "Is it the shadows?" and a man says to her, "Shhh." We all listen more.

More noises come from outside then. Horrible noises. It is shouts and the shadow things and the worst screams ever.

The door opens with a bang. It is a surprise, a big one. The Badhbh man is there. Why did he come? All his clothes are blowing with the wind. "Close the door!" someone shouts. The Badhbh man tries to close it but the wind makes it hard. It is too late. The big wind is already come in. It blows on all the fires and one, two, three, four, all of the fires go out.

It is very dark and everyone is shouting lots of noise all around. Someone screams. The door shuts and the wind isn't coming in any more. All I can see is Una's special sword doing the glowing. She has it out just a little bit so we can see. Someone bumps me and I say "Ouch" and I don't know who it was. It is so much smoke and I am coughing. The boy is crying again or maybe it is a different one. We need to make the fires quick before the shadow things come.

"Who has the flint?" says a voice. "Quickly." Someone is shouting at the Badhbh man and lots of other shouting.

"All the children to the far wall," says Una. She says it loudest so everyone can hear. Everyone moves back and I do too. Only the Badhbh man doesn't move. He stays by the door.

"I have f– flint," I say. I am a Hawk so I always have some. I take it out from my belt pouch.

"Why didn't you say?" shouts a man from Clann-na-Bruthaich who I don't know and I can't see him properly because of the smoke.

"I did s– say," I tell him, which is true.

"Well light the bloody fire, then," he says.

There is no reason to be mean. I go to the fire that is closest and go on my knees. Everyone is watching me and I have to be quick. My hands are shaking. I do not want everyone watching. I am not good at doing the flint. I hit it on the steel but I can't do it hard enough. I keep trying. There is a bit spark but it is not a good one.

"Out of the way, let me do it," says the man. He takes

the flint from me and pushes me away. It is rude of him to do that so I do an angry face at him.

He tries to light the fire but it is hard for him to do it too. He stops when he hears the sound. It is a horrible sound that is like strangled. It is a shadow thing, I know it. It is outside and it found us. The Badhbh man is at the other end of the nursery by the door and he takes out his sword. It is a special one too which does glowing. He moves it in a circle around him and says something quiet. Then he cuts both his arms with the sword. He is bleeding. I think maybe he did it to kill himself because he is scared of the shadow things but he is not dead. He wipes his blood on the sword and it glows more red. He moves the sword in a circle again and then hits it in the ground where is stays wobbling. A big circle glows all around him. It is magic, I know it. He did the blood magic. I have never seen it before and I cannot even believe it.

"What are you doing?" Una shouts to the Badhbh man. "You should be helping all of us, not just yourself."

The Badhbh man closes his eyes. He does not say anything. I was watching the Badhbh man and I forgot about the shadow thing. It is coming in now, under the door. It is like black water moving. The man with the flint sees it and does the flint even faster but the fire will not start. The shadow thing is inside. It goes to the Badhbh man and it tries to get him but it can't because of the circle glow he made. The Badhbh man should kill it with his sword to help us but he doesn't. All he does is watch. The shadow thing moves away from him. It is going to get us instead.

"Stay back," says Una to all of us. She steps forwards two steps and takes out her sword and holds it in front of her. The sword is very bright light glowing and the shadow thing goes straight for it. Una waits until the shadow thing is just about to get her and then she slams the sword down.

The shadow thing explodes. The scream is the worst sound I ever heard in my life. I put my hands over my ears to stop hearing but I can still hear it. All the parts of the shadow thing disappear in the air and then it is gone. Una did it. She is brave, not like the Badhbh man.

The boy who was crying before starts crying again. He does not like the sound of the shadow thing dying is what I think. Then he is running and he runs all the way to the door and opens it and goes outside. He shouldn't do that. It is not safe to be outside.

"Stop him!" someone shouts.

I do it. I run after the boy. Being the hero is helping and brave and I am good at doing that. When I pass the Badhbh man, I grab onto his sword in the floor and pull it hard. It comes away and the circle around the Badhbh man goes. His eyes open big.

"No!" he says, and he tries to grab his sword back but I have it now and I am too quick out of the door. If he will not use it to help people, then I will use it to help people.

Outside it is a lot of wind. There is fighting sounds

and screams. The screams is the shadow things being killed which is good and also people being hurt which is very not good. I hope my Clann-a-Tuath are not hurt and my friends are not hurt too like Jaime and Aileen and Maistreas Eilionoir and Crayton. Please don't let the shadow things get them.

The Badhbh man's sword has light so I can see a little bit but I cannot see the boy who ran away. I look around for shadow things. I cannot hear them close but maybe they are hiding and will get me.

"Crying boy!" I shout because I do not know his name. "W– where are you? You have to come back— in!"

I hear him. He is crying but only a quiet bit. I go around the side of the nursery wall and he is on the ground behind a barrel. He is hugging his knees and his head is down.

"Come on, you boy," I say, and I pull on his arm to make him stand up.

He does a louder cry and pulls his arm away and will not move. Hmmm. This is a tricky one and difficult.

I pat the boy on his head which is to be kind. He doesn't look at me so I go down next to him.

"Are you scared of the sh– shadow things?" I say. He nods his head. I do not tell him that he is wrong to be scared because I am kind and being nice. "Look, I have a m– magic sword. It will stop the shadow things so you don't need to be— scared."

He lifts his head then and looks at the sword. His eyes are shiny colour. "Can I hold it?" he asks to me.

I think about it and then I say yes. I give him the sword and he holds it in two hands. He is not crying now which is good. "It is good to be b– brave," I say. "Shall we go back in now? It is— safer inside."

The boy nods and we stand up. I let him hold the sword even though it is too big for him and he has to do dragging. We turn the corner and I reach to open the door but I pull back just in time. There is a shadow thing on the door. It nearly got me.

"Get back," I say to the boy. "G– give me the sword!"

"I'll get it," says the boy. "I am brave now."

He swings the sword but it is too heavy and he lets go. It does not hit the shadow thing. It lands on the ground. The shadow thing slides down off the door and is blocking so we cannot get the sword.

"Run!" I shout.

I grab the boy's hand and we run. The shadow thing chases us. I am not good at running. The boy is faster. He is pulling my arm. It is hurting but I have to go fast fast fast.

We run all the way around the nursery in the circle and there is the door again and I have to open it quick. The shadow thing is nearly so close to us and it is hard for my fingers to do the door open. Come on come on. The door opens and we fall inside. It is light in the nursery from the fires. They are lit again so the shadow thing cannot follow us in. Someone shuts the door so the wind does not put the fires out like it did before. My breath is hard and lumpy.

"Where's my sword?" says the Badhbh man. He is standing over me. He is very cross. "You had no right."

"I l– lost it," I say, but that is only a little bit true. I know where it is. It is outside, of course. Then I have the idea. Lenox said I couldn't fight the shadow things because I did not have a weapon but if I get the Badhbh man's sword again then I do have a weapon.

Being the hero is helping people, like I helped the boy who was crying and ran away. Now I am going to be the bigger hero and help the other people too.

I stand up. Someone is giving a cuddle to the crying boy. Everyone else is looking at me.

"I have to go now," I say. "I'm going to be the hero."

I open the door and go back out into the dark.

JAIME

CRAY PARRIES THE FIRST FEW STRIKES OF THE *SGÀIL*'S sword, but none of us can get close enough to destroy it. More shadows drift towards us, forcing Aileen and me to switch our focus onto dealing with them. Aileen slays two and I take out a third, but more keep coming. I know what they're after: our weapons. People are being disarmed all around us, and the *sgàilean* are rising from the ground. There's only one thing worse than an army of *sgàilean*, and that's an army of *sgàilean* with swords.

Cray, Aileen and I fight with our backs pressed against each other, hoping to protect one another by staying together.

"Ah!" Cray cries as the *sgàil*'s sword nips his shoulder. He manages to land a blow with his spear and the *sgàil* bursts into smoke, but already another *sgàil* has picked up the sword and Cray is once again under attack. I'm distracted by a *sgàil* of my own. It takes me four attempts to hit it. When I look back, Cray is in a tugging war; a *sgàil* has a hold of the opposite end of his spear and is trying to pull him off balance. Aileen has taken over defending us against the *sgàil* with the sword.

"Jaime, I need you!" says Cray.

I crouch under his arm to sweep at where I imagine the *sgàil* holding his spear must be, but my thrusts hit nothing. Cray tumbles forward in a head-first roll and is pulled away by his spear.

"Cray!" I shout.

Aileen kicks at the hilt of the sword in front of her. The sword falls from the *sgàil*'s grip, and Aileen slashes with her hook. We dash through the *sgàil*'s disappearing wisps in the direction Cray was taken.

The body of a man being dragged in the opposite direction almost collides straight into us. I catch a glimpse of ginger beard. Donal. Aileen sees him too.

"Help him. I'll get Cray," she says.

I don't want to leave her – and I don't want to abandon Cray – but if I don't save Donal, no one will. I run after him, trusting that Aileen and Cray will be able to look after themselves.

I chop at the grass in front of me as I run in case there are hidden shadows lurking there. Donal has managed to get to his feet, but he's unarmed. He has his back to me, so doesn't see the *sgàil* that has picked up a discarded sword. It rises, preparing to stab him from behind. I launch myself at it and jab with my own sword, destroying it just in time. Donal turns at the sound of its dying scream and looks from me to the fallen sword.

"You did good, lad," he says, ruffling my hair.

He bends down to pick up the sword, but it is snatched away by another *sgàil* before he can grab it. The *sgàil* swings it with unrestrained force and lands it deep in Donal's side. Donal's eyes widen on impact and he drops to his knees.

"No!" I shout.

I strike at the *sgàil*. It dodges my sword with ease and launches a counter-attack. I stand over Donal's fallen body and defend us as best as I can. Everything Cray taught me about sword fighting – posture, stance, grip – disappears from my head. It's taking all my concentration not to drop my sword. The *sgàil* drives its weapon at me again and again. My arms are tiring, and beneath me, Donal is fading fast.

There's a surge of cold up my back. A *sgàil* is on me. I open my mouth to scream, but the wind is knocked out of me. The *sgàil* pushes me forward with the force of a tumbling boulder. I turn as I fall to avoid being impaled on the other *sgàil*'s sword, but it still makes contact, slashing my left arm from my shoulder to my elbow. I crumple to the ground. My head is full of noise and thorns. Blood from the wound on my arm pools in front of my eyes. I watch as the soil sucks it away.

Out of nowhere, the Badhbh's voice drifts into my mind. *Blood magic is fed by blood. The more blood you feed it, the more powerful it becomes.*

I wonder... From where I'm lying, I lift my sword to the cut on my arm. I cover one side of the blade in my blood, and then the other. At first, nothing happens, but then the blood starts to disappear as if the sword is *absorbing* it.

I'm so distracted, I almost forget about the threat of the *sgàilean*. I turn my head as the armed one swings its sword directly at my face. A hand reaches out and grabs it just in time. Donal holds on to the blade with trembling fingers, its edge digging into his palm.

"Move! I can't hold it for much longer," he says through gritted teeth.

I squirm to one side. Donal lets go of the blade and it sinks into the earth. The sword I'm holding twitches then starts to hum, and it glows much brighter than it was before. While still in my hands, it lunges at the *sgàil*, as if acting on its own accord. In the same stroke, it also tears through the *sgàil* that pushed me over and then a third that I didn't even know was there. All of them disappear with ear-shattering shrieks. There's no doubt in my mind: the sword has changed. It starts to vibrate so fast it makes my hand burn. I fling it to the ground, then crab-scramble to Donal. He's still alive. I whip off my cloak and press it into his wound. He winces. I take his hand and place it on the cloak.

"You're going to be all right," I say. "Just keep applying pressure."

I prod at my own wound. It hurts like crazy but doesn't look too deep. I rip off my sleeve and – with one end one held tight between my teeth – tie it above the cut to slow the bleeding.

Whispers to my left. More *sgàilean* are coming. My sword is where I left it, glowing brighter than ever. I reach for it and feel its power the moment my fingers curl around the hilt. Whatever magic the Badhbh instilled in it has been warped and intensified since the blade came into contact with my blood. A raw, unruly energy pulses through it, which is both terrifying and impossible to resist. The sword is a part of me now; for better or worse we're connected. The sheer power of it shivers through my wrist.

One thing is certain: the sword is as hungry to kill as the *sgàilean* are. I lash out at four approaching *sgàilean*, unaware if it is me controlling the sword, the sword controlling me, or a combination of the two. Either way, we destroy all four in one mad flurry. Their death smell scorches my nostrils and I roar at the sound of their departing screams.

I tighten my grip and raise the sword high into the air. A wild crimson glow pulses out of it, bathing me in its light. It acts like a beacon, causing *sgàilean* to flock towards it from all directions. Hundreds of shadows, speeding towards me, all intent on my death. My breath races at the speed of a raging bull. I'm clutching the sword so tight my fingers feel like they're on fire. I close my eyes, focusing on nothing but the whispers as they draw nearer, nearer. The sword thrums in my hand.

I slowly count to three, then I open my eyes and I strike.

AGATHA

I FIND THE BADHBH MAN'S SPECIAL SWORD STRAIGHT away. It's on the ground where the crying boy threw it. I pick it up. The shadow thing that was here before has gone away. I run to the loch. When I see it I can hardly even believe it. It is a battle and a big one. Moving lights are all around the loch which are red and pink ones from the other weapons that the Badhbh man made. And it is black black shadow things trying to get the people and screaming. I cannot see Crayton or Jaime or Aileen. I run to find them and help them. I will get the shadow things. I am not afraid.

Someone is running towards me and they are holding a Reaper tool. It is a long stick with a blade on it for cutting the crops. It is what the Reapers use, I know that. It is a magic one now and it is glowing. Does the person need help? I can help them. I cannot see the person. Oh, oh – it is not a person. It is a shadow thing

that has the Reaper blade. It comes at me and swings it.
I do a jump backwards. The blade nearly cuts my face
it is so close.

The shadow thing's other hand is a claw in all directions trying to grab at me and tear me apart. I swing the
Badhbh man's sword at it but the shadow thing is too
quick and it is too hard to do it. When I move the sword
to get it, it is already gone.

It has both of its shadow hands on the Reaper blade
now and it lifts it high. I put up the Badhbh man's sword
and the blades hit together. It is a big crash with sparks
and my arms wibble. I fall onto the ground on my back.
The shadow thing swings the Reaper blade from the side
and hits the sword out of my hands. Then it moves the
Reaper blade up into the air again. It is a pink line sharp
in the sky. It is going to get me and I will be dead. I cannot
stop it. The blade moves fast towards me. I close my eyes.

Something grabs my shoulder and pulls me backwards. It hurts where it grabs me. It is a different shadow
thing which has got me and it is pulling me away. The
only good thing is that the Reaper blade did not kill me
but the bad thing is this shadow thing has got me now
and it will kill me instead. I hit it with my hands but it
holds on harder. I am bumping on the ground so fast
and all of me hurts. There is screams around me and
shadow things disappearing and falling people and horrible smell and it is too loud in my ears and my eyes and
I cannot stop or make the shadow thing let go.

My bottom is wet and so is my back and my legs and

I am splashing wet all over and then under water and I cannot swim and I will drown. The shadow thing lets go. It feels like my shoulder falls off when it does it. I sit up. I am in water and wet all over. Milkwort runs out of my pocket and into my hair. He does not like it in the water. He nibbles on my ear which means to tell me to be more careful. I tell him sorry and stroke him.

I am in the loch. Where did the shadow thing go? And why did it bring me to the loch? Shadow things do not like the water.

Sun-Leaf, says a voice in my head. I turn and Thistle-River is next to me. He says he hopes he did not bite too hard.

It wasn't a shadow thing that pulled me away, it was Thistle-River!

You saved me, I say to him in my head. He tells me my life was in danger so he helped me the same as I helped the deers. I say thank you to him and I say it again because I mean it a very lot.

I stand up and look all around. The loch is full of the deers. Outside the loch there is fighting everywhere. Lots of shadow things have got the special weapons which makes them even more worse. I want to help but I do not have a weapon any more and I wasn't very good at doing it with the weapon anyway. I need a plan which is helping without having the weapon.

People are running and the shadow things are chasing them and getting them. It is too horrible to see it. Why do they not run into the loch? If they come into the water then the shadow things cannot get them.

One of the running people is Aileen. She does not have a weapon and the shadow things are going to get her.

"Come into the—   loch!" I shout. "Aileen! Qu– quickly!"

She doesn't reply. Maybe she doesn't hear me. Then I see why she can't come into the loch. There are shadow things all around it and they are stopping people coming in. I don't know how Thistle-River got past them. It must be because he was running so fast. This is so bad and it was not the plan. If Aileen and the other people cannot go into the loch there is nowhere safe for them to be. How can I make the shadow things go away? I am thinking hard for the clever plan.

The shadow things do not like fire and they do not like water. That is what I know. Also they do not like rain. The Nice Queen Nathara told me that. It is because rain is water. If it rains the shadow things will go away. I look at the sky. It is dark and some clouds but it is not raining and I cannot make it do that. I have to have a different thought. Then I get one.

Can you help me? I ask to Thistle-River. And then I say *please* for the manners. Thistle-River says that yes he will help and asks what I need him to do. I tell him my plan. It is for all the deers to make it rain with splashing. If they splash big ones all around the loch, the shadow things might think it is raining and go away.

Thistle-River thinks it is a clever plan. He lifts his head

and does three loud deer barks. The other deers do it the same, all around the loch. They are looking at me now. *Follow me and make big splashing*, I say to *Thistle-River*, and I start running in a circle around the edge of the loch. I run as fast as I can and I stamp hard with my feet to make the splashes. Thistle-River does it too and then the other deers do it as well. They run faster and make bigger splashes with their hooves. They are all running past me and the big splashes go over me and I'm wet. It is harder for me to run with all the deers running as well and harder for me to see with the water on my head.

Then one is next to me that is not a deer. It is a bull and it is Crayton's bull and it's called Bras. He stops and goes lower which is asking if I want to go on his back. I do want to go on his back so I climb up and I hold on to his hair with my hands. He starts running fast. I scream because it is fun to be fast. All of the deers and me and Bras are running now in the circle around the loch and there is so much splashing and water. My ears are full with the stamping. The water from the loch is raining on the shadow things and they don't like it and they move away. It is my plan and it is working. The shadow things go away in all directions and the people with weapons get them easy because the shadow things are confused. Crayton is one of the people doing the fighting with his spear. He is good at fighting and gets lots of shadow things and is strong. There is lots more horrible screaming which is the shadow things being stabbed and disappearing.

The deers slow down running and so does Bras. I say thank you to Bras and get off from him into the water again. It is cold on my legs and I am shivery pimples. The people with no weapons come into the loch and they are safe. I knew my plan was a clever one.

"Agatha, you genius!" says Aileen. She comes to me with lots of splashing and hugs me. It is a nice hug and I like it. "It was you, wasn't it? That got the deer to chase the *sgàilean* away from the shore?"

"It was!" I say. "It was me," and I am smiling.

"Hang on, what's that?" Aileen points behind me. There is one light that is brighter. It is a weapon I think but it is more red and more bright. It is down by the other side of the loch.

"I don't— know," I say.

We walk towards it but stay in the loch so the shadow things don't get us. The person with the weapon holds it in the air high.

"Is that—?" asks Aileen. She doesn't finish it what she was going to say. The strangle sound that is the shadow things gets louder. They have seen the bright sword too. All of the last ones go to it quick all together. I cannot see who it is that has the bright sword because they are covered in too many shadow things that are black swirls and screaming explosions. The sword is doing flashes and cuts so so fast and it is getting them. It is getting them all.

Too many screams that are loud and horrible and then the last one goes and there is no more screaming. It is quiet and not as dark as before. The wind is the only sound blowing. I can see the person who is holding the bright sword now. I cannot even believe it. It is Jaime. I wave to him and smile but he doesn't see me. He is wobbling. The sword drops from his hand and he falls to the ground.

JAIME

When I open my eyes, Aileen is there. She's saying something, but I can't focus for long enough to work out what. Everything is such a blur. Did I really just kill all those *sgàilean*? It was like I was in the centre of a tornado, one that was intent on my destruction. But the sword... The sword took over. I don't know what happened. It didn't feel like it was me, yet at the same time, I've never felt so alive.

My head is still full of the *sgàilean*'s death screams; they linger like a painful echo at the back of my mind. I'm on the ground. Did I fall? The ground is so uneven. There was something else, someone else... *Donal*.

"Where's Donal?" I ask, ignoring whatever it was Aileen was trying to say to me. "He was hurt; they have to help him. He was right here. He needs help, he was bleeding, he—"

"Cray carried him to the sickboth," says Aileen.

"He's still alive. I think he's going to pull through."

That's all I needed to hear. While there's life, there's hope. And Cray – he's alive too.

I'm so tired. I close my eyes.

I feel like I could sleep for a hundred years.

AGATHA

EVERYONE IS CHEERING. ALL OF THE SHADOW THINGS are gone and we did it. I shout too. It is a loud noise I make that isn't words. It is just noise because I am happy and it's fun.

"Thank goodness you're safe," says Maistreas Eilionoir. She grabs my fists and squeezes them. "You're not hurt?"

"No," I say. My head is pounding a lot of hurt because of talking to the deers but I do not say that one.

"It was a hard-won fight," says Maistreas Eilionoir, "but we did it. We lived to tell the tale."

I nod my head yes. Maistreas Eilionoir gives my fists one more squeeze and then goes to someone else and squeezes their fists as well. It is what everyone is doing. I wanted Maistreas Eilionoir to tell me I am the hero but she didn't. Other people talk to me and grab my fists but no one tells me I am the hero. Maybe they didn't see the clever plan when I did it with the deers to make the splashing.

"So you decided to disobey my instructions to stay in the nursery," says Lenox. He looks tired but his smile is not a cross one.

I do my pretty smile for him. "I was doing lots of helping," I say.

"I'm glad you're all right, Aggie, even if you are terrible at doing what you're told."

It is still night-time and everyone is tired from the fighting but there is lots to do. Some people were hurt by the shadow things and the Herbists are making them better. The Stewers give out bowls with drink in. A woman gives one to me and I drink some. It is hot and makes my tongue ouch but also it is sweet and juicy nice. Other people pick up the bodies of the people who are dead. It is sad that they are dead. They put them next to the loch in a line. Lots of people help them do it. Tomorrow we will say goodbye to them. *"Caidil gu bràth"* is what we will say which is "Sleep forever with peace."

After, it is time for everyone to go to sleep. Not forever, but with the peace.

"Today will be a day of celebration," says Kenrick. "A celebration in honour of our fallen clansmen. A celebration of our victory over the *sgàilean* and a celebration of what we can achieve when our two clans work together. The Badhbh, here beside me, assures me that the *sgàilean* are no longer a threat. They have been destroyed and will never return." There is lots of cheering at that and fists in the air. "To our friends from Clann-a-Tuath, I say this: you have helped us defend our enclave and helped protect our beautiful Isle of Skye – our *shared* home. I met with my clan this morning, and it has been agreed that we will reciprocate your help and support you in reclaiming your enclave, by whatever means necessary. May Clann-na-Bruthaich and Clann-a-Tuath forever be strong!"

Everyone shouts again because they agree. It is very good what he said and means we can go home. Maistreas Eilionoir stands up. She is going to speak too. I have not finished eating morning meal yet but it is not allowed when they are talking. I put in one more mouthful quick before she starts. It is a big one. Crayton is sitting next to me and he laughs when he sees me do it.

"Thank you, Kenrick, and thanks to everyone here," Maistreas Eilionoir says. "It is no secret that all we have truly wanted since coming back to this island is to return to our home, to the stability and familiarity of our own enclave. We long for it, we have fought hard for it, and we will fight again if necessary. Knowing we have your support fills our hearts with courage. We have always considered Clann-na-Bruthaich our allies, but from this day forth, we also consider you our friends." People cheer and fists in the air again when she says it. Then she says, "Last night was a testament to what we can accomplish together. We are here today, sharing morning

369

meal, because of each and every one of you. That is the way of our clans. We fight. We survive. We thrive."

Maistreas Eilionoir sits down and there is more cheering. I look at everyone around me happy and smiling and then I know it. Maistreas Eilionoir is right when she said we did it together and it means that everyone is the hero. We were all brave and did helping and that is what is being a good clan. I am the hero too because I helped the crying boy and I had the clever plan to make the deers do the splashing but I do not need everyone to tell it to me. I know that it is true.

After morning meal it is time to say goodbye to the deers. They are my friends and I like them but they want to go back outside the enclave. That is where they live. They will be safe there now the shadow things are gone. They walk together through the enclave and everyone waves at them. When we are at the Lower Gate, the Moths open it and the deers go out. I say a special big goodbye to Thistle-River.

We will meet again, Sun-Leaf, Thistle-River says to me. He bows his head and I bow mine too. Then he does two loud deer barks and runs off into the trees. I hope it is true what he said that we will meet again.

It is time for the celebrating. Everyone goes to around the meeting tree which is a black one now. It was Jaime who burned it. Some people play the pipes and I do some stamping. Someone starts saying an *òran* and everyone joins in with the chanting. It is the one about the giants called Faolan and Eòsaph. I have heard it a lot of times.

Faolan and Eòsaph were the brothers but they didn't like each other so they fought with big hammers. That is why the Skye island broke off from Scotia because Eòsaph hit the ground so hard and it cracked a big one. I say some of the words but I can't remember all of them. Remembering isn't my best one.

It is fun to hear the piping and the *òran* and do the stamping with my clan but then it reminds me of something and I have to leave. I walk away to the wall and go up the steps to the top. It is cold with the wind but also there is sun a bit and it is nice on my face. Skye island is pretty this morning. It is a bright one with the sunshines on the grass. Milkwort comes out and sits on my shoulder so he can see it too. He thinks it is pretty as well. I walk a long way around the wall looking out all the time.

"Hey, Aggie, what are you doing up here?" I turn around and it is Jaime who said that. I knew it was him because I know how his voice sounds. I don't know why he is on the wall, though.

"I'm a— a Hawk," I say. "I'm looking out and being a— good one."

"Didn't you want to join the celebrations?"

I shake my head no. People are still playing the pipes. I can hear it. The music and everyone happy made me think of when Jaime had to marry the girl from Raasay. That was when all the bad happened. That's why I came to the wall to look out, to make sure the bad doesn't happen again.

"Why are y- you here?" I ask Jaime. He is not a

Hawk, so it is not his duty to be on the wall looking out.

"I just felt like getting away for a bit," he says. "It's nice up here. Peaceful."

"Yes," I say. "It is." Then I say, "You got so— many of the sh– shadow things, Jaime. You were the— the best one." I saw him do it. He shakes his head but doesn't say anything. "It's good that the shadow things are gone now," I say. I smile a big one. I want to make him smile as well. When he sees my smile he does a big smile too. Jaime is my good friend.

"Did you hear it when Kenrick said he will help us get our e– enclave back?" I say.

"Yes."

"That is a good thing. I want to live there again now."

"Me too."

"Do you think the B– Badhbh man will help as well?" I ask.

"I doubt it. He's a coward. The Bó Riders might, though. Cray's going to go back and ask them."

"The Bó Riders are coming— here?" I say. "To S– Skye?"

"They might. That'd be good, wouldn't it?"

"Yes, J– Jaime, it would be very good."

The bull people are from the mainland. One thing I thought is that maybe my father is a bull person. If they come here I can ask them a secret that is who my birth father is.

Milkwort goes from my one shoulder to my other shoulder so he can see Jaime better. Jaime strokes him on the top of his head and he likes it. There is a bandage on Jaime's arm where one of the shadow things hurt him with a sword. He is very brave.

"Can I ask you something, Aggie?" Jaime says to me.

"Yes, you can," I say.

"Do you ever think about what happened to us in Scotia? And in Norveg?"

I nod my head yes. "I think about it— lots of times," I say.

"How does it make you feel?"

I have to think about that. Then I say, "Sometimes sad a lot. I feel sad about Lileas, and about the b– bull riders when the— wildwolves got them, and also that the N– Nice Queen Nathara was— dead."

"And how do you stop that from consuming you? From filling your every thought with darkness?"

Hmm. That is a confusing question. "Good things happened— too," I say, which I don't know if it's what he asked me. "We rescued our c– clan and we did it. And we met C– Crayton and the bull people who are our friends and did— riding on the bulls. The good things make me more happy when I think of those ones."

"You're right." Jaime still looks sad.

"It's okay to be sad sometimes too," I say.

"That's true. Although I'm not sure I do feel sad. I don't know what I feel."

I think of what can make Jaime happier. Doing hugging makes me happy sometimes. "Do you want me to h– hug you?" I ask him.

"Sure, that'd be nice."

I hug Jaime, a big one.

"Thanks, Aggie. Maybe we can talk about it again sometime?"

"You can talk to me when— whenever you want, Jaime," I say. "I like talking."

Jaime looks at me. His eyes are wet and he smiles. "You're very wise, Agatha. You know that?" he says.

I smile when he says that. I like that he called me wise because it means clever.

"What's that?" Jaime says, and he points. His face is frowns.

I look at where the point is, which is at the forest. There's something walking out of the trees. It is an animal – a black one with white hair – a horse I think it is. Also someone is riding it.

"It's a— a— girl," I say.

"She looks exhausted," says Jaime. "Or dead."

He's right. The girl is forward on the horse. Maybe the shadow things got her. "We should h– help her," I say.

I run to the steps that go down from the wall.

"Wait," says Jaime. "Her face... I think—"

He does not say all the words. I am gone away down the steps. Jaime stays looking at the girl from the wall. I should have hit the chime. It is the First I should have hit, once at the bottom which means I have seen a person but I don't know who is it. Should I go back and hit the chime? Hitting the right chimes and quickly is being a good Hawk. But it is only one girl. It is not the enemy. She needs help and I am helping. That is important too.

I am at the Lower Gate. There are no Moths here. They are with the pipers being happy is what I think. I am not a Moth so I am not allowed to open the gate but I know how to do it. You have to take off the metal part and pull the wood handle in a circle. If I open it only a little bit I can go out and help the girl. The gate will not be open a lot for enemies to come in. I take off the metal bit. It is heavy.

"Agatha, what are you doing?" says Jaime.

He is at the top of the steps and coming down from the wall. I think he will make me stop opening the gate but I don't want to stop so I do it more quickly. I want to help the girl. I do the wood handle in the circle and I go out.

"Aggie, wait."

The horse is closer now and it stops. It is black all over except for the white stripe on its face and its long hair that is white as well. I walk to it. The girl sits up on its back and looks at me. She has a tattoo on her face.

She is a deamhan.

My mouth goes open shocked.

The tattoo is a bird and it looks like a dead one. There is a hand on my shoulder. It is Jaime. He is breathing fast from running. We both look at the deamhan girl.

"Hello," she says. I don't say anything and Jaime doesn't say anything. "Sigrid," she says, and she points at her chest. I think that is her name, "Sigrid". On her wrist there is a metal bit like a chain. "I am friend. I help you." She speaks our language funny like Knútr the nasty deamhan spoke it funny.

"What do you mean?" asks Jaime. "Where have you come from?"

Before she can say the answer, the arrow is in her body. Her face is all surprise and pain. She slips off the horse and goes down. Jaime is quick and catches her before she hits the ground.

Who did the arrow? There. There is another deamhan by the trees. He is sitting on a big white animal and is holding a bow. It was him who fired the arrow, I know it. We have to get back to the enclave.

Jaime holds the girl's head and presses on her chest where the arrow is. His hand is all red.

"I don't— I don't—" he says.

I can't stop looking at her. Blood is in her mouth and it comes out onto her face. It goes over the bird tattoo and it looks like the bird is bleeding. The girl tries to say something but it is hard to hear the words. I lean in closer and then I hear it.

"Danger," she says. "Bad men coming."

A NOTE ON THE LANGUAGES

The "old language" spoken by some people in Scotia and on Skye is, for the large part, Scottish Gaelic. Occasionally, I modified words and made alternative choices for artistic reasons or in order to aid the reader; I take full blame for any errors or inconsistencies.

The language spoken by the Norvegians is a fictional one, inspired by Old Norse. Much of Sigrid's idiosyncratic slang also stems from Old Norse.

ACKNOWLEDGEMENTS

The problem with acknowledgements is that you have to write them so far in advance, you end up missing out all the people who work on the book post-publication. Consequently, I'd like to start by thanking all the people who *weren't* mentioned in the acknowledgements for *The Good Hawk*, but have done wonders in helping it soar: Rebecca Oram for being a PR ninja, Jo Humphreys-Davies, Josh Alliston, Bridie Shepard and the whole sales team at Walker Books (absolute legends, every one of you), Sara Marcolini for making the Italian translation such a wonderfully collaborative process, Emma Caroll, Mel Darbon, Emily Stratford for the phenomenal song, Imogen Russell Williams, Georgie Carroll from Walker Books Australia, and Rachel Fogden at the Down's Syndrome Association. I'd also like to give a huge thanks to all the booksellers, bloggers and librarians around the world who have championed the book and encouraged children to read it – you are the real heroes of this story.

Onto *The Broken Raven*, and my first thank you is to my editors, Annalie Grainger and Susan Van Metre, for continuing to steer my writing with such enthusiasm and wisdom – you make these books what they are. Megan Middleton, you took over the reins like an absolute pro when Annalie went on maternity leave; you're such a vital member of this team. John Moore, thanks for continuing to be awesome, along with Jamie Tan, Gráinne Clear, Helen Mortimer and Anna Robinette. Being published by Walker is like being a part of one big, loving family and I feel very privileged to have been welcomed into it with such open arms. Special thanks to Denise Johnstone-Burt and Jane Winterbotham.

To my agent, Claire Wilson. You continue to be my biggest supporter (maybe second biggest, after my mum) and my greatest defender. Thank you for always being there for me; I couldn't be more grateful.

Violet Tobacco, you worked your magic and created such a striking and atmospheric cover for this book – I adore it. And thanks to Margaret Hope for your wonderful creative vision.

Another big hug to my favourite smasher Donna Bryce-Macleod and her sister Heather Macleod for keeping me on track with the additional Gaelic in this book.

Shoutout to all my friends, old and new – those from school, my uni crew, CSSD and CPS buddies, my CBeebies family, my new author friends, and all those I've collected from various acting jobs over the years... I can't thank you enough for your messages of support and the way you've hollered from the rooftops about my books. You're amazing, and I'm so lucky to have you in my life. Same goes for my extended family of cousins, aunties, uncles, and everyone in between.

Mum, you finally got a book dedicated to you! Hope you'll stop hassling me about it now ;) Padge, keep working on the theme tune – I'm sure Hollywood will be calling you any day. Grandma, it's another "fantasy" book, I'm afraid... I'll try and write something with less "made-up things" in it next time. Thanks for showing it off to your friends all the same. Tom, Lils and Sprogger – I know it must be hard to have such a ridiculously talented sibling, but I'm afraid I just can't help it. Seriously though, I'm so proud of all three of you. Iluvallthepeplinmyfaml.

Rich, I don't need to tell you how brilliant you are, but I'm going to tell you anyway. You're brilliant. There isn't no one more hek brimmin I'd rather have by my side.

And finally, the biggest thanks of all is to you, the reader. Thanks for picking up this book and for wanting to continue Jaime and Agatha's story. I hope Sigrid has also won a place in your hearts. There's more to come, and I promise you, it's going to be one hell of a finale.

JOSEPH ELLIOTT is a writer and actor known for his work in children's television, including the hit series, "Swashbuckle". His commitment to serving children with special educational needs was instilled at a young age: his mother is a primary school teacher specializing in SEN, and his parents provided respite foster care for children with additional needs. One of his first jobs was working at a holiday playscheme for children with learning disabilities, and he went on to work as a teaching assistant at Westminster Special Schools for nearly five years. Agatha was inspired by some of the incredible children he taught during that time, particularly those with Down's syndrome. Joseph lives in London. Say hello to him on Twitter: @joseph_elliott.